PRAISE FOI

MW00852589

"One part Heathers and M
and Jeffrey Dahmer, Krist
title in the juiciest, goriest way imaginable. It's a deep plunge into
madness and murderous frenzy for the pure hell of it. At the same
time, it is intricately clever in the way it delivers its carefully
calculated doses of eye-popping brutality. *Full Brutal* is a damn good
hardcore horror novel."

—Bryan Smith, author of
68 Kill and *Depraved*

"Kristopher Triana goes *Full Brutal* in this vicious portrait of a high
schooler, through all the traditional rites of passage—first seduction,
loss of virginity, first blackmail, loss of humanity, and that most
important rite... *last* rites, and lots of them. You will never forget the
unflinching world seen through Kim's eyes, in all its glorious
derangement. Triana follows up *Body Art* with another morbid
display of shocking depravities, carving his name deeper into the
dripping upper echelons of the splatter elite."

—Ryan Harding, author of *Genital Grinder*
and co-author of *Header 3* and *Reincarnage*.

"*Full Brutal* is one of the best books I've read in a long time. I loved
it. Extreme horror is in good hands."

—Kristopher Rufty, author of
Something Violent and *Pillowface*.

"*Full Brutal* is like *American Psycho* through a *Mean Girls* filter, except
cheerleader from hell Kim White makes Patrick Bateman look like a
well-adjusted gentleman you'd really like to get to know. Arguably
Triana's finest and most disturbing work to date, and I'm a little
terrified to see how he's going to outdo this one in the future."

—Chad Stroup, author of
Secrets of the Weird

"As violent and sadistic as it is wickedly satirical, *Full Brutal* will leave
you feeling disgusted, degraded and filled with contempt for
humanity. I loved it."

—John McNee, author of
Prince of Nightmares

FULL BRUTAL

KRISTOPHER TRIANA

BAD DREAM BOOKS

ISBN: 978-1-961758-00-1

BAD DREAM BOOKS

Originally published by Grindhouse Press June 12, 2018

for Nana
who loved a good horror story

"People speak sometimes about the 'bestial' cruelty of man, but that is terribly unjust and offensive to beasts; no animal could ever be so cruel as a man, so artfully, so artistically cruel."
— Fyodor Dostoyevsky

"I carried it too far, that's for sure."
— Jeffery Dahmer

PART ONE

UP THE DUFF

ONE

I'd heard that losing your virginity was a big deal. All the girls at school who'd had their cherries popped said it was a life-changing experience.

And I needed a change in my life.

I was so tired of the stale routine of my world. Every weekday before dawn I would get up, make myself presentable (a girl has to look good, unlike the slobs we call boys), skip breakfast, and head to the bus stop. There I would exchange meaningless small talk with the other sixteen-year-olds, the drones. We'd talk about music, clothes, boys and Netflix shows. We'd share stories about our lives that everyone had already read about on Facebook and Instagram. Then we'd be hauled off to the eight-hour prison of high school, the mind-manipulating monotony machine where one's personality goes to be trampled to death.

There was a time when I would spend the hours after school with friends—my squad—but for the last month or so I'd become listless. It wasn't that I hated people. I was just happier when they weren't around. Well, maybe not *happier*, but at least less miserable. I'd grown weary of the same brats and bitches babbling about their fucking makeup, their clothes and their boyfriends, as well as fucking their boyfriends. And as for the boys in my life, they existed, but I had little use for them too. They were all just hairy flesh-bags to carry redundant hormonal responses, belching out testosterone-fueled lies and flexing their incomplete, teenage bodies like mannequins in a sporting goods store.

I was slender and pretty. I took good—*very* good—care of myself, so I got the attention a young woman is supposed to need. My grades were excellent and I had a solid social circle. Father made an exorbitant amount of money and we lived in a house far bigger than the two of us needed, with me having my own floor with a private bathroom, entertainment room, office and small yoga gym I'd made out of the spare bedroom. I had the sort of life every girl my age wants.

And I hated all of it.

It was just so unbearably banal. My stupid, little American-pie life had been lived millions of times; so much so that I saw it as an anti-life, a stale rerun for the sorry bimbos who had never dared to step outside the lines drawn for them by their peers. Even the thought of teenage rebellion made me want to wretch, as it too was an exhausted cliché. How the fuck would dressing myself in Hot Topic clothing and listening to The Misfits be any less conformist than my cheerleader uniform and Beyonce? Wearing all black was for the weak, smoking weed for the lazy, and partying for those who were too afraid to be alone. If I really wanted to rebel, I would have to abstain from such convention.

But I wasn't going to abstain from sex.

Not that I was particularly interested in it. I had never let a date go beyond kissing, and even that didn't give me a spark. Whenever I kissed boys I felt like I was just sucking on a snail. It was wet, wiggly, and sort of gross. I wasn't a lesbian, but I still didn't really like boys. I had just been going out with them because that was what a teenage girl did, just like all the other crap I had trapped myself with—school, friends, cheerleading, and my shit-stain hometown in general. I guess I was sort of asexual. I honestly never gave intercourse much thought, at least not until I decided to lose my virginity.

"It changes you," Amy said.

We were walking home from the bus stop on a sunny but cold day in March. She lived around the corner from me, and our close proximity, age, and general lifestyle had made us friends—best friends, according to her. She'd made that clear with the two necklaces forming one heart. One she gave me as a gift for Christmas, and the other she wore around her pale, elegant neck.

"Changes you how?" I asked.

Amy pulled her long hair out of its ponytail and fluffed it as if she was accentuating what she was saying by giving herself bed head.

"It just makes you a woman," she said. "It's like suddenly your childhood is gone, and the whole world just looks all different."

"You really get a whole new perspective?"

"Sort of. It's hard to explain to those who haven't felt it."

I held back a groan. She wasn't being specific enough. I liked to know all the details of a thing before I launched myself into its lap. "But it's a change for the better?"

She looked at me as if shocked by my lack of understanding. "Oh, god, yeah."

It had only been a few days since Amy had *given herself* to her boyfriend, Brian, and she wouldn't shut up about it. I think she unloaded all of her thoughts on the matter on me because I was her BFF and therefore the only one she told, not wanting to be deemed a slut even though she and Brian had been a serious item for almost four months, an eternity for a teenage couple.

I had my hands in the pockets of my coat and was peeling one of my cuticles back. I was excited to eat it once Amy and I parted ways.

"Does Brian have a new perspective too?" I asked.

She gave me another strange look. "I don't know, Kim. I mean, like, he's a *guy*. You know how they are about sex and stuff."

I did, and yet didn't. Not to the same degree she did. Amy was the more popular of the two of us—in fact, I had leeched off that popularity and had really just become popular by association—and she had had many boyfriends. While I was attractive, Amy was absolutely stunning. She was blond to my brunette, creamy-skinned, and fuller in the chest than I was. If I was a rose, she was a flower garden. So whereas the hounds sniffed around me, they raced toward her like a thrown Frisbee. I wasn't jealous of Amy though. She was just the older sister figure when it came to our duo. That's why I always came to her with my questions.

"Well," I said, "was he a virgin too?"

Amy's face soured and she turned away. I'd upset her.

"What?" I asked.

"That's just not the kind of thing you ask."

"Why not?"

She huffed. "It just isn't, okay?"

"Okay, sorry."

But I wasn't sorry. I enjoyed pressing Amy this way, especially because we were friends, which made it easier for me to get away with it. She would forgive me for crossing boundaries that would get other girls' hair pulled out by the roots. Passive aggression was a sport I often played, a delightful pastime just like manipulation, sarcasm and suggestion. My friends were not exempt from these games, though they didn't know I was playing. If anything, they got the heaviest assaults of all.

"So," she said, mellowing now, "do you think you're going to go all the way with Derek?"

I snorted a laugh. "We're not serious."

Derek was one of Brian's friends and we all had double dated, and then he and I had gone out solo to a movie, which was a comfortable first date for me because it meant we could hang out for two hours without speaking to each other. Since then we'd gone on two more dates, which were adequate but I had spaced far apart, and I had attended some of his games' after parties, but only as a group night out. Derek was an adequate male—a member of the basketball team, fit and trim, a good sense of humor. He was the latest in a string of swinging dicks Amy had tried to pair me up with, always wanting to be the matchmaker. To me, she came off more like my pimp (not that I ever let Derek get anywhere).

"He's a catch, Kim. And he really likes you. Brian says he won't shut up about you."

"Sounds like a stalker."

She rolled her eyes jokingly. "You don't like anybody."

Amy laughed, not knowing how right she was.

Luckily, Father came home later than usual, for I'd gotten wrapped up watching free internet porn and lost track of time, so I didn't get started on dinner until after six. It was Wednesday, so I made my special lasagna, like every Wednesday when he wasn't away on business.

Thanks to Amy, sex had been on my mind all afternoon. I was

also taking comprehensive sex ed in school as part of life management; of course sex ed was also taught to younger students, but this was sort of a refresh that was obviously inserted into the curriculum now that those of us in the 11th grade were on the threshold of getting it on. So I understood the mechanics of sex, but had not really seen it in action, only faked in movies. I had seen some pornography, but mostly as part of a giggling, slumber party crowd sneaking a peak at pictures of naked men online. I had never watched anything hardcore before.

Finding free videos was surprisingly easy. Most websites even had categories I could choose from—*threesome, anal, blowjob, step-mom* (what the fuck, right?), *gay, Asian* and many more. So I clicked on *teen*, thinking it would be the most appropriate for someone my age. Of course it just meant the girl was a teen, or was at least trying to pass for one (many had tattoos and giant, fake tits revealing them to be many calendars past their high school days). The forcefulness of the men surprised me. There was none of the sweet talk or pressure boys applied when they were trying to get their hand under my skirt. The guys in these videos just seemed to *take* sex. The girls were willing, but they didn't seem to be *having* sex so much as they were having sex *done to them*. And the intercourse was almost violent in nature. It was fast and hard—mixed martial arts, only wetter and more awkward. Seeing genitals up close was repellant enough, but seeing one slam in and out of the other at close range made me wince.

Do people actually get off on this?

I decided to search different categories. Finding one marked *amateur*, I clicked on it and scanned a few of the videos, thinking it might be sex for beginners like me. These movies were made by people who were not sexual amateurs, but rather amateur filmmakers. Most of these videos were milder in nature, the majority being recordings and photos of couples who just decided to film themselves doing it in their own beds.

There was a banner at the top of this page, with a connecting link in blue letters.

Upload Your Own.

Apparently the page's followers provided all the content for this category.

I watched these clumsy fools for a while, then moved on to some of the more intense stuff just to satisfy my curiosity. I watched men shoot their sperm on women's faces, wondering why either of them would want to do such a thing. It wasn't offensive to me or even gross; it just seemed weird and pointless. I watched people put their tongues into someone else's asshole and thought the same thing. I scrolled and clicked and rolled my eyes. Nothing I could find seemed the least bit thrilling, until I clicked on *bondage*.

I expected to just find videos of the light and fluffy tie-up games husbands and wives desperately resorted to once they got tired of fucking each other the normal way. I expected to see lace wrist wraps and blindfolds. What I got was so much better.

I saw both women *and* men being degraded and abused. There were clamps and chains and vinyl. There were electric prods used on buttocks and clothespins clamped onto nipples. Women didn't just suck dick, they had their faces *fucked,* sometimes until they threw up. And the asses were whipped until they were as pink as hams. The physical abuse was enticing, but the way the masters stripped the slaves of their humanity was what made me slip my hand down into my jeans. My pussy had grown wet while watching a woman hung upside down from the ceiling being spit on by two men. There was a metal ring strapped to her mouth to force it open and they kept hocking up loogies and spitting them down her gullet. Then they crammed both of their cocks into her mouth at once. As her mascara ran I felt my clit swell and I rubbed it with my middle and ring fingers, flicking it back and forth like a card in bicycle spokes. I had never been into masturbation, having never been excited enough by anything to engage in it. I had touched myself before, and sure, it had felt good, but nothing erotic had been going on in my mind; I was only curious about my own body. But now I was being fed sincere thrills via the computer screen. Somewhere, at some time earlier, people had gathered together to degrade someone, and as a further disgrace they had recorded it to share with others, and now the video's journey had led it to my wide, staring eyes. I found it all so incredibly delightful.

Maybe there was something to sex after all.

I came *hard.* My body shook and I shrieked out loud. It was my first ever orgasm—a powerful, surprising awakening. I sat there for a moment, shuddering, shocked by what had just happened, what I had just done to myself. My crotch was sopping wet, so I slid out of my jeans and panties and walked to the bathroom to clean myself up. I then cleared my browser history and got started on dinner, finishing just as Father's car pulled up in the driveway.

I opened the front door for him and he kissed my forehead and hung his keys. I helped him out of his coat, feeling the winter cold that still clung to his clothes.

"How was your day, Father?"

He nodded. "Good. How was school?"

"Fine."

Like the dinner, this little exchange was a scheduled ritual, only this one was not restricted to Wednesdays alone. There was a lot of routine when it came to our relationship, which I found very comfortable and reassuring. With Mother dead some seven years now and me being an only child, our bond may have been important but it was not something we obsessed over. We had our set ways and that was that. His love was mechanical, a repetitive system that brought neither highs nor lows but maintained a controlled level, steady as a dead man's flatline. As a daughter, I reciprocated in a fashion that was identical, and therefore adequate.

He went to the closet to put away his shoes and I brought the filled plates out to the dining room where I had already set the table. He poured each of us a glass of chardonnay. I had purchased fresh flowers and used them to fill the vases. The candles in the centerpiece were lit. To most people these would be the sorts of things added for special or even romantic occasions. But this was how we always ate, yet another part of our routine. Father preferred classy dining and it was a taste I too had come to appreciate. One should take pleasure in their meals.

"Is your homework done?" he asked as he sat down.

"Yes," I lied.

Usually I did have it done by now, but I'd burned too much time pleasuring myself. I would finish my assignments in my room before bed so he would not see me working in my office.

"That's good, Kim. You're a good girl."

Father leaned down and smelled the lasagna, his favorite. The flames of the candles reflected in his glasses. He was tall and lean with thinning hair, but there was a reserved nature to him that was masculine and old fashioned. Despite being a businessman, he still seemed rugged and chiseled, a tamed wolf. He sat up straight and cut into a segment of the dish. I watched his face for signs of approval, and when he nodded I began eating. It was important to me that I kept Father well fed. Not that he was some brute who would smack me around if his dinner was served cold. I did not aim to please him out of fear but out of a mutual respect. This was our home, and a home is built on a foundation of basic principles. We had scripted our own code of conduct over the years and had adapted to the changes that had been thrust upon us by fate's brute force. As bored as I was by the routine of my own life, I felt routine between Father and I was essential, as if it were the only rope tossed to us as we swam in quicksand.

TWO

The next day I got serious. Not that I thought there would be much to do. I was a pretty young woman. It certainly wouldn't be difficult for me to get laid. There was Derek, as well as other boys I'd dated but had never let get anywhere. I could call on any one of them to take care of this for me. On top of that I had a school full of raging lotharios to choose from—jocks, emos, nerds and everybody else with a set of nuts. Boys want sex at all times and will even fuck a total stranger if she looks good enough. Finding a partner would be easy for a girl like me; too easy, in fact. I think that's why I decided not to go with any of them. Losing it to one of these high school hard-ons would be yet another exercise in monotony. It was what every other girl did. It's not that I wanted to be different. It was that I had decided to have my cherry popped because I wanted a change in my life. Making that change in a completely generic manner would defeat the whole purpose.

I had to get creative with this if it was going to have the desired effect.

It wasn't until fifth period the idea came to me. Ironically enough, it was in the middle of life management class, during another sex ed presentation.

"There are many different types of birth control," Mr. Blakley said. "There are pills and injections women can take . . ."

He rattled off more but I zoned out on the words as I watched him walk back and forth before his desk. Mr. Blakley was one of the younger teachers at school. He was in his early forties and good looking for his age; not strikingly handsome but well put together and clean cut. Everything about him seemed trim and neat—his build, beard, and demeanor. He wasn't exactly the object of schoolgirl crushes, but as far as faculty went he was a top pick.

As I sat listening to him talk about spermicidal suppositories, the idea came to me with sudden, doubtless clarity. Losing my virginity to a boy my age would be the very definition of banality, but a sixteen-year-old girl losing her virginity to an adult—and a teacher at that—would be an unconventional, drastic move. It would be a dark and dirty thing with all the makings of a game-changer. I didn't want it because it would create a scandal, upset Father, or any of those other attention-seeking acts the bad girls do. I wouldn't tell anyone, not even Amy; not because I would be ashamed, but because sharing the experience with others was not what it was about. I wasn't trying to fit in with the other girls who had gone all the way and I certainly wasn't looking to draw attention to myself.

I was just so tired of being alive.

Fucking my teacher sounded like a great idea.

If losing my virginity would change my life and give me a new perspective, then losing it to Mr. Blakley would turn the volume of that change all the way up until feedback screeched through my brain. Maybe it could deafen the black thoughts that liked to circle through it like a carousel of misery, the mute button being hit on my daily daydreams of suicide and self-mutilation, of peeling back my skin and eating it.

"Condoms are the best way to prevent pregnancy and protect against sexually transmitted diseases at the same time," Mr. Blakley said. "Remember they're always available for free at the nurse's station."

A few quiet snickers floated from the back of the class where the punks lurked. Mr. Blakley glanced at them and the snickers died out. Watching his eyes narrow, I felt a warm rush grow through me. Now that I had chosen him as my fucker, I was finding his authority over the classroom very attractive. I shifted my thighs beneath the desk, my pleated cheerleader skirt rustling softly against my skin.

A boy two rows over raised his hand. Mr. Blakley pointed at him.

"Um," the boy said, "what if we don't like the way condoms

feel?"

He didn't seem to be playing class clown. If anything he seemed to be using this opportunity to brag about his prowess by implying he'd already had sex. Judging by his blackheads, cheap clothing and cheaper haircut, I suspected this was a lie.

Mr. Blakley didn't flinch. "Well, Tommy, maybe try different ones."

Having said what he wanted to say, Tommy leaned back into his seat and stayed quiet for the rest of the class. And as the time for the bell to ring drew nearer, I stirred and cracked my knuckles under my desk as I pondered how I would go about this. Having seen porno, I thought I understood what men wanted, seeing how the industry was almost universally catered to them—not the bondage stuff, at least not for most people, but the standard hardcore. The women all came off so strong in those videos, but I assumed anything that popular must be right.

When at last the period ended I took my time gathering my books so all the other students could file out first. Once the room was empty, I set my eyes on Mr. Blakley, but he was seated at his desk, jotting notes in his planner. I slung my book bag over my shoulder and put a sway in my hips as I walked toward him, hoping my cheerleader outfit would have the same effect on him it had with boys my age. A few steps in, he looked up at me and smiled politely until he saw the look on my face.

I could have waited to form some sort of plan. I could have studied him for a while or even teased him with winks here and there or brushed up against him to gauge him. But there was a fresh urgency to my need now, and I doubted taking the slow road would yield any better results than the straightforward sexuality I'd learned from those videos. I thought of the *teen* category specifically then, and how it was almost always older men banging the girls. Maybe it had something to do with men wanting to relive their youth, or maybe it was based in a deep-seated need to dominate the innocent. Either way, it was a porn genre of its own for a reason, and I was going to use that to my advantage.

I was biting one corner of my lower lip when he looked up at me, the position of my mouth flirty and suggestive. I knew from seeing Amy do it. His face went slack for a moment, and then he regained himself, but in that brief moment I caught the arousal hiding behind his eyes. I knew right then and there I would have him, that he would soon be between my legs, thrusting us to a higher plain. The power of my own sexuality, which was still a relatively new ability, filled me with a sense of strength as I leaned over and put my hands on his desk, cocking one hip, tilting my head, and brushing one side of my hair over my ear.

I let the silence linger so he would have to be the one to break it.

"Yes, Kim?" he said, his voice low, the tone neutral.

"Hi, Mr. Blakley," I said. "I just want you to know how helpful the sex ed classes have been for me."

I saw him swallow. "Yes, well, I'm glad. You've done very well on all of your tests, as usual. And your homework is always—"

"I have an idea for homework," I interrupted. "I think an example of applied learning would be very helpful, don't you?"

His face reddened, darkened. I hoped I hadn't stepped too far too fast. There was a new vibe coming off Mr. Blakley now, one that reminded me he was my teacher and could cause me a great deal of grief if I pushed this in a direction he didn't want to go. The last thing I wanted was to jeopardize my stature as one of the school's honor roll golden girls.

"What are you saying, Kim?"

Now I was the one to swallow hard. A tingle went through me, part fear and part titillation. In a way, the fear caused my anticipation to deepen. I felt like a high-stakes gambler with it all on the table, a daredevil about to jump a dirt bike over flames.

"I'm saying I'm a virgin." I cowered a little, still testing the water.

His eyebrows rose and he crossed his arms in front of his chest. This made him seem armored and I wasn't sure how to take that.

"Well," he said, "I think that's a good thing for a girl your age."

Shit, I thought. *I walked right into that failure.*

"But," he continued, "when the time is right, you'll know. Just pick the right boy."

This could be taken two ways. He could be giving me the *make-sure-it's-someone-you-love* bullshit, or he could be suggesting *he* might be a good choice. Time was running out. The next class would come in any minute. I leaned in further, my face closer to his, and whispered.

"Mr. Blakley, I don't want a boy to fuck me. I want it to be a man."

I heard the air catch in his throat. The redness returned to his face and his eyes fell to his desk. Before he could regain his composure, I started toward the door. He looked ready to say something, but just as he stood to do so, a group of students walked through the door and I was able to slip past them and into the hall, leaving my planted seeds to germinate in Mr. Blakley's mind until tomorrow.

<hr/>

That afternoon Amy invited me to go out with Brian and Derek to go see the comic book movie of the month. I found superhero films to be incredibly redundant and obtuse but figured going would help get my mind off my exchange with Mr. Blakley. I was obsessing over it, rerunning it in my head like an old TV show marathon. While I was confident, there was still a nervous tremor. He could easily report my behavior to the principal, who would relay it to Father. That would disrupt the routine I had with Father and derail my academic stature. Plus I could be suspended, a thought that chilled me. I knew if I made it through the next few hours without getting a phone call, I would be in the clear. It would mean Mr. Blakley hadn't mentioned the incident to anyone, which would also signify his interest. Getting through those hours would be a lot easier surrounded by the noise of my friends and the blurry battles of yet another Marvel movie.

I went home, changed into tight black jeans and a gray cardigan, put on one of my mother's necklaces and applied fresh makeup. I texted my father, telling him I was going out tonight. Thursday was leftovers night anyway, so I put Sunday's turkey chili leftovers into the Crock-Pot to warm, chopped some celery and put it into the fridge, and placed a bottle of wine and a sleeve of low sodium crackers on the counter. Then I slipped into my coat and took the short walk to Amy's house.

Amy drove us in the new Honda Civic she'd received as a sweet sixteen present. It still had a lingering echo of new car smell, and she wouldn't let anyone eat or drink in it. She even told me she refused to have sex with Brian in the backseat; she was okay with having sex in cars, just not on her own upholstery. She put on an Ariana Grande album and I stared out at the evergreens that lined the roadways like sentries. It was sunny again and I found myself mourning the fading winter. Soon it would be warm and the leaves would return to the trees, and then the heat would slither back and soil everything. I hoped we would at least get a few more days of cold gloom and bad weather; not the kind that brings snow days where people can go sledding and drink cocoa, but the miserable days of sleet that seals car doors and creates black ice, of snow that caves in roofs and piles so high in the street that it turns into gray barricades you can't see past to make a secure turn.

"So," Amy said, "are you excited to see bae?"

I mentally gagged. "Don't call Derek *bae*. In fact, don't call anyone my bae."

Amy giggled. "You have to have somebody to call your own, Kim. Someone to treat you good and shower you with gifts and all that."

And shower you with other things, I thought, thinking of the *facial* category on the porn sites.

"I like being single," I said.

"Don't you ever want to get married?"

"Jeez, Amy, it's a little early to be talking about that shit, isn't it?"

"I'm just saying."

"Are you going to marry Brian?"

"I don't know," she said. "I'm low-key in love with him."

She giggled again and her girlishness sickened me. I hoped her brakes would fail and we would slam into the back of another car and spin upside-down into a ditch, horribly mutilating her while leaving me unscathed.

"Everyone always says we'll only be young once," I said. "We have our whole adult lives to be married."

And stay as miserable as every married couple seems to be.

"Well just how long do you plan to play hot to trot?" she asked. "I mean, like, if you're going to do what we were talking about, you need to find someone to do it with. It can't be just anybody. You want it to be special. You want it to matter."

She was going into the big sister role with more gusto. Sometimes it seemed like I was being given the sort of redundant lectures usually reserved for parents.

"I know," I said, thinking of Mr. Blakley. "It'll matter."

She waited for me to say more. I didn't.

We met the boys inside the theater. They were playing air hockey and while they acknowledged our arrival they didn't bother to stop playing. Brian had just gotten a haircut and I could smell the cologne coming off him in waves whenever he moved. He was fit and wore tight clothes to make sure everyone knew it. Derek was dressed nicer than usual, likely in an effort to impress me. When we had last gone out he made sure to pull out my seats for me, help me with my coat and open every door for me even when it was awkward. His chivalry was outdated and laughable, and it amused me even though I made no mention of it. It was such a pathetic nice-guy move, the kind of behavior that comes off as desperate and sends a guy into the friend zone faster than the crack of lightning. But while Derek played the gentleman for the first part of our dates, he always got grabby near the end of them. I had never let him get further than up my shirt, and his hands had been clumsy on my breasts, squeezing more than caressing, and giving no love to the nipples. His kisses were like tonguing a cup of rice pudding, always accompanied by his unwelcome erection pressed against my side, a kitten nudging to be petted. Even with sex on my mind, I didn't plan on letting Derek get anywhere with me tonight. I wouldn't leave with him or sit alone with him in the theater so he could touch me in the dark. The thought of teasing and confusing him with frigidity was more arousing to me than anything we could do together.

Annoyed by the way Brian kept slapping the puck around instead of fawning over her, Amy turned to me.

"We should get some popcorn and stuff," she said.

She was pulling one of her power plays. For one thing, we would be walking away without them, and for another thing, we would be paying for our own snacks. This was meant to make Brian feel inadequate, for it underlined the old cliché of the guy paying for everything if he expected to get something in return.

Brian stopped the puck. "Hold up."

But Amy kept on walking. She could be a cold bitch when she didn't immediately get her way. It was one of the few things I genuinely liked about her. I kept up with her and, as we headed toward the candy display, we heard the boys trotting after us. When they caught up they tried to laugh it off but the fear of having blown it lingered on their faces.

"Just wanted to finish the game," Derek said.

"That's okay though," Brian added. "We don't need to."

"Good," Amy said, instantly back to her cheery self. "Buy me some snacks?"

"Sure!"

Brian grinned and it amused me to see how easily Amy had manipulated him. He was now excited and grateful to be allowed to spend money on her.

"You want anything?" Derek asked me.

I had a different game to play with Derek. "I have my own money."

He seemed to deflate. "Are you sure? I mean, like, I'd be happy to, you know?"

"I'm good."

He put his hands in his pockets and put on a smile. He even tilted his head to let his dark hair hang over his forehead, making him look even more handsome.

"It's good to see you," he said.

Of course we saw each other at school every day, but that's not what Derek meant. I had to fight the urge to say something cold. I couldn't be *too* bitchy. Derek was playing the nice guy, but he was a jock, not a nerd. He wouldn't put up with me being shitty unless I spliced that shittiness with a glimmer of hope when it came to him getting his pecker wet.

"Good to see you too," I lied.

We ordered our popcorn, drinks and chocolates and Derek jumped in and paid for mine before I could. I allowed this but didn't show any appreciation. He carried the soda tray and popcorn tub and still managed to open the door for me when we got to our theater.

"Such a gentleman," Amy said.

A shit-eating grin filled Derek's all-American face.

I managed a smile by picturing them both hogtied while I pissed on their faces.

The movie was recycled drivel and the boys ate it up. Amy seemed to like it as much as any other movie, but for her going out to the movies had nothing to do with the movies themselves. It was a social thing, a staple in the life of white suburban teens with generous allowances. More importantly, it got her out and *seen* with her popular boyfriend and squad, in her newest outfit and shoes, giving her more opportunities to flaunt her superiority even outside the halls of our school.

Derek had held my hand during part of the movie, and I allowed this for a short while before I shifted and let him go. Later he put his arm around me, but the arrangement of the seating made it too awkward and uncomfortable and he gave up.

The movie ended, and I turned my phone on as we walked outside, having turned it off for the show. As I waited for the screen to come back to life my friends talked about the colorful nonsense they'd just seen.

"So," Brian said then. "You ladies wanna take this party elsewhere?"

When I looked at Amy she gave me a glance filled with mischief, like she was going to go along with this obvious setup to try and force me and Derek together out of a sort of inside joke if nothing else. Like a lot of girls, we had a code around boys for these sorts of moments. When looking right at each other at times like this, if one of us brushed our hair behind our ear that meant *yes*, but if we blinked three times it meant *no*.

I gave Amy the winks and the bitch tugged a lock of her hair behind her ear.

She could suck off Brian any time. This wasn't about that. This was about her further pushing me into Derek's lap. Perhaps it had something to do with our discussions about sex and serious relationships, but I knew it was mostly Amy wanting this pairing she'd made to work out. It was about her being a good matchmaker. It was about her being fucking right.

I decided to answer Brian before she could.

"Maybe if it was the weekend," I said. "We should be getting back, with school tomorrow and everything."

I enjoyed the disappointed look that fell over all of their faces. And now that my phone was awake it buzzed, alerting me of a missed text. My fears of Mr. Blakley telling on me resurfaced, and I stepped away from the others to check the message. I heard Brian trying to change our minds but ignored him as I read Father's text.

Father: *Dinner was very good. Did you do your homework before going out?*

I texted him immediately with the lie he wanted to hear. I could finish my homework before bed.

"Just got a message from my Dad," I said. "If it was up to me I'd go with you guys, but he wants me home. Parents, right?"

Defeat washed over the boys (fathers are teenage boys' kryptonite) but I could sense Amy's annoyance. She knew my relationship with Father and the freedom he allotted me. And it was only eight o'clock. We stayed out later than this on school nights all the time. She knew I was full of shit, but now she understood how serious I was about bailing on the guys, so she didn't press it any further. She pulled the cold bitch routine all the time with other people, but rarely with me. I was her precious BFF, after all. We were sisters in her mind and she cherished the idea of that. It was part of her little Norman Rockwell, perfect-girl-life delusion. This cemented her to what she perceived as our bond and made me exempt from her signature selfishness.

"Sorry, boys," Amy said. "Maybe some other time."

She stepped into the tease role with a downright savage elegance. She did not push blame onto me, but rather formed an alliance, allowing us to blow kisses that gave the boys ideas for a next time while still breaking their hearts. When we parted ways Derek leaned in to kiss me for the first time that night, and I gave him my cheek.

"I'll call you," I lied.

We got into Amy's car, leaving them standing in the parking lot like the stupid dicks they were. I expected Amy to be mad and give me one of her lectures, but she seemed laid back, even happy.

"It's good to keep them waiting sometimes," she said.

"I hope Derek brings something to read. Cause he's going to wait a long time."

The headlights cut through the darkness as we headed for home, the hollow of night seeming to call me into it with silent promises of something equally dark to come. I could only wonder what it was, when it would arrive, and what I needed to do to obtain it.

"Just don't be too harsh with Derek," Amy said. "I don't want things to get awkward for Brian and me."

"Don't worry about it."

"I mean, if you don't like him I'll accept that, but keep in mind he's my boyfriend's best friend. He's in our squad, so he'll be around. You don't have to go out with him, but don't like, you know, make him an enemy."

"I won't."

I said it in a way that made it seem like I would do that for her sake, but in reality I just liked the idea of slowly poisoning what little there was of this anti-relationship I had with Derek. I was curious to see just how much I could torment him with a finely tuned combination of emotional abuse, leading him on and then neglecting him completely. If he thought I was just playing hard to get, then I could leisurely pick him apart. If properly timed and executed, I might even get him to fall in love with me just because I was so hard to get love from. He was already very into me. An obsession could be triggered if I gave just enough to take it all away again. Watching bondage porn had given me a taste for degrading others. I felt this was a good way to start on the real thing.

THREE

Mr. Blakley didn't report me.

I went through the first four periods without being called to the dean's office or, worse yet, being sent to talk to a guidance counselor. So while I was nervous throughout the day, it was not out of fear of being punished, just pre-game jitters.

And it was certainly a game now between my teacher and I.

That was why I decided to dress a little more provocatively today in a tight, red dress that ended north of the knee. Amy always called it my *do me* dress. I usually reserved it for going to clubs and the occasional cocktail party. This was its debut at school, and from the looks the boys were giving me I was confident it would have the desired effect, giving Mr. Blakley a message as equally clear as the one I'd given him the day before.

Just in case I needed more ammo, I had a back-up tactic.

When fifth period came I hurried to life management class, nearly skipping from the growing heat in my chest. I was the first person to enter the room, and Mr. Blakley glanced my way, took a deep breath when he saw how I was dressed, then dropped his eyes back to his planner without a word. I went to the desk closest to the front, directly in front of his desk, and made a big deal of crossing my legs and tugging at the sides of the short dress. I took out my cherry red lipstick and hand mirror. As I applied a fresh coat, I looked in the mirror but watched Mr. Blakley watching me from the corner of my eye. I rolled the tip of the lipstick over my lips slowly, then popped them a few times before putting everything away as the rest of the class piled in. A few of the plain-Jane girls gazed upon me with bottomless jealousy, and the bad boys that always sat in back of every class made no effort to hide their leers. I wondered if I could get Derek to beat them up for me. He was much taller than those two, and wider in the shoulders. I doubted he would have any trouble. It could also be a valuable test of his devotion. I pushed the thought from my mind though, not wanting my focus to waver.

"Good afternoon, class," Mr. Blakley said.

I did not join the murmured return of a greeting. I kept my eyes on him, watching in a predatory manner, a stalker, a jungle cat. His body language was off and he was making an obvious effort to avoid looking at me. I could almost smell his trepidation. Adventure hung between us by a taut rope.

"Today we're going to watch a video," he said. He reached into his desk, brought out a remote and turned on the mounted television. "This will fill our class—half of it today and the other half on Monday."

The TV turned bright blue as the DVD player whirred to life.

Mr. Blakley had made no mention of a movie the day before. This would completely avoid discussion. Plus, he could turn off the lights, making it easier for him not to look at me. He was fighting it, trying to avoid and deny it. It was cute. He put on some Lifetime Channel teen pregnancy movie and the class leaned back, most of them planning to zone out, draw or even catch a few winks. Mr. Blakley leaned forward in his chair, his head down. He attached a book light to one of the binders on his desk and started grading papers. There was not much for me to do now except wait.

When it was close to the end of the period he stopped the movie. Half of the class groaned like zombies when the light came on and the sound of shuffling book bags filled the room as Mr. Blakley came forward with a stack of papers in his hands. He went to the girl in the front left of the class and handed her a stack, then the boy next to me.

"Okay, weekend homework," he said.

When he reached me he tried to put the stack on my desk instead of handing it to me, but I reached for them and let my fingers slide down his wrist and over his knuckles. He hesitated for just a moment, then released the papers and moved on to the next student until we all had sheets to pass back through the class. He then went over to his desk and leaned against the front of it.

I saw my opportunity.

As he told the class about what pages of the book we'd need, I uncrossed my legs, opened them, and waited for him to notice I hadn't worn any panties and had shaved my sex clean.

He did, and luckily the class was getting out of their seats and didn't notice the way he stared down at my pussy. I kept my legs open for a few seconds, then crossed them again and inched my skirt back down so no one else would see. Mr. Blakley came back to himself, flustered. Sweat was forming on his temples like grease. He seemed as if he wanted to address the class in some sort of goodbye, but instead he just stood there and stared down at the carpet. I got out of my chair and took my time gathering my things as the classroom emptied out.

A pang of frustration went through me when some nameless guy approached me, his backpack slung over one shoulder, his leather jacket as gaudy as his earrings.

"Hey, Kim," he said.

There was only so much time before the next class filed in. I didn't have time for this bozo. I gave him a warning look, one that cautioned him that his pride was dangerously close to an open flame.

"Can I talk to you out in the hall?" he asked, giving me a dipshitty grin.

"No."

His smiled faltered. This wasn't the first asswipe to hit on me today. Never underestimate the power of a red dress.

"Hey, just give me a chance to—"

"I said fuck off, you little nobody."

He blinked. He even glanced to Mr. Blakley as if to ask him to punish me for my foul language. But our teacher had gone back behind his desk with other things on his mind.

"Fine," the guy said. "Nevermind, jeez."

He took his time walking out and my eyes threw hot daggers into his back. My mind screamed *get the fuck out* on a loop and I realized my teeth were grinding. When at last he was gone, I approached Mr. Blakley.

He put up a hand to halt me. "Don't."

I waited for more.

"I don't know what kind of joke you're playing," he said. "But it's gone far enough."

"It's no joke."

"Don't toy with me, Kim. I've let it slide so far, but . . ."

"If you were going to punish me you would have done it by now. Besides, if you told on me then they would be on to us when we started fucking."

He still hadn't made eye contact with me.

"I know this is some kind of prank," he said. "Did you make a bet with your girlfriends or something? You all think it'll be funny to tease the teacher, is that it?"

I glanced toward the doorway. It was empty and would be for a few more minutes, so I walked around the side of the desk. I took Mr. Blakley's hand and ran my fingertips over the knuckles.

"Look at me," I said.

He slowly lifted his head and when his eyes met mine I slipped his hand under my skirt and slid one of his fingers across the lips of my vagina. I had already moistened just by thinking about doing this.

I stared into his eyes. "Still think I'm joking?"

Mr. Blakley sucked in a deep breath and, while he didn't move his fingers, he also didn't pry his hand away. I slid the finger some more, digging just the very tip of it inside me so he could feel my tightness, and watched him redden before he sat up and pulled his hand away, afraid of being caught. He rolled his chair out and stood up.

"I'm a married man."

I wondered which one of us he was telling.

"I don't care."

"Your only a . . . just a . . ."

I reached into the open pocket of my bag and took out the folded piece of paper with my number on it and handed it to him.

"Mr. Blakley, this is happening."

I made a point to have no plans even though it was Friday night. This new game was all the entertainment I needed. I charged my phone and kept it on me the entire afternoon. Though I busied myself with homework and preparing dinner, the memory of how I'd made my teacher tremble in his seat kept coming back to me, and

I found myself wondering if he smelled or even licked the finger I'd put to my sex, if he jerked off as soon as he could or tried to fuck his wife before his daughter got home.

Caitlin was her name. She went to the same high school and was one year behind me. I only knew her name because everyone knows when a student is the child of a teacher. It's like watching out for a prison snitch. She seemed like a nice, friendly girl, sweet in that blushing tween kind of way. If not exactly pretty, she was very cute, but still sort of growing into her own skin. I had never thought much about the girl until now. Mr. Blakley's daughter being one of my classmates only sweetened the misdeed. It made it feel dirtier, meaner, like this was some sort of betrayal.

Night fell and Father came home. We ate in comfortable silence, and when I offered him seconds he accepted.

"I'll be going out of town for a while," he said.

This wasn't uncommon. He was an executive and often traveled for work. He always brought me back little gifts, usually something locally made he found in downtown shops, and not some mass-produced, airport kiosk crap.

"Where to?"

"Phoenix. The trade show."

"It's not in Boston this year, huh?"

"No. Boston inflated their prices enough to send the show elsewhere."

"Well, you'll enjoy the warm weather."

"That I will."

When dinner was over Father retired to the den to half watch sports while reading the paper. I cleaned up and went upstairs to my loft. I went to my computer, wanting to watch more humiliation bondage but uncomfortable doing it with Father home. Instead I decided to do a search for extreme, violent films. I ended up scanning through horror blogs, making notes of the films that came up the most often—*Nekromantik, Martyrs, Splatter: Naked Blood, The Human Centipede, The Guinea Pig* series and *A Serbian Film.* When I was done, I went onto Amazon and ordered all of them with the private credit card father had given me, and added a few other movies Amazon suggested based on my selections—*The Burning Moon, Ichi the Killer, I Stand Alone* and *Cannibal Ferox.* This killed some time, but it wasn't even nine o'clock yet. I got up and paced around my level of the house. I thought about taking a long bath to collect my thoughts but didn't want to be in there if and when Mr. Blakley called. I could have popped on a movie or flipped through a magazine, but I didn't. I just walked around my bed and looked out the windows, cracking my knuckles.

My phone rang at eight forty-five.

I closed my bedroom door and let the phone ring a few times before picking it up.

"Hello?"

I heard background noise, like a crowded bar.

I recognized Mr. Blakley's voice. "Kim?"

"You know it is." There was only noise on the other end. "What took you so long?"

He hesitated, then: "I'm not going to call you from my cell. I had to find a payphone. That's not an easy task these days."

I waited for more.

"I'm still not sure about this," he said. "You're what, seventeen?"

"Sweet sixteen, actually."

"Jesus."

"Don't worry. It'll be consensual."

"Not in the eyes of the law. It's called *statutory rape*, Kim. This doesn't just put my marriage and career on the line, but also my freedom."

"You worry too much, Mr. Blakley."

His voice changed a little. "Call me Bob. Any girl who puts my hand under her dress can call me Bob."

"Did you like having your hand on my pussy?"

"I . . . I did. Yes."

"Do you want to touch it again?"

"Yeah."

"Do you want to put your mouth on it?"

"Oh, yes."

"Do you want to put your cock inside of it?"

"I . . . yes. Very, very much."

I paused. "Well, then?"

"It's just . . . I have a family."

"I know that."

"I love them all. I love my wife."

"Doesn't matter to me one way or another."

"It's only that . . . I don't know, I really need . . ."

"You don't have to justify it to me. Just tell me where you want to meet."

He fell silent for a moment and I listened to the patrons of the bar.

"I told my wife I was going out for drinks with some co-workers. That buys me a couple of hours."

"That should be enough time."

"Do you have a car?"

"Yeah."

I didn't tell him I would be borrowing Father's. Even just mentioning a parent could make Mr. Blakley chicken out.

"Do you want to get us a room?" I suggested.

"We can't do that!"

"Why not?"

"That sort of thing can be traced with credit card bills. And it's a public place on top of that."

"Where then?"

"We should meet somewhere where you can leave your car and get into mine. Then we can drive somewhere secluded."

"Fine by me."

He breathed a sigh of relief. I guess he expected me to object to this or have reservations of my own. But I was not remotely worried about it, even though it was everything a teenage girl is not supposed to do. In fact, that was what I liked about it most of all.

My teacher gave me the name and address of a gas station and made me promise I would tell no one where I was going. I agreed and told him to stop being ridiculous. I went on my computer and looked up the distance. It would take me twenty minutes to get there. He told me he would be parked behind the store in a blue sedan and I should wear something hooded and do my best not to be seen.

I started getting ready even before we got off the phone. I put on my pink panties with the white lace on the sides, pulled on my tightest Levis, and put on a sweater without a bra. I touched up my makeup and hair, and then stood looking in the mirror for a moment, just savoring the anticipation.

Father looked up from his paper as I entered the den.

"You look nice," he said.

"Thank you."

"Going out?"

"Yeah. Amy and the girls are at the plaza doing some shopping. Thought I'd join them."

"You have your credit card or do you want some cash?"

"I have the card, thanks."

"Okay then. Keys are on the hook."

I walked over and kissed him on the forehead. He patted my shoulder and then went back to reading the economics section as his only child went out to get fucked by a grown man.

FOUR

His car was tucked behind the dumpster of the Circle K, in a spot the light of the streetlamps didn't reach. As I walked to the car I heard the doors unlock, and I lifted the handle and got inside. He was sitting there, his breath making white puffs in the cold night air. It was strange to see him in his jeans and sneakers, a t-shirt on beneath his jacket. He seemed flustered as he started the car and we pulled out of the lot.

"You're not wearing a hoodie," he said.

"They mess up my hair."

"We need to take every precaution." He shook his head. "I can't believe I'm even doing this. I must be nuts."

"So where are we going?"

"To the trails out near Big Rock. I know some that are less traveled. We can park there if the coast is clear."

We drove on, not saying much. Thinking of the girls in porno movies, I reached over and put my hand on his crotch and started rubbing the lump in his jeans. He kept his eyes on the road but a sort of nervous smile came across his face. I kept rubbing until I could feel he was fully hard and then I scooted closer in the seat and started sucking on his ear lobe.

His words were whispers. "Oh, Jesus, Kim."

I popped the button on his jeans and unzipped his fly, opening the folds. He wore generic, boring white briefs. I reached inside and felt his manhood stand at my touch and his chest shudder against me. I had never felt a dick before. The softness of his cock's skin surprised me, as did the plump rivers of veins running through it. The head had the shape and texture of a cooked mushroom, and an unruly web of hair surrounded the base of his shaft. I had thought cocks looked ugly on camera; they looked somehow worse in person. It seemed big to me, but I had no previous dicks to compare it too, only the ones I'd seen in videos, which was not the same as seeing one in the flesh and holding it in your virgin hands.

"Put it in your mouth," he said.

This surprised me. He was suddenly assertive, his arousal canceling out his nervousness. It excited me because it made me feel like this really was going to be a life altering experience, whereas up until this point it had just felt like a high stakes game of manipulation. His hand went to the back of my head and he gently guided me down into his musky crotch. Shadows hid his genitals and his cock was not only hard but twitching, making me think of those vibrating video game joysticks. I had seen a lot of blowjobs online, but wasn't sure that gave me enough information to do it correctly. I figured it couldn't be all that difficult. I opened my mouth and took in the head of his dick. His hand ran over my head like he was patting me to sleep, but then he pushed my head down and his pelvis forward, and the rest of his cock entered my mouth and I gagged as it hit the back of my throat. I shook my head to get loose.

"Watch your teeth," he said.

I caught my breath and put him in my mouth again, closed my lips around him, and started going up and down like the girls in the videos. It was like sucking a long, rubbery thumb. I did this for a minute and he shuddered like an abused dog.

"Okay, okay," he said, moving his hips to slide himself free. "That's enough." He seemed almost afraid and I wondered if I had done something wrong. He was breathing heavy, flustered. "We're almost there, baby."

I didn't like him calling me *baby*—it sounded too personal and sweet—but I didn't say anything. I could still taste the salt of his cock sweat and wondered if I was supposed to like it. As with so many things, I felt only numb indifference.

He drove us past the front of the park and around to a worn path lined by tall, yellowed grass. The drive was smooth until we reached a fork and moved onto a trail of rougher terrain just wide enough to fit the sedan through. We circled around into a thicket and he pulled into a spot beneath the spidery shadows of dead tree limbs, then parked and turned off the engine. He gripped the wheel for a moment and stared straight ahead as if we were lost at sea. I could sense the doubt clouding him, threatening to take him away from me, so I reached for his still exposed cock and gave it a squeeze.

"Okay," he said. "Climb into the back."

I slid between the gap in the front seats and when I got to the back I started undoing my shoelaces. Mr. Blakley sat for another moment of contemplation, then got out of the car and slid both of the front seats all the way forward. By the time he opened the door to the backseat I had slid out of my jeans and coat, and the gust of cold air made my skin come alive with goose bumps. I was already wet from the thrill of all we had done so far—all this dirtiness and danger and the summoning darkness of the woods. This all felt so grim and filthy; somehow evil. When he saw me sprawled out in his backseat, he actually licked his lips. He got in and hurried out of his coat, and then his hands and mouth were all over my body. He stroked my thighs and squeezed my breasts beneath my sweater, his fingers large and warm. My nipples hardened and dimpled at the touch of his tongue. He pulled at my panties so hard that I heard them tear, so I raised myself up so he could slide them off, and his face dove into my sex.

Based on how much he had enjoyed oral sex, I expected to like it, but as his tongue entered me I started to wonder if all oral sex was just to excite the man. He made every effort to stimulate my clitoris and he worked my pussy with his finger as well as his mouth, but it didn't do much for me. I wanted to get to the sex itself. This foreplay felt like it slowed everything down, and the ennui of it irritated me.

"Put your dick inside me," I said, not bothering to do so in a seductive manner. I stated it not with allure or as a command, but almost like a plain statement of fact, like I was reading from a dictionary.

Mr. Blakley lowered his jeans but kept them on, and seeing him like this struck me as comical and I had to stifle a laugh by clearing my throat. Women look rather beautiful naked (provided they aren't pigs or trolls). Men, on the other hand, just look gangly, hairy and awkward, like they've been made from the less desirable scraps left behind after the creation of women. His legs were pasty in the moonlight, his dick pointing at a curve like a fleshy compass above an unbalanced nut sack. He pulled off his shirt, revealing the soft handles of his belly and a happy trail of black hair.

Then he was on top of me.

And then he was inside me.

After all his lectures about condoms, he didn't use or even mention one. He just rushed in raw, and I let him do it. We didn't speak. He just slid in and out. I felt myself opening and closing, my body contouring around him as he moved. It felt invasive, even a little painful, but this was the big moment. This was the life changer. I wouldn't allow myself to drift off mentally to avoid the bodily irritation the way I did at the dentist. In a way this reminded me of going to my Ob/Gyn, just not as cold and sterile. There was heat to this invasion, and an extreme intimacy that made me more uncomfortable than being in the stirrups. I hated hugging, and this was like getting a sweaty bear hug while someone played where I peed. There was actually another human being *inside of me*. Wet mud sounds came from our genitals. His breath smelled bad and he was making an ugly face. It all bordered on the grotesque.

After about thirty seconds, he groaned and held his position, his dick all the way up inside me. I felt it pulse a few times, and then he rested his face into the nape of my neck, air from his nose burning against my skin. It wasn't until he retreated off me I realized he had already come. It was all over as quickly as it started, and aside from a dull ache between my legs, nothing had changed. There had been no great epiphany, no enlightenment or even cheap hallucination.

Maybe the life changing effect is delayed, I thought, *like time-released medication.*

Mr. Blakley sat back against the seat with my legs still snaked around him. He wouldn't look at me. I wasn't sure what should happen next, if I was supposed to do something or not. I decided to stay stoic, thinking no move was better than a wrong one. Eventually he spoke, but still kept his eyes on the floor mats. He seemed nervous and ashamed, and that made me smile to myself.

"I've been with one woman for the last twenty years," he said. "I just got excited."

I wasn't sure what he meant by this, so I stayed silent.

"It's just you're so young and pretty," he said. "A woman's body changes after two kids. You're so firm . . . so . . . *tight*."

His compliments confused me. He didn't seem to be flattering me, but rather trying to explain something. *He's making excuses*, I realized. *It's supposed to last longer. Not just in the videos, but in real life. He popped off too quickly and now he's embarrassed.*

It was more arousing than anything else he had done. His self-disgust in this moment of failure made me want to touch myself and so I did, and when my hand went to my sex I felt a sticky, snot-like trickle coming out of me. I held my fingers up to take a look at his runny, little seed.

"Jesus," he said. "I can't believe I came inside you." He looked at me now with tensed eyes, the crow's feet showing themselves. "Say something!"

"What do you want me to say?"

"I don't know, just don't play the mute. I know it wasn't great and I'm sorry. It's been a while. My wife and I don't have sex much anymore. Maybe if we did I wouldn't have done this."

He's making it her fault. God, I love this.

"A man has needs," he said. "And you came at me so hard."

Now it's my fault too. Funny how men aren't much different than boys.

But this didn't anger me. Instead it made me horny. Mr. Blakley was panicking now and I found his anxiety to be a real turn on. His sweat made him look older and bloated and he kept running his hand through his hair. The man was trying to squirm out from under a rock he had dropped onto his own head, and watching him unravel like this made me proud of what I'd done to him. I knew now I had the power to make a grown man's body betray his heart. I'd made him take something away from himself, made him cave, and this caused him to lament by his own volition. Now I was watching him rapidly cycle through the stages of grief. He'd failed his wife, failed his family, and even his act of betrayal was a failure in and of itself. He'd fucked a teenager and had done it *badly*.

"Damn it!" he said, punching the back of the seat.

He put his head in his hands. A moment later his face shot up.

"You know what," he said. "I don't have time for this. I have to get back."

"That's it?" I asked, just to hurt his male ego.

His face crumpled. "I told you, I got overexcited. It's been a long time and . . ."

He trailed off and then put his clothes back on. I wiped my hand on the cushions when he wasn't looking and dressed myself. In a few moments we were back in the front of the car. We didn't speak again until we were out of the woods and back on the road.

"Again, I'm sorry," he said. "I know this was a letdown."

I didn't reply.

"Was this really your first time?" he asked.

"Yes."

"You didn't bleed."

"Did you want me to?"

"Jeez, Kim. What kind of thing is that to say?"

"Then why'd you bring it up, Mr. Blakley?"

"Would you please not call me that? It makes me feel like a pedophile. Call me Bob."

"Why did you bring it up?"

"I was just surprised is all. I wouldn't expect a virgin to be so forward about sex."

I looked at my nails to express my boredom with him. "My hymen already broke because of cheerleading. That's why I didn't bleed."

He looked back at the road. "Okay. Well, I don't know what else to say except I'm sorry it wasn't a better experience. I don't think anyone's first time is what they expect it to be. I know mine wasn't."

I didn't take the bait and ask him about it. Instead I crossed my legs and stared out the window. It had started to rain. The wetness in my panties had grown cold and uncomfortable and I was ready to be home and away from him, to take a contemplative bath and see if the life-changing epiphany would come or if I would have to wait until the next morning for my amazing new perspective to hit.

"I would have done it with you again if there was more time," he said. "But Simone will be suspicious if I'm out too late. I'm a homebody. She was surprised enough that I wanted to go anywhere in the first place."

"It's fine," I said. "We're done, Mr. Blakley."

"You've got that right. We never should have done this. Honestly, now that it's all out of my system, I'm pretty sick over all of this. I just want to go back to my normal life and forget what just happened. You need to forget about it too, and keep your mouth shut, understand?"

"What's there to tell?"

He looked at me with a hardened jaw, and it made me scoot further away from him. He pulled over onto the shoulder of the rural state road that led out of the forest. There were no other cars, no streetlights. He put the car in park and turned to me, putting his finger in my face.

"I'm not fucking around here, Kim. I will *not* have my family, career and livelihood jeopardized by some careless little girl who thinks everything is just a game. Don't you *dare* breathe a word of this, you understand me?"

I wanted to push him a little more just to see how crazy I could make him, but I was startled by how fast he had gone from apologetic to angry. The illusion of safety a student has around a teacher suddenly vanished, and I realized then just how little I knew the man.

"I won't," I said. "I won't."

"You'd better not. Remember that, Kim. You'd *really* better not."

He stared at me until I looked away. He put the car in drive and sped us out of the dust and into the long, black throat of the night.

FIVE

The morning brought nothing new. I certainly did not feel any different, except for a slight soreness between my legs. The world seemed just as stale and empty as always, and the misery of the sunshine as it poured through the blinds of my bedroom window made me groan with discontent. Early daylight always hurt my eyes and made me antsy. It made the house look dusty and highlighted every small imperfection, making me want to scrub and clean and curse. The light threatened me with the warm spring that was coming no matter how hard I wished it away. It filled me with indignation.

After I'd gotten home, I had soaked in my tub for a long time in candlelight. I felt gross and wanted to wash, but also wanted the sauna-like meditation this offered. The night's events played through my mind like a movie; I felt detached from it, like it had happened to someone else while I had sat there watching and laughing with a mouthful of popcorn. But it was no movie. I had actually fucking done it. At last I'd experienced sex, and had found it to be overhyped. But there was a good part to it. The shame, humiliation and regret Mr. Blakley felt when the dirty deed was done was exhilarating for me. His anguish far exceeded his cock when it came to my own enjoyment of the night.

It was then I decided I would only have sex with married men, preferably ones with children. Fucking some guy who had nothing to lose from doing so would only make him happy, and that would irritate the piss out of me. The real pleasure lay in making them give in to temptation, making them hate themselves for it, to live with both the fear of being discovered and a terrible, crushing guilt that would never fully fade. I knew some men were selfish pigs and wouldn't feel remorse at all, but those with children, especially small ones they could risk losing custody of, would be almost guaranteed to have a breakdown.

These poor bastards would be my prey.

Though awake, I stayed in bed until almost noon just thinking about it all. When I finally got up, I went downstairs to find Father gathering his golf bag. He wore a stupid white hat with a puff on top, loud pants, and a blinding, checkered shirt.

"Good morning, Kim," he said. "Did you get anything good last night?"

That weekend I avoided Derek's calls, went shopping with Amy for real, and watched S&M porn whenever Father was out. The bondage videos got me curious, so I started researching types of knots, sex toys for S&M, and the strange outfits that often came with this play. While scanning Google for bondage articles I came across one about a serial killer named Dennis Rader, better known as B.T.K—which stood for *Bind, Torture, Kill*. The article came up because of the killer's M.O. of tying up his victims before torturing them to death. This pulled me into a wormhole on Sunday afternoon, reading about various serial killers. I found their behavior quite fascinating. There was a primal need to these people (almost always men) that made them compulsively destroy others, compulsions that held sexual implications as much as they were motivated by rage. It made me wonder just what made them so different from people like me, who had similar desires but did not behave as violently.

Along with B.T.K, I was particularly fascinated by the story of Albert Fish, a man who had invited a ten-year-old girl to his niece's birthday party and then led her to an isolated house where he strangled her and butchered her body. He took home several pounds of her flesh with him, which he made into a stew he devoured over the course of several days while masturbating. As a side dish he ate his own feces, while also flagellating himself with straps made of leather and nail-studded paddles whenever he wasn't shoving needles into his groin and rose stems up his urethra.

The other case that intoxicated me, along with the wine I sipped while reading, was that of Edmund Kemper, who started his killings when he was just a year younger than I was; that drew me into his sordid tale, and his horrific deeds kept me there. At fifteen, Edmund shot his grandmother in the skull before gunning down his grandfather. He was an animal torturer in his youth, burying cats alive and then displaying their body parts in his room like trophies. After a stint in a psych ward, he emerged as a monstrous, six-foot-nine man and started killing young women. He took pictures with his dead little trophies, and disemboweled the girls and fucked their body parts and viscera. He had a particular fondness for fucking severed heads, and even enjoyed this act with his mother's head after hammering her skull in and raping her decapitated body. He then shredded her larynx and stuffed it down the garbage disposal because he felt she had bitched and yelled quite too much while she was alive. Kemper's story sent me into a hot bath where I furiously masturbated, using the massage feature on the removable showerhead.

I did not hear from Mr. Blakley that weekend, and I did not reach out to him. I also didn't tell Amy anything—not just being secretive about Mr. Blakley, but about having lost my virginity at all—as I had no real desire to share with anyone. I kept hoping my new outlook on life would suddenly wash over me like a dizzy spell, but my view remained the same—bleak, pessimistic, dark as a bear's asshole. I was more bored than ever because my big hope to relieve my boredom through meaningless sex had been a stunning letdown. For a while that hope had been an exciting distraction from my daily stagnation, but now the drudgery had returned even stronger than before.

But I did have new daydreams now, ones revolving around making disgraces of men. I still desired Mr. Blakley, but in a different way. I had broken him down, but doubted I had ruined him. My fantasies transformed. I imagined luring him into an affair and doing everything I could to get him caught by his wife. While it would be delightful to see his career ended and to watch him cry in court, I didn't want that to happen because it would negatively impact me, derailing my life and image. I only wanted to wreck his family and end his marriage, not so I could have him all to myself but rather to play an intricate role in his self-destruction. It would almost be like making him commit suicide (and who knows, maybe he actually would when things fell apart). And once his family hated him, I would be gone. I would never sleep with him again, though I might tease him a little at school, or anywhere else I could torment him.

I was in a good mood on Monday. It was the first time I would see Mr. Blakley since he'd fucked me. In the morning I kissed Father goodbye before he left for his trip, and he thoughtfully took a cab so as to leave me the car. I had my own key on my ring, along with ones to the house and a fake key that was actually a pocketknife, which Father had bought me for protection. I put lavish curls in my hair and wore the blue top that brought out my eyes and headed for school, taking the Volvo instead of the bus. Getting through all the classes I had before fifth period was nerve wracking, but I focused on my schoolwork to try and keep my mind off everything else. I didn't have a plan for what I wanted to do when I saw him; I was just excited to watch him squirm.

I saw his daughter at lunchtime.

Caitlin was just leaving the line with her tray, so I got up with my own, which I had just sat down with, and waited for her to find a seat. She didn't seem to be meeting up with any friends, and my own hadn't arrived yet, so I followed behind her until she sat at one of the tables. Her hair was in a ponytail and she wore a sweatshirt with *PINK* written on it. There was an innocent cuteness to her, accentuated by her petite frame and braces.

"Mind if I join you?" I asked.

She looked up at me with wide eyes. We weren't exactly strangers, as both of us were involved in extracurricular activities that took place in the gym, but I was popular and older. Sitting with me would be an honor for a grunt like Caitlin Blakley.

"Of course not!" She beamed.

I sat across from her and glanced at her food. It was mostly junk—pizza, fries, a cookie. It was a wonder she was still thin and not covered in zits.

"I'm Kim White."

"Yeah," she said. "I know. You're a cheerleader. I really hope to make the team next year. My name's Caitlin."

She didn't say her last name, trying to hide the fact she was the spawn of faculty.

"Yeah, sure, I've seen you around the gym. That's great you want to be a cheerleader," I said, feigning enthusiasm. "Are you any good?"

She blushed. "I hope so. I take gymnastics, and I took dance all through childhood."

"Really? That's good. You know, I started in ballet."

This was true. When my mother was alive, she had been obsessed with turning me into a music box princess.

"Wow," Caitlin said. "I did some ballet when I was real little, but I didn't like it as much as other types of dance. It hurt my feet and my back."

"Well, no pain no gain," I said.

"Yeah, I guess so. My balance is pretty good now though."

"That's very important. Crucial really. People don't realize how dangerous cheerleading is. Those boys on the field think their sports are a big war, but they're wearing all sorts of protective gear. We're being thrown upside down in the air with nothing but a skirt, in a field or on hard gym floors with no mats. We could get seriously injured, even paralyzed. It happens."

She looked at her pizza. "Scary, huh?"

"Yeah. But maybe that's half the fun."

I winked and she smiled as she picked up the slice of pizza. I let her chew for a minute and sipped my diet soda.

"Maybe I could help you," I said.

Her mouth fell open. "Seriously?"

"Sure. I mean, if you want."

"Oh, absolutely!"

"I figure I could teach you some moves so you'll be ahead of the other girls when try-out time comes."

Her fingers went to her parted lips. "Oh, Kim, that would be amazing!"

I laughed warmly, like a new friend would. She had no reason to distrust me. I was not one of those popular girls who publicly bullied the less fortunate.

"I mean, why not, right?" I said. "It'll be fun. Besides, it's up to us cheerleaders to pass the torch, you know?"

She smiled like a damned idiot, on the verge of squealing.

"When do you want to start?" I asked.

She could hardly sit still. "Oh, like, whenever you want."

"Well, no time like the present. I can come by your house this afternoon."

Mr. Blakley kept his eyes on his papers as the class filed in, totally ignoring me. He played the rest of the movie and barely interacted with us at all. The second half of the film was sappy and derivative, with the teen girl struggling to deal with being young and knocked up. It ended just in time for the bell to ring, and while I had thought about being the last one out again, instead I decided to play things cool and not interact with him, at least for now. We did not make eye contact even once.

After school I drove to Dick's Sporting Goods to buy a pair of pompoms for my new friend Caitlin, finding a pair that closely resembled our team's maroon and gray combo. I'd told her I had plans early in the afternoon, but would be by around five, figuring Mr. Blakley would be home by then. Amy called while I was driving home.

"What are you up to?"

"Just heading home."

"You have the whole place to yourself," she said. "Don't you think you should invite your best friend over?"

I cursed myself for not sending her call to voicemail.

"Um, not tonight, okay?"

She sighed. "Why not?"

"I have to catch up on some reading, and I haven't worked out in days."

"Oh, big deal. I say we drink some wine, eat cookie dough ice cream, and binge watch *Pretty Little Liars*."

"Maybe tomorrow, okay? He'll be gone for weeks, Amy. There's no rush."

"Oh, all right." She huffed, but then turned warmer. "You know what we should do? We should have a party."

"No way. No parties in my house."

Father would have hate that, and frankly I have would too. I did not trust people enough to have them in my house with little supervision. The thought of a party filled me with paranoid visions of drunken teens raiding our medicine cabinet, screwing in Father's bed, and having sticky fingers when it came to small valuables.

"Just a small one," Amy said. "Just our close friends."

"Just *the boys*, you mean."

"No, I don't. Sure, I mean them, but also our squad—Dakota, Brittany, Tanner and maybe Ashton."

Christ, the most popular kids in school. It was so nauseatingly Amy.

"I don't think so . . ."

But then a thought shut me up.

Caitlin.

If I worked on cheerleading with her and developed a strong facade of friendship, and then invited her to a party with these high school celebrities, she would be spellbound and would do just about anything I asked of her from that point on. She would become my new pet, circling my feet each day, asking what to do next to earn her kibble.

"*Buuuuut?*" Amy said, sensing my change of heart.

"Okay. But we keep it small and invite only. You can invite your guests and I'll invite mine."

───────────◆───────────

I got to the Blakley house a little before five. It was a modest, two story home, smaller than my own and with not much of a yard. The sight of Mr. Blakley's sedan in the driveway gave me a warm flash, as did the sight of the silver Hyundai beside it. I hoped it belonged to his wife.

I checked my hair and got out of the car, the new pompoms in my duffle bag along with my own. I had changed into my cheerleader uniform and wore knee high socks to emphasize my youth. I'd even put my hair in pigtails.

The doorbell rang.

The woman who answered smiled wide when she saw my uniform.

"Oh, hello!"

"Mrs. Blakley?"

"Yes, you must be Caitlin's friend."

She seemed even more excited to have me there than Caitlin was. She was the mother of an aspiring cheerleader, after all. These women live through their daughters and will do anything to gain an inside track. My return smile was genuine. Things were going far better than I ever could have hoped.

Mrs. Blakley stepped aside and let me in. She had dyed blond hair and her roots were beginning to show. Her face was pretty but there were lines forming around her eyes and stretched out across her forehead. I could tell she had once been thin; while she wasn't really fat, she had never lost all of the baby weight. After Mr. Blakley's comment about how tight I was, I imagined her pussy as a gaping tunnel of loose viscera.

Stepping into the living room, I saw the house was clean and yet cluttered, with clothing draped over the backs of chairs and magazines and remotes scattered on tables. A cartoon was on the television and a boy of about five sat before it, surrounded by action figures and letter blocks. He did not look away from the screen as I entered.

"Can I get you something to drink?" Mrs. Blakley asked. "Lemonade? Soda?"

"Um, sure. Diet soda is good, thank you."

She led me around a wall toward the kitchen. Mr. Blakley was sitting at the table, eating a sandwich while grading papers.

"What's your name, honey?" the mother asked me.

"Kim. Kim White."

Mr. Blakley looked up at me and instantly froze with tension. A blob of peanut butter squeezed from his sandwich and fell onto one of the papers with a splat. He did not move. His stare was unwavering; the man didn't even blink. His wife was bent into the fridge and did not notice this awkwardness, and when she came up with a can of soda he looked back at the table as if he were still working. He even moved his pen around for effect.

"Bob, this is Kim. She's a friend of Caitlin's, a cheerleader."

He looked up and nodded like he was meeting me for the first time. "Hello."

"Hi, Bob," I said.

This familiarity made Mrs. Blakley glance at me and then at her husband.

"I'm in his class," I said. "He's always very laid back, and he told me to just call him Bob."

She was surprised. "Bob, I didn't know that."

"Well," he said, "I think it makes the students feel more comfortable."

I admired the speed of his cover up.

"He's a great teacher," I said. "Especially when it comes to our sexual education."

His wife was turned toward me, which gave Mr. Blakley a chance to scowl in my direction. The rage that soured his face made my nipples harden, giving me an inexplicable craving for a rare steak.

"Well," his wife said, "why don't you just call me Simone."

She put her hand on my shoulder and I grinned at her with the same lips that had sucked off her husband the night before.

"Okay, Simone."

"I'll just get Caitlin down for you."

She moved past me and out of the kitchen. She was on the other side of the wall now, and I waited a moment before following her. Mr. Blakley stared at me and I stared back, winked, and then blew him a kiss. His face was on fire as I walked away to join his wife in his living room, in his house, where his little boy was playing and his only daughter prepared herself for me upstairs. The moment Simone called up the stairwell I heard fast footfalls above, and then Caitlin rushed down the stairs, dressed in a gymnast leotard which made her look younger than her fifteen years.

"Hey!" she said, all smiles. "I heard you come in, I just wanted to change first."

"Cool. You ready to rock?"

"Absolutely!"

I gave her a best buddies smile and put my bag down on the top of the couch and opened it up. When I gave her the pompoms her face lit up like a fireworks show. Simone was still standing with us, a bit of mist in her eyes. Joy had just walked into their house, promising the near-future fruition of their dreams. There was an instant trust here, a sisterly kinship I didn't even have to earn.

"These are for you," I said.

Caitlin bounced on her toes and gave me a hug that was hard for me to endure, but I did not let my mask break. Simone, not wanting to impose on our moment, stepped back around the wall. Caitlin was saying something to me now about the backyard setup, but my ears were tuned to the kitchen where Simone was whispering to her husband, telling him how nice of a girl I was.

We spent the afternoon in the backyard and continued working even after it was full dark, using the porch light to make our flips and splits. Caitlin was actually very good, but I didn't praise her too much. I wanted her to feel like she needed my help. I gave her criticism in a constructive manner, firm but not cruel. I told her what she was doing right, but put more focus on what she needed to improve upon and even change. She eagerly agreed when I told her we should practice regularly, thanking me profusely for my time and wisdom.

Around eight-thirty we came back inside. Mr. Blakley had gone upstairs, but Simone was in the living room, sitting in a recliner that gave her a view of the yard through the sliding glass door. When she saw us coming she turned her attention toward the television, but Caitlin and I both knew she had been watching us most of the evening, and once we were inside Simone stood to greet us as if we'd been away for months.

"How'd it go?" she asked, more to me than her daughter.

"Good. Caitlin has a lot of talent."

Simone's face was prideful, almost smug. For some reason it made me think of how Mr. Blakley had complained about her not putting out enough for him. It made sense to me. I had a real hard time trying to picture this woman having sex. She was too much like a TV mom—kindly in a schmaltzy way and rendered sexless by that very pleasantry. It was as if she'd had kids via the stork. I imagined the sight of a hard cock would make her faint.

"Well," she said, "we're just so appreciative of you helping her, Kim. If there's *anything* you need from me to help things along, you just name it."

"Thank you, Simone. But it's my pleasure, really."

Her smile revealed a gap between her front two teeth. "You know, I held off on serving dinner so you two could keep working. Why don't you stay and eat with us?"

I'd been hoping for this. "Oh, I wouldn't want to impose."

"Nonsense. We'd be happy to have you."

I pretended to mull it over for a second before answering. "I'd love to."

I was tempted to ask if I could take a shower first, so Mr. Blakley could picture me naked and glistening, but I figured I'd save that card for a future visit. I was already so ahead. It would be best to ration out my aces. Caitlin invited me upstairs to change. She and the little boy's bedrooms were open, but the third bedroom door was only open a crack. It was silent inside. Caitlin changed in her room and I changed in the bathroom, putting on the tight jeans and shirt I'd brought along in my bag. There were two toothbrushes in a cup on the counter, one pink and the other small with Batman logos on it. I used them to scrub the sweat out of my crotch and then put them back. When we got downstairs the rest of the family was sitting with a meatloaf steaming in a tray. Mr. Blakley sat with his elbows on the table and his hands locked under his chin, his son beside him marching a Ninja Turtle across the tabletop. The chair on the other side of him was empty, so I sat down in it, scooting it closer to him.

As we ate, Simone grilled me about the cheerleading team, our coach Mrs. Morrell, and my background in the sport, rattling off so many questions I could barely eat. Occasionally Mr. Blakley would glance over at me, probably trying to convey some sort of warning, but I ignored him. His unhappiness was palpable, and his wife picked up on it.

"Is your meatloaf okay, honey?" she asked.

He looked up as if he'd just bobbed out of freezing water. "Yeah. Great. It's great."

There was a hint of annoyance in her eyes, but she put it aside to continue the cheerleader talk. Caitlin jumped in from time to time, but for the most part her mother dominated the conversation, much as I suspected she dominated her daughter's pathetic life.

When I saw an opportunity to change the subject, I did. I turned to Mr. Blakley.

"Bob," I said, "I have a question, about what we were talking about in class the other day."

Mr. Blakley stopped chewing. He stared at his food, picking at it. "Oh?"

"Yes. It's about semen."

Simone stirred uncomfortably. "Oh, my," she said, looking toward the boy.

I feigned worry. "I'm sorry, is this not . . ."

Mr. Blakley turned to me, his tone firm. "It's not appropriate dinner conversation, Kim. Maybe wait until tomorrow, in class."

"Oh, no, no, it's fine," Simone said. "Let me just take Dalton to the living room with his food. He can watch some cartoons."

I was the cheerleader. In this house I could get away with what others couldn't.

"Simone," Mr. Blakley said, "you know he won't eat if he's watching TV."

"It's *fine*, Bob."

There was a subtle edge to her voice as she escorted Dalton toward the living room, carrying his plate. Caitlin watched them go, and with her attention turned away, I reached under the table and gave Mr. Blakley's crotch a quick rub. His fork clanked on the plate and I took my hand away just before his daughter looked at him. He couldn't get up from the table just yet. He would be avoiding my question and ignoring important company. For this his wife would eviscerate him, later on when they were alone. The sound of a Sponge Bob cartoon carried from the living room as Simone came back to the table.

"Okay," she said. "You can go ahead, Kim."

I batted my eyes with innocence. "I was wondering how it operates. Is it true the sperm from a single male will attack other sperms and even set traps for them, to try to keep them from the egg?"

I saw Caitlin shift in her seat. Simone drew her lips tight.

"Yes, that's true," Mr. Blakley said, keeping it at that.

I went up a gear. "Well, I also wanted to know about stimulation."

The whole room seemed to come to a halt, six lungs stopping.

I gave him the doe eyes. "How do both partners get the stimulation they need, especially if the sex doesn't last long?"

I was *really* pushing it, I knew. But I couldn't resist. The tension was a thick, raw thing now. It writhed in the secret corruption Mr. Blakley and I shared. Simone forced a smile. Caitlin's face was a strawberry. I had the whole damn family now.

Mr. Blakley was curt. "That's not the sort of thing I teach in class, and you know that. We study safety and reproduction. That's it."

I feigned an embarrassed little laugh. "I'm sorry. This is all foreign to me. It's just been on mind . . . since Friday."

I let the reference to our date linger like a stench. Caitlin jumped in, willing to say anything to not have to hear her father talk about sex anymore. "So, Kim, do you want to try and work on jump drills and V-ups next time?"

"We could do those. Maybe some straddles too."

Mr. Blakley had had enough. He stood. "I, um, need to get back to grading those papers."

"You've been at it all afternoon," Simone said. "How many papers do you have to grade?"

"I'm just a little swamped, okay?"

He took his plate to the sink and rinsed the remains of his dinner down the disposal.

"Well, all right," Simone said.

He had to pass by me to get to the stairs.

"Goodnight, Bob," I said, grinning like the reaper. "See you tomorrow."

SIX

He was ready for me the next day.

Mr. Blakley avoided the topic of sex during class, sticking to information about the post-coitus reproductive process. Just as the period ended, he approached me.

"Kim, see me after class."

He waited for the rest of the students to leave, then gave me his best death stare, his face like granite, eyes piss holes in the snow. He stood close and pointed a finger just an inch from my face.

"Just what do you think you're doing, you little bitch?"

His use of profanity made me giggle.

"You think I'm fucking around here?" he asked.

"No. I just think you're cute."

"I'm not cute, you goddamned slut, I'm pissed off. How dare you come to my *house*. Are you insane? You want to fuck with me, I'll show you who you're fucking with."

He opened a folder on his desk and slid a sheet of paper over to me. It was a referral, the kind you take to the dean's office when a teacher wants you to be reprimanded. I'd never received one in my whole life.

"Are you kidding?" I asked.

"Do I look like I'm kidding?"

"What are you writing me up for?"

"Being disruptive and inappropriate in class."

"What? I never did anything like that."

"Well, I say you did, and they're not exactly going to ask your classmates about it, now are they?"

I glanced at the paper. He had quoted me as using bad language and making crude sex jokes.

"You want to play whore," he said, "then I'm gonna discipline you like one. You're an honor roll student. I know how important your permanent record is to you. Unless you cut the shit you'll be seeing a lot of these."

I held the paper up and slowly tore it in half.

"You just earned another one," he said.

"The hell I did. You're not going to do this to me, Mr. Blakley."

"Oh no?"

"No. Your wife and daughter want me at your house as much as possible. They have big, pretty, pompom dreams."

"Enough trips to the dean and you'll be off the team. One way or another, you won't be around my house and family anymore."

I laughed. "Yeah, but *you'll* be the one to have caused that. Students get a copy of each slip. I'll show this to Caitlin today and work up some tears, telling her I'm worried that *you'll* get me booted off the team. How do you think your family will take it when I stop coming over to help Caitlin because I'm so afraid of you?"

Mr. Blakley fell slack, cornered.

"Here's how it's going to be," I said. "You're not going to write me up for jack shit. In fact, I'm excused from all homework and get automatic 'A's from here on in. And you're gonna be a total sweetheart to me when I come over."

He didn't say anything, just stared.

I patted his shoulder. "Don't be so grumpy. You be good and there might just be some more pussy in this for you."

Seeing his fists ball, I stepped back, relieved when a pair of girls walked into the room.

I made plans with Caitlin to practice on Thursday. Amy was pushing to have the party that weekend, but I wanted more time to work on my prey, to gain her complete trust and obedience. I told Amy I wanted to give our guests more notice, and we settled on having the party two weekends later.

Mr. Blakley and I ignored one another at school, and when I went over to his house on Thursday he was conveniently absent. Something told me he would be working late more often and would be having a lot of teacher's meetings. But he couldn't bail every time I came over. It would raise questions. In addition, I decided to drop by unannounced now and then.

My extreme horror movies arrived and I did double features every evening in my room, getting tipsy on chardonnay and fingering myself to scenes of violence, torture and rape. I was in the middle of watching the infamous baby scene in *A Serbian Film* when my phone rang. It was Derek again. I'd talked to him a little at school but only in between classes. If I didn't pay him some attention soon he would either start whining or give up on gaining my affections all together, and I didn't want that. I wasn't sure what I needed him for, but it never hurts to have a lap dog.

I paused the movie but kept my hand in my panties.

"Hello, Derek," I said.

"Whoa, hey there, Kim," he chuckled. "I thought you might be avoiding me or something."

I rubbed myself but kept my voice normal. "I have no reason to do that."

"What are you up to?"

"Just watching a movie."

"Oh yeah? Which one?"

"*A Serbian Film.*"

"Oh. Foreign, huh?" He sounded bummed. Derek wasn't exactly keen on other cultures. "I didn't know you liked those. Say, maybe we could go to a movie together tomorrow?"

I slipped two fingers inside my sex and slowly curled them as I imagined using a chain to hoist Derek up over my bed. I was in the mood for play. I was also hungry, and didn't feel like cooking.

"Why don't we get together tonight?" I said.

"Really?"

"Unless you're busy."

"Oh, shit no."

"Why don't you pick me up and we'll go get something to eat."

After ending the call I changed clothes but didn't bothering dolling myself up for him, not wanting to give him the impression I wanted to impress him with my appearance. Dressing down and wearing little makeup would be like an insult to our date, a hint at a friends-only relationship.

He got to my house at six-thirty in his Dodge Charger. He was dressed in his Sunday best sans tie, his hair was full of product, and he smelled like a freshly mopped floor. We made small talk as we headed into town. There was a light crawl of fog in the streets and a layer of gray in the early night sky. He asked me where I wanted to eat and I told him I didn't really care, and the schmuck took me to an Applebee's, not exactly the best way to impress a girl. We ordered and, bored with the small talk, I decided to make things interesting.

"Say, Derek. What's the kinkiest thing you've ever done?"

He blinked, sniffed. "Whoa . . . Um . . ." He chuckled again, a boy suddenly thrust into a woman's world. "Um . . ."

"Never mind," I said. "You don't have to tell me."

He dove for the save. "No, no, I want to. I was just, you know, surprised."

"Don't you like surprises?"

"Hell yeah." He sat upright in the booth, all strutting cock now. "You bet I do."

"So then spill it. What's the kinkiest thing you've ever done?"

He took a moment. "Well, I had sex with a girl in—"

"Who? What's her name?"

"Cassie Boone." His ex-girlfriend, the sort of neutral girl you forget about the moment you meet her. "Don't spread it around school, but we had sex in public sometimes."

"Like where?"

"Well, the beach . . ."

I rolled my eyes. "You ever tie her up?"

He paused. "You mean, like, with ropes?"

"Ropes, handcuffs—anything."

The dumb chuckle again. "Is that what you're into?"

"You keep answering my questions with questions."

"Fine—no. I never tied her up."

"Did she ever tie you up?"

"No."

"How come?"

He shrugged. "I dunno. Just never came up. I don't think she was the type."

"Are you the type?"

The deep voice again. "I could be."

Before he could get too confident, I shifted. "Is Brian the type?"

"What?"

"There you go again with the questions."

"But why are you asking me about Brian?"

"Just curious. Did he tell you he ties up Amy?"

"No. Do they really do that?"

"They might. I don't know. But don't you *dare* say anything."

Again with the damned chuckling. "Okay, I won't. What are you talking about all this for, Kim?"

I was merely planting seeds in my garden of shit. "I dunno. No reason, I guess. But hey, anyway, I don't know if Amy told you yet but I'm having a party the Saturday after next. Hope you'll be there. It's gonna be lit."

"You know it. Yeah, I heard your old man is out of town."

"Don't call him my old man. That makes my skin crawl."

"Okay, sorry, I didn't mean nothing."

It was no big deal. I just liked keeping him walking on eggshells.

Our food arrived and we talked about school, potential plans for college, and all the inane shit teenagers talk about, the kind of monotonous drivel that made me zone out and daydream about cutting myself up and driving screws into the thumbs of my friends. Derek couldn't have been more boring if he was a documentary on pinecones. He was bereft of any individualism, a carbon copy of every other home-team-rooting, flip-cup-playing, chest-bumping meathead in all of the clichéd little suburbs of our cookie cutter country. As he babbled on to combat any possible moments of awkward silence, I imagined hammering knitting needles up into his nostrils to give him an old fashioned lobotomy. I wondered if anyone would even notice a change in him afterwards.

When we were finished he paid the bill and we went to his car. He tapped his hands on the steering wheel. "So what now?"

He had a goony look on his face, and I didn't think about what I did next. It was almost reflexive. I grit my teeth and swung, punching him in the jaw, making his head snap to the side and bump against the window.

"Ow! What the fuck, Kim?"

Part of me hoped he would hit me, but he didn't. He put his hands up but only to protect himself. I knew I couldn't have hurt him that much, but he looked emotionally devastated, and that was stimulating and wonderful.

"What the hell was that for?" he asked.

"Just having some fun."

I put my hand on his leg and scratched my nails on his jeans in a playful manner. The shock on his face made it worth having gone out tonight.

"You *hit* me."

"Did you like it?"

His face paled. "What? Why would I like it?"

"You wanna hit me back?"

"What? No, you're a girl."

"But fair is fair. An eye for an eye."

"I'm not gonna hit you, Kim!"

I swung at him again and he blocked the first blow but I came at him with my other hand, pounding his forehead. It probably hurt me more than him, but he fussed and winced, so I started smacking him in the face.

"Stop!" he cried.

"Make me." I had slid over in the seat, climbing onto him. "Come on, faggot."

He tried to grab my wrists but I was too nimble from cheerleading, my movements fast and fluid. I was nearly in his lap now. Grabbing his hair, I bent his head back and he groaned in pain as I gave him another smack across the mouth. He pushed me and I hit the steering wheel, honking the horn, and I moved between his arms and straddled him, laughing. He was still going for my wrists when I began to grind my crotch against his. I stopped hitting him so he wouldn't be distracted, and he blinked at me, unsure what was happening.

"What are you . . .?"

I put a finger to his lips. "*Shhh.*"

I rolled my hips and pushed into the lump in his jeans. He mellowed but kept breathing heavy, the stupid look on his face filling me with bloodlust. Derek seemed confused and uncertain, but he was clearly enjoying this part, as I could feel him hardening beneath me. When he dared to reach up for my breasts I smacked him again but kept riding him. Derek didn't know what to do and that amused me, so I slid off of him and whispered in his ear.

"Take out your cock."

"We're in a parking lot. Let's go back to your house."

"No. It's here or nowhere."

"Someone will see us."

"Maybe; maybe not. Take it out."

He looked around and I could see the pink marks on his face where I'd hit him. We were parked near the back of the building where there was little light, and the car's windows had fogged, creating a snowy illusion of privacy. He was still hesitant, but a stiff dick has no sense. He undid his belt and in a moment his hard-on flopped out like a beached dolphin. It was a bit longer than Mr. Blakley's but had an ugly mole in the center of it. I took it in my hand and started jerking him off. I did it fast and hard and his legs shuddered, feet wiggling.

"Holy shit," he said.

I kept going. I still had zero desire to have sex with Derek. This wasn't about sex—at least not for me; this was about dominance. I was giving him pleasure, but was also inflicting pain and making him fear me while still being aroused. I was taking control of him.

"This is it for tonight," I said. "So tell me when you're getting close."

A few moments later he was moaning and his eyes rolled up. "Oh, yeah. I'm gonna come. Don't stop."

I stopped immediately.

His eyes snapped open. "Come on, come on!"

He grabbed my hand and put it back on his dick. I pulled away and smacked him.

"What the fuck, Kim?" He grabbed his twitching cock. "What're you doing?"

"Make me finish you," I said.

He gave me the same dumb look he'd been giving me since we'd started. "You want me to . . . ?"

"*Force me* to finish you."

I'd reached Derek's breaking point. He went red and reached for my hands, thrusting them toward his flapping genitalia in a fit of frustration. I writhed away and that's when he grabbed my hair and started lowering my head to his crotch. At last my loins began to stir.

"You want this?" he asked.

"For Christ's sake, don't ask, faggot, just take."

As he tried to force his way into my mouth I snapped my teeth at him, so he grabbed a fistful of my hair and jerked off with his dick pressed to my face. His sperm splashed hot on my cheek, one big glob spilling down to my lips. I slurped it into my mouth and the taste was like hot snot. Derek wobbled there on his knees and his grip on my hair loosened, so I got up and spit his own cum into his face.

"Aw!" he yelled, wiping it away with his sleeve.

My crotch was on fire, but the whole scene was so absurd I started laughing hysterically. Derek looked at me as if I was playing with my own excrement.

"What the fuck is wrong with you?" he asked.

"Says the guy who just came on my face."

"I was trying to . . . you know . . ."

"Yeah, yeah. But this is our secret, understand?"

"Oh, yeah, sure."

"Yeah, right. Like you kept fucking Cassie on the beach a secret?"

He looked away, shamed.

"I'm serious, Derek. If you tell this to *anyone*, and it gets back to me, I will break down and cry date rape."

Derek tensed. "Whoa, wait a minute, you said that—"

"We ate dinner and you took me home. Nobody's gonna believe I finally did anything with you anyway. They'll be more likely to believe you forced yourself on me. Just be good and there might be some more fun in this for you."

Now I had two swinging dicks at my command.

SEVEN

"You're doing great!"

Caitlin smiled with her whole body. We were practicing on the trampoline in my backyard. The day was warm and sunny and it seemed to make her extra bubbly.

"I can't believe how much I've learned," she said.

I helped her down and she took a long drink from the water bottle. Her nubile body was glistening with sweat, her dirty blond ponytail coming loose. She was flushed and it made her look younger, a rosy-cheeked girl on Santa's lap.

She took her inhaler from her gym bag and puffed it.

"How's your asthma, anyway?" I asked.

"Oh, it's okay."

"Cheerleading takes the wind out of you, you know?"

"It's not as bad as it used to be. I can manage."

Her cuteness made me want to bury her face into my snatch until she suffocated to death. Instead, I nudged her with my elbow in a chummy fashion.

"You're gonna be a shoo-in next year."

She moved in closer. "Thanks to you."

"Hey, not just anybody would be able to do what I've been teaching you. You've got talent and discipline."

"I've been working on the routines you gave me every day. My mom has been helping me."

"Simone's great. She's so supportive."

We sat down in the lawn chairs.

"Your mom must be so proud of you too," Caitlin said. "You're so successful."

"Oh, well, my mother's dead."

Caitlin crumbled as if she'd hurt her chest. "Oh, gosh. I'm sorry, I didn't know."

"It's okay. It was a long time ago."

"What about your dad?"

"Yeah, he's alive. You just haven't seen him because he's out of town. I'm an only child, so the house has been all mine."

Her eyebrows rose. "Wow. That's so cool. My folks would never leave me alone. They act like I'm just a little kid."

"I had a nanny when I was younger, but when I turned twelve Father said I was ready to handle the house on my own when he goes away. It gets lonely sometimes."

It was true I'd been left alone since I was twelve, but loneliness was an emotion I had never had nor understood. I was just throwing Caitlin some bait.

"Well, hey," she said. "Maybe I could spend the night some time." I looked at her but stayed silent. I saw the doubt fall over her and watched her back paddle. "I mean," she babbled, "you know, like, if you ever want to. I know you don't need me to, I didn't mean it like that. I know you have plenty of friends to hang out with. You're so popular."

"Yeah," I said with a sigh, "but you know, I didn't just *become* popular. It's something you have to work at, just like cheerleading and schoolwork."

She nodded. "I guess so. I wouldn't know."

"I'm going to help you with that too. Just remember, it's hard work. Sometimes you have to do things you don't want to."

"Kind of like when you have to work out, even though you just want to lay around and watch Netflix, right?"

"More than that, Caitlin, more than that. Remember, there's more to being a cheerleader than just backflips. You represent all the girls of the school. If they don't look up to you, and even envy you, then you'll never make it."

I savored the self-doubt I'd put in her eyes.

"Don't worry," I told her. "I'll show you the way."

"Thanks, Kim. You're the greatest."

She is so easy to tame, I thought. *You'd think I had her on a shock collar.* The mental image of that made me giggle, so I shifted the conversation.

"Anyway, I appreciate you wanting to keep me company, Caitlin. But I don't think your folks would like you sleeping over with my father being out of town. They might think we were going to sneak over some boys."

Now it was Caitlin who giggled.

"What?" I said. "You've never sneaked around with a boy before?"

"I dunno. Not really."

"No boyfriends?"

"No. I mean, you know, I've been on dates, but nothing serious."

She crossed her hands between her legs, feet bobbing them up and down.

"You ever *do* anything with them?" I asked.

Her eyes went wide but she was still smiling. "Kim!"

"Come on. I'll tell you what I've done. It's scandalous."

"Oh my God." She started to laugh in the way young girls do.

"Just between you and me," I said. "What do you think, that I'm gonna tell your mom or something?"

"You'd better not!"

Now I laughed. "So come on, what was his name?"

She looked away, shook her head. "No, no."

"So . . . are you still, you know, a . . ."

"Kim! You're so bad!"

But she was laughing, jittering like she was about to jump up and down at any second.

"Can you keep a secret?" I asked.

She nodded. "Sure."

I leaned in close and she did the same.

"I just lost my virginity," I said.

Caitlin put her hands over her mouth. "You did?"

"Yeah. And to an older guy."

"Nu-uh."

"It's true."

"Was he a senior?"

"Nope. Older."

"Whoa. So, like, college?"

"Well, he's certainly an academic."

She wiggled in her seat and then blurted it out. "I dated a boy for a while and I used to let him, like, feel me up."

We were having a bonding moment I doubted she'd had with anyone else. From the way she acted, I sensed this was the first time she'd told anyone other than her diary.

"Now who's bad?" I teased.

"Hey, we went out for months before I let him."

"Did you feel him up too?"

She blushed again.

"Dirty girl!" I said.

"I just used my hand. And he's the only boy I ever went that far with."

"So what ever happened to this stud?"

"Oh, you know, we just decided to break up."

This probably meant she'd been dumped. Probably because she only gave him her hand.

"What about your guy?" she asked. "Do you still see him?"

"Yeah, all the time."

"So are you guys, like, serious then?"

I pretended to mull it over. "Well, *he* sure takes things seriously. Between you and me, I'm just having fun right now."

"Wow, that's so cool. You call the shots."

"Totally."

We gushed for a bit.

"Can I ask you something?" she said.

"Sure."

She hesitated but I knew what was coming.

"What's it like to go all the way?"

I told her everything Amy had told me, all the bullshit about how it's a life changing experience and how nothing is ever the same afterward. I spoke of tenderness and passionate closeness, a joining of two souls in the ultimate expression of love. It was all high, magic talk and she hung on my every word, eyes unblinking.

"Wow," she said. "It sounds so romantic."

EIGHT

I woke up early on Friday because of discomfort. My breasts were tender for no real reason. I hadn't been playing with them and neither had anyone else, but it felt like they'd been pinched and bruised, and I went to the bathroom to look at them. They appeared normal, but even the movement caused by walking around made them ache. I put on one of my more supportive bras, wondering if this had something to do with my period. It wasn't due for another week.

When I got to school Amy was standing by our lockers with Brian and Derek. I had seen Derek around school of course, but we kept our interactions short and didn't change our behavior in front of friends. We didn't speak of what happened, but we didn't turn cold to one another either. It was as if it had never happened, or at least that's how we acted. I was confident he hadn't opened his mouth, not even to Brian, for if he had, Brian would have looked at me funny before collecting himself.

"Everybody's stoked for the party next weekend," Amy said.

Brian put his arm around her. "Totally. Don't worry, Kim, my brother can get us some twelve packs."

"We should have some good snacks," Amy said. "Maybe we can order some pizzas. And we'll need a great mix too. I'll make a playlist for us."

It was my house, but this was going to be Amy's party. That was fine by me. It meant less work on my part, so I could focus on more important things, like bonding with Caitlin and her mother and stressing out Mr. Blakley. I had continued to miss him in my visits to the house and I wanted to rectify that. He was due for some emotional torture.

Amy continued. "You know, Kim, you still haven't told me your guest list. Who else are you inviting?"

"Mandy and Summer will be coming."

They were two other cheerleaders. I wanted as many as possible there for Caitlin. I hadn't invited her just yet, but I knew she would be there.

"Mandy Clark?" Amy asked.

"Yeah."

She snorted. "Well good, I can finally ask her if that's acne or just scars from dodging the coat hanger for nine months."

Brian blinked at his girlfriend. "Damn!"

"I didn't know you hated Mandy," I said.

"I don't," Amy said. "She's just a skank. But if you want to invite her . . ."

"There's also another girl who I'm sort of showing the ropes to, for cheerleading."

Amy smirked. "You're teaching now?"

"Just more to add to the old college application."

She moved on. "Okay, well, Tanner and Dakota will be there. Brittany has some family thing she needs to get out of. Ashton says he could swing by but he wanted to bring some friends."

"No."

Ashton was an extremely popular senior—a star running back with shaggy hair and a smile that dropped panties. Given half the chance, Amy would have torn hers right off for him. Only I knew how bad she had it for him. She was still involved with Brian and insisted her crush was harmless, but every time she was around Ashton she fluttered like a crackhead butterfly. Even if she didn't really want to make a move on him, getting him to our party would be a broad power stroke for her. Amy was already one of the greats in our grade, but this would add another notch to her gun belt (or possibly headboard).

"He's not going to bring a lot of people," she said. "Just one or two."

"I don't want anyone I don't know in my house. I know Ashton. He's wild enough without having his crazy friends around."

"He has college friends, Kim. *College.*"

"Not in my house."

Amy was about to object, but she could see I wasn't going to budge on this. She'd already convinced me to have a party. She knew when to settle, at least with me.

"Okay, I'll tell him to come alone. Not sure if he will though."

"That's, like, ten people," Derek said. "Not much of a party."

"It's big enough," I said. "The people who matter will be there."

I went by the Blakley house later that afternoon, unannounced. My breasts were still hurting so I wouldn't be doing any exercises, but I figured I could still run Caitlin through the drills. Mainly I wanted to see Mr. Blakley, to torment him in one way or another—maybe tease him by slowly eating a banana or making some more double entendres around his wife and children. I hadn't decided what I was going to do yet. Some things you just improvise.

This time it really paid off.

His car was in the driveway but Simone's was not. I parked and walked up the steps and rang the bell. The house was quiet. No cartoons or voices. I heard muffled footsteps on the stairs, and a moment later the door came open. Mr. Blakley was still in his school clothes but his tie was loose, shirt halfway unbuttoned.

His eyes were like rusty nails. "They're not here."

"Where'd they run off to?"

"Simone took Caitlin and Dalton to see her sister."

I smirked. "Having a lovers' spat?"

"No. They're just visiting today, and I like some alone time now and then."

I stepped up. "Well then I came at just the right time."

He put up a hand. "Oh, you have got to be kidding me. You are *not* coming in."

"Hey, you said you wanted to make that lame sex up to me, right? Now's your chance, Mr. Blakley."

"Damn it, I'm not playing this game with you."

I tried to nudge my way in, pressing my breasts up against him. He wouldn't budge at first, but then there was the sound of people talking across the street and Mr. Blakley panicked and hurried me inside and closed the door.

"The last thing I need is my neighbors seeing you here," he said.

"Oh, I'm here all the time. No one will know the difference."

I wasted no time pulling my shirt over my head and Mr. Blakley sighed but kept looking at my breasts and body. I tossed the shirt, kicked out of my shoes and fluffed my hair.

"You really need to leave," Mr. Blakley said. "They could come back at any time."

"That just makes it all the more exciting."

"You really are nuts aren't you? If we get caught . . ."

I walked up to him and grabbed him by the belt. "The sooner you get on with it, the sooner I leave."

I undid his buckle and fly and slipped my hand in. Despite how he felt about me, his dick had a different opinion. His posture relaxed as I took hold of his growing erection, and I used it to guide him toward the stairs.

He muttered as we walked up. "This is bad. You should go."

When we got up to the landing I kissed his neck, slowly went down on my knees and took his manhood in my mouth, knowing how he liked that. He put his hand on my back, helped me up, and tried to guide me toward his bedroom.

"Not in there," I said.

"What?"

I pointed to Caitlin's room. "Fuck me where your daughter sleeps."

His chest rose and fell. "Kim . . . come on . . ."

I unbuttoned my jeans and wiggled out of them and my panties. Standing there naked, I turned to show the soft, white peach of my buttocks. His pants were taut at his knees, his erection pointing toward the ceiling, still slick with my saliva. He hoisted up his pants so he could walk toward me, and when he got to me he slid his hand beneath my sex. I let him touch me for a moment, then took him by his tie and led him into the room.

Caitlin's bed was unmade and there were some clothes and books scattered about. One of the drawers of her dresser was partly open, revealing balled up underwear and her A-cup bras. I reached in and took out a pair of her panties, pink with little ladybugs on them. Mr. Blakley watched as I slid them on. I turned around and bent over the dresser, pulling Caitlin's panties to one side to expose my glistening sex.

"Stick it in me, Daddy."

He did.

We didn't get caught.

To my surprise, Mr. Blakley lasted longer than he had a couple of weeks ago. The physical aspect of sex still felt weird to me, but the wrongness of what we were doing prickled me with a lustrous ecstasy. I called him Daddy the whole time he fucked me, but he refused to call me Caitlin when I told him to, so I reached between our legs and squeezed his balls and threatened to stop fucking him until he did. Her name was like acid in his mouth. He spit it out. This time when he climaxed he pulled out, and when I felt that first sperm hit my back I moved out of the way so his load spattered across his daughter's dresser, much of it sprinkling her drawer full of underwear. The look of self-loathing on his face when he realized what he'd done was something I would cherish always.

I patted my sex dry with her *PINK* sweatshirt and then gathered my things while he cleaned his crotch in the bathroom, murmuring to himself. When I put on my jeans I skipped putting on my panties and stared at his open bedroom door as I held them in my hands. He was still in the bathroom with the door closed. I could try and sneak my underwear under the bed in the hopes Simone would find them. I certainly wanted to ruin his marriage. But the problem there was he might just crack and tell her about me. It was unlikely he'd admit his mistress was a teenager (if I were him I would claim it was some woman my own age), but I didn't want to risk it. My degradation of Mr. Blakley had become much bigger than a mere assault on his marriage. Besides, I didn't want the game to end just yet, not when I had so many more cards to play.

I drove off feeling light and relaxed. I was looking forward to bathing, and my breasts hurt more from having Mr. Blakley's hands all over them, but I was still high from the escapade. I had a terrible craving, so on the way home I stopped at the grocery store and bought a sirloin steak for myself for dinner, which I ate rare with no sides.

NINE

The weekend was uneventful. It went by in a blur of watching abuse porn, hanging out with Amy and Dakota, reading a biography of the female serial killer Aileen Wuornos, and tidying up around the house. I thought about the coming party, about Caitlin and Mr. Blakley, and even about old shit-for-personality Derek. There were all sorts of ideas and plots swirling in my head like a toilet's flush.

On Monday morning I felt bloated and exhausted. I hadn't slept well because my bladder had kept me up. I'd been peeing more frequently, but now it was getting ridiculous. I wondered if I had a urinary tract infection. I'd had them before and they'd given me similar problems. I made a mental note to pick up some concentrated cranberry juice. If that didn't clear things up I'd make a doctor's appointment to get some antibiotics.

After brushing my teeth I slipped out of my nightshirt, and the soft cloth irritated my nipples. When I looked at them, I saw that the areola had darkened.

"What the fuck?" I asked the mirror.

When I slid out of my panties I saw I had some spotting, which I felt confirmed my suspicion of an early period. I changed into a dress so jeans wouldn't squish my puffy stomach. I felt gassy, even a little nauseated, but I loathed the notion of missing school. I had perfect attendance so far this year and I wasn't going to blow it on water retention and cramps. There was a basketball game coming up and I hoped I would feel well enough by then to cheerlead, but knew I'd go through with it regardless.

It was cooler out today, gloomier. It soothed me. I had downloaded a Halloween sound effects album and I listened to it on the way to school, repeating the tracks that were all screams and rattling chains. When I arrived, I saw Dakota standing on the sidewalk, talking to a long-haired boy named Zack. He was the kind of guy that could always be found in detention or hanging out in front of gas stations. When they saw me approaching, Zack whispered something to Dakota and then wandered off, hitching up his jacket like he'd just walked off the set of *Grease*. Dakota had just been to the salon and her black bangs were infuriatingly perfect. She was looking more like a Kardashian every day.

"What's up?" she asked.

"Not much." I rolled me eyes toward Zack. "What was that all about?"

"Hey, don't judge. Zack was hooking us up for the party."

"Hooking us up?"

Dakota wasn't a heavy drug user, but when she partied she went all out. She would bump lines of coke when it was around, but painkillers were her drugs of choice. The rest of our squad wasn't that into drugs—just a little weed here and there. Amy had dabbled in pills herself, but had not enjoyed it. I refrained from drugs with the exception of the Adderall Dakota sometimes got me for when I was cramming for exams.

"Zack's got all kinds of connections nowadays," she said. "He's gonna get me some O.C.s."

I was always surprised at how careless Dakota could be when it came to taking pills. Oxycontin was supposed to be as addictive as heroin but she never seemed concerned about taking it. She was a pretty girl with a curvy body. She would likely get fat when she was older, but at seventeen she was only plump in the right places. This made her very popular with the boys. She was an honor-roller like me and was even involved in highbrow afterschool activities like Odyssey of the Mind and advanced physics. She was book smart as well as street smart. All of this made it even stranger to me she wasn't worried about drugs derailing her life. I could only guess there was some deep, inner pain she was desperate to dull. Maybe she was yearning to shock her parents to get their attention, or maybe she was trying to wash away the memory of being molested by an uncle. It was just a curiosity of mine—I certainly didn't give a shit about her. If anything, I was rooting for the pills to break her down, leaving a pathetic waste of woman where a promising human being had once stood.

"Any other stuff you want for the party?" she asked.

When I thought about my guests I had an epiphany that gave me chills.

Dakota stared at me. "Are you okay?"

"Yeah, fine. Just a little tired, didn't sleep too well."

"I'm sure Zack can get you some Trazodone or Ambien."

"You should be a pharmacist, you know that?"

She batted her lashes. "No way. I'm gonna be a doctor so I can write scripts."

"Well, I think I'm good. Booze is enough for my party." But it wasn't. Not now. "I've got to get to class," I said. "I'll see you later."

We parted ways and I went off to catch Zack.

I did not want Dakota to know about what I was going to ask him for. They were drugs I had heard about many times, as did every teenage girl, the ones they always warned us about.

Zack hadn't gone far. He was standing just outside of L-wing, sneaking a cigarette before the morning bell. *Christ*, I thought, *if he was any more of a cliché he'd be a cartoon character*—messy hair, too many earrings, a t-shirt of the black metal band *Ghost* poking out from inside his leather jacket. I could imagine him at forty, still tacking up rock band posters to the walls of his one-bedroom apartment overlooking the highway, his only savings account in a Mason jar—pennies put aside for a half hour with a Craigslist escort now and then.

"Hey," I said.

It being the first time I ever deigned to speak with him, he looked at me incredulously.

"Yeah? What?" he asked.

"I want to make a special order, on the down low."

His yellowed teeth formed a rictus grin. "Honey, that's the best way to deal."

"I'm having a party in a few days," I said.

Caitlin's face grew bright, her little braces twinkling like tinsel.

"You really ought to come," I said.

"Oh my gosh, yes! When is it?"

"It's on Saturday night. Mandy Clark and Summer Scott will be there." She knew the cheerleaders. I had taught her to learn about them all so she could better buddy up to them. "So is Amy Heidnik and few of my other close friends."

"Oh, man. This is so freakin' awesome."

Caitlin didn't know the importance of playing anything cool. She never even made an effort to hide her excitement. I had learned a way to make someone like you was to mimic their gestures and expressions, but deftly and not in a mocking way. It gave the illusion of familiarity and kinship. I made subtle impressions of her smile, her jittery body language, and her wide, excited eyes.

"There'll be some boys there too," I said. "Brian Wheeler and Derek Schechter, for starters."

"Right, Derek's on the basketball team. I've seen him play. He's really good."

"So you can make it?"

"Of course I can! Oh my god, what should I wear?"

I put a finger to my chin. "Hmmm. Something that makes you look, well, more *mature*, if you know what I mean. Why don't you come over here early and I can give you a makeover?"

"Oh, Kim, this is so cool. Thank you so much."

She surprised me by coming out of her chair and wrapping her arms around me. I held back bile.

"You're such a good friend," she said.

TEN

The house was set for the party. I had wine ready and some bowls of nuts and Chex mix, and as a gag I put out a bowl of condoms. This would get a laugh out of everybody, but it would also get their minds on sex, which was important. Brian and Amy stopped by to drop off the beer, and I had already picked up my drugs from Zack. To top it all off, Father's liquor cabinet was fully stocked.

Caitlin came over at six, two hours before the official start of the party. She was wearing jeans and the *PINK* sweatshirt I had cleaned my pussy with when I had last fucked her dad. A bag was on her shoulder.

"I thought I should dress down for when I left," she said. "My folks think I'm just spending the night so we can work on drills and stuff. For some reason my dad *really* didn't want me to, but my mom made him. There's no way I was gonna tell them about the party."

She opened her bag and took out the dress. It was new—still with tags and stickers. I was impressed by her taste. It was a slick-looking, sleeveless blue dress with a low neckline. It was also small, so it would be tight.

"Nice job, Caitlin," I said, and meant it.

"I used all of my babysitting money I'd saved to get it. I brought high heels too, is that too much?"

"No, no. Heels drive the boys crazy. I'll wear a dress and heels too, so you won't be the only one."

"I'm kinda nervous."

I'd told her how important it was to make a good impression, that these were high caliber guests who could make or break her when it came to being a cheerleader and a popular girl.

"This is a test," I said, "just like any other. You need these people to think you're cool. That means you can't act girlish, okay? Don't shy away from trying new things if everyone else is doing it."

"I won't. I trust you, Kim."

My stomach filled with insects.

We put some curls into her hair and I did her makeup for her. I'd never seen her with anything but a little mascara on, and the extra touches of lipstick and soft eyeshadow really highlighted her best features and accentuated the fact she was budding into womanhood. She looked nearly seventeen instead of fresh out of her training bra.

"You look hot," I said to her reflection in the mirror. "Dang girl, you look *movie-star* hot."

She giggled, aloof in her dazzling new world. Caitlin was so grateful, so innocent. She was more than a sweet girl; she was, at her very core, a good human being.

I put on a dress, but not one as tight as hers, not just because I was still having stomach cramps, but also because I didn't want to attract as much attention as she would get. When Caitlin came out of the bathroom in her dress, I shook my head.

"What?" she asked.

"The dress is perfect, but we need to do something about that."

I pointed at the panty lines showing through the thin material.

"Oh," she giggled. "Oops."

I went to my dresser and pulled out a thong and tossed it to her. She slid her panties off—yellow with fucking little *bicycles* on them—and put mine on. Stepping into the heels turned her toned, gymnast ass into a ripe plum.

"How about a little drink?" I asked. "To soothe the pre-game jitters?"

She squinted. "Oh, um. I dunno. I want to be on my A-game. I don't want to get drunk and make a bad impression."

"You'll be fine, Caitlin. Besides, everyone is going to get a buzz on tonight. You don't want to stand out by not drinking."

"Well, yeah, I guess that's true. But I've only ever had a wine cooler before."

"No problem. You and I can have a glass of wine to start off, and the rest of the night I'll be the one to serve you, okay? That way I can monitor how much you're drinking so you don't have to stress about it."

She let out a breath, relieved. "That's a good idea."

Caitlin puffed her inhaler in preparation for the night, and we went downstairs for our first drink.

The party was going strong by nine-thirty.

Even Ashton the football hero had shown up, which turned Amy's mood around. She'd been pissy for the past hour over my having invited a nobody like Caitlin to drag down the squad goals of her party. Now she was bimbo-level bubbly, openly flirting with her crush, the two glasses of chardonnay lowering her inhibitions, much to Brian's chagrin. I would have to monitor the situation when I could. I did not want a fight to break out, no matter how happy I always was to see blood spilt. This party needed to be jovial and non-threatening so nothing would derail my plan. I didn't even want to hit the smallest of speed bumps.

Taylor Swift was playing and Dakota was dancing with Brittany, Tanner doing the white-boy two-step beside them. When I glanced at them, Dakota was staring at me in admiration. She did this often, and whenever I caught her she smiled cutely and looked away. I introduced Caitlin to the cheerleaders, and the four of us chatted for a while, Caitlin glowing with her second glass of wine in her hand. I was keeping them small. I didn't want her to end up with her head in the toilet. She was gabbing it up with Summer, who seemed to genuinely like her, and while Caitlin's childlike excitement was obvious the other girls seemed to find her enthusiasm endearing. She was maintaining good conversation; I was very proud of her.

"I'll be right back," I said, showing them my empty glass.

For the first time that night, I left Caitlin's side. She'd been clinging to me like a tick, but now she felt secure in a new circle of potential friends. As I poured myself some more wine, I eavesdropped.

"Kim's been just the best," Caitlin was saying.

"You've picked a great coach," Summer said. "Based on what

she's told me about you, you're bound to make the team next year."

Mandy lowered her beer. "The competition is rough though. You have to practice hard and be willing to do whatever it takes."

I smiled so wide it hurt. *Mandy, I could kiss you.*

I left them in the kitchen and entered the dining room where Brian and Derek were standing, drinking their cheap beer and talking about nothing. Amy fawned over Ashton as he talked to her about football, a sport she had no true interest in. Brittany wandered in from the living room and made her way to the beer cooler in the corner and had Brian take a picture of her with it.

"Tag me on that," she said.

She and Brian stared at his phone while he uploaded the photo, and I saw my chance to pull Derek away without anyone noticing. Taking him by his shirtsleeve, I took him to the doorway leading into the kitchen.

"What's up?" he asked.

I nodded my head in Caitlin's direction. She did not see us.

"What do you think of Caitlin?" I asked.

He looked her up and down and I could see the glaze of alcohol in his eyes. I wondered just how many he'd had. I'd introduced them, but they hadn't talked much. Caitlin's focus was on Summer and Mandy, and Derek's seemed to be on Coors Light.

"She seems nice, I guess."

I leaned in to whisper in his ear. "Look at that ass."

He chuckled, but he looked. "You're fuckin' weird, Kim."

"You think *I'm* weird? That girl is a *freak.*"

He looked at me. "No way."

"Just look at the way she's dressed, Derek."

He was silent for the moment, still looking at her. "Seriously?"

"I shit you not."

I sipped my wine and Derek took a long pull on his bottle.

"So, why tell me?" he asked.

I faked a small laugh. "You moron. She's crazy about jocks. She wants to be a cheerleader so she can be closer to guys like you all the time."

He took another gulp of beer, emptying it.

"I'm gonna get a stiff one," I said. "Come with me."

I led him through the crowded dining room and into the den. He looked around, admiring it, his buzz revealing itself. Putting down my wine glass on the cabinet, I opened it up, taking out a bottle of

Jack Daniel's and mixing it with some cola. I poured us a tumbler each and Derek knocked his back. I poured him another.

"About the other night," I said. "I just want to say I'm sorry if it freaked you out."

"Are you kidding? Of course it freaked me out."

"I know, I know. I really am sorry. I just thought I should explain."

He waited, took another sip of his drink.

"I was just curious about kinky sex," I said. "That girl, Caitlin, she was the one who told me about it. She's really, really into it and told me a lot of guys like it. I think I was just doing it wrong."

His brow furrowed. "You mean that girl is into . . ."

"Caitlin likes it rough. She digs it when guys take charge and dominate her. She gets really into it when guys force themselves on her, you know? That kind of thing isn't for me, so I thought I'd try being the dominant one. I guess it was too intense for you."

"Well. I guess I liked *some* of it," he said, defending his male ego. "But I think I'd rather be the one in charge."

"See, I thought you would say that. You're a big, strong guy; the manly type. You should be the one calling the shots."

A boozy grin came across his face as he stepped up to me. "So . . . you wanna . . ."

I patted his chest. "Easy, tiger. This isn't about you and me. This is about you and Caitlin."

He blinked. "Caitlin?"

"That's right. She's got the mad hots for you."

"Really?"

"Why wouldn't she? She's a basketball freak and you're a star player, and a very handsome one, I must say."

He stood up a little straighter, grinning. "But isn't she, like, a sophomore?"

"She's the most grown up sophomore you'll ever meet, if you know what I mean."

He glanced down the hall toward the kitchen and sipped his drink. "What'd she say about me?"

"That she's seen you play a bunch of times, and she thinks about you when she's in the shower."

He nearly spit his drink. "Holy shit."

"That's why I'm telling you. I know things haven't really been working out with us, and that's okay. This chick is ready for you,

Derek. You just have to *take* her. That's the way she wants it. She plays the whole innocent virgin act, but that's all part of the game. She likes to feel like she's a sweet little girl being dominated by a big, tough guy who refuses to take no for an answer."

Derek finished his drink. Sweat was forming on his brow.

"Go say hello to her," I told him. "But don't mention this conversation. It'll ruin the game."

He stood there a moment, mustering up some nerve, and then put the empty glass down and headed toward the kitchen. With him gone, I went into the cabinet and took out the small tin. Before opening it, I glanced around to make sure Derek hadn't come back. I was alone in the room.

I had already crushed the two Klonopin down into powder. Zack had assured me that doubling them up would make them just as strong as Rohypnol. I'd told him I wanted them for my own problems with anxiety, so he wouldn't think it was strange I was asking him for a drug so associated with date rape. I poured the powder into my wine glass and swirled it, then left the room.

Derek was standing with Caitlin and Summer when I entered the kitchen. The rest of the party had made its way out to the back patio where a joint was being passed around. Brian was jumping on the trampoline with Ashton, so I figured things were okay on that front.

"I'm *baa-aack*," I said in singsong.

Caitlin's face was all happiness and I took her empty glass from her and gave her the one spiked with the pills. She took a sip. I had sampled it and found the pills had virtually no taste, just as I had read.

"So how long have you been working on cheerleading?" Derek asked her.

He was doing the twenty-questions crap guys do when they can't be interesting.

"Just about for forever," she said.

"She's so talented," I added. "Wait till you see what she can do."

I gave him a sly wink when no one else was looking.

Summer said: "She really knows her stuff."

Light sparkled behind Caitlin's eyes. The door she'd been scratching at had been swung wide open, and everyone on the other side was welcoming her with open arms. She was an actress landing her first starring role, a long-time girlfriend at last getting an engagement ring. I had taken her into a land of dreams and promise, where all of her hard work would finally pay off.

I looked up, pretending I was being called from the patio. "Excuse me for a second."

I went out back and Amy cheered when she saw me.

"She's a little drunk," Brittany said.

I laughed. "Hell, she's turnt."

I joined the inane party chatter for a few minutes, talking about TV shows and teachers and such, and then poked my head back into the kitchen and called for Summer. When she came out I talked to her about Caitlin and her prospects, and Summer agreed the girl had a lot of potential, that she was very sweet. I kept the conversation going now that I'd gotten her outside, which would leave Derek with Caitlin. They were alone in there for about twenty minutes before Brian leapt through the crowd and went back into the house on a quest for more beer. Amy followed, Dakota swaying behind them, her body language telling a tale of narcotics. It was getting colder out, so once the weed stopped going around everyone began to shuffle in.

When I came into the living room Derek was still talking to Caitlin. She had her back to the wall and he was leaning into her, one hand on the wall behind her. I hoped to get by without her noticing me, but she looked my way and then excused herself from Derek. When she got to me I saw how bleary-eyed she was. Her words slurred.

"Heeeey, Kim."

"How's it going over there?"

Her brow furrowed. "Um, okay, I guess. Derek's being very . . . um . . ."

"That just means he likes you, Caitlin."

She tried to smile but it was painful, forced. "Yeah, but . . ."

"Remember, making friends with the jocks is just as important as making friends with the cheerleaders. You know how popular he is. I would have thought you'd be mad excited that he's into you, especially because he's a senior."

"Oh, it's pretty cool. It's just that he's being kinda . . . *forward.*"

I scoffed. "You expect him to send you little love notes? This isn't junior high, Caitlin. You need to grow up."

My curt criticism jolted her and I worried that she might start to cry.

"I'm sorry," she said.

"He's cool, he's good-looking . . . I mean, don't you think so?"

"Yeah, totally."

"Then remember what we talked about. No being a little girl tonight. You have to be open to new things, and that means new *guys* too."

"But, Kim, I just . . . I just met him." She was woozy now and having trouble getting her sentences together. "You don't mean . . ."

"I brought you into the fold, Caitlin. Don't let me down. Don't fucking embarrass me."

The hurt that flushed her stoned face would keep me high most of the night.

"I won't," she said. "What do you think I should do?"

It was hard not to show how happy I was. Caitlin had become my molding clay. She would yield to me and let me shape her into whatever I wished.

"Just roll with it," I said. "Guys like Derek like to lead, so let him. You can trust him; believe me. I've known him for years and he's not a bad guy. Just loosen up and see where the night takes you."

"Okay."

"And remember what I said about new things."

She hesitated, then said: "But what if he wants to . . . you know . . ."

"You're not a *total* virgin, Caitlin. And the last thing you want is for anyone here to think that you are one. You've already jerked a guy off. But like I said, this isn't junior high. Don't blow this by not blowing him."

She took a deep breath and when she moved she fell toward me and I had to stand her upright.

"Sorry," she said. "This wine has gone to my head."

"Yeah. I say you've had just about enough."

She smiled. "Thanks, Kim. You always look out for me."

I guided her back into the kitchen where Derek was talking to Ashton, and poured Caitlin a glass of water to make her think I was trying to sober her up. Amy came in at just the right moment and batted Ashton's arm playfully.

"You wanna play flip-cup?" she asked.

"Turn up!" he yelled.

Caitlin was watching them, so I turned my head to Derek and whispered in his ear.

"You should take her upstairs," I said. "Second door. Guest

bedroom."

He grunted like a caveman and slurped his beer down. He put the bottle on the counter and walked up to Caitlin and slid his arm around her waist. It startled her and she looked at him, then me, and then she forced a smile. When his hand slid down to her butt, she didn't push it away.

ELEVEN

About twenty minutes after I'd whispered to Derek, he and Caitlin disappeared. He'd managed to sneak her away. I turned the music up just in case, Amy's old school rap getting people even more amped up. Some were dancing, others playing flip cup, all having a blast. The house was nice and loud, the party small but jumping. I had stopped drinking and was carrying a party cup filled with gold ginger ale so people would think I had a beer. I wanted to be sharp for whatever came next, for it could be anything.

I was tense. I kept expecting Caitlin to come running down the stairs half dressed and bawling, or Derek to come down to tell me she'd passed out or thrown up. But they didn't. They stayed up there for a good forty minutes.

"Where's Derek?" Brian asked from the head of the dining room table. It was covered in upside down cups. "I want to beat him next."

I shrugged it off. "He must be around here somewhere."

"You wanna play?" he asked.

"No, I'm buzzed enough as it is."

He was trying to egg me on when I heard footsteps on the stairs. My breath caught in my throat. I walked into the living room just as Derek came down. His fly was open. He grinned at me, his eyebrows going up and down. His skin was pink and not just because he was drunk.

"You were right," he said. "She really does play the virgin."

My pulse quickened. "Were you forceful?"

"Oh yeah. Mad forceful. She struggled but she was, like, really weak about it."

"So, did you go all the way?" I asked, nudging his arm like I was one of the guys.

He snorted, his face growing redder. "Hell yeah. It was way live. I did her real good too—she's passed out now."

Brian called from the dining room. "Hey Derek, get your ass in here!"

Derek looked at me as if waiting for permission, so I patted him on the shoulder and he followed the sound of the flip cup game. I went upstairs. The drunken prick had even left the door open when he'd walked out. I could see Caitlin lying on the bed, naked but for her bra. I tiptoed my way in, passing by the trail of her shoes, dress and panties. There was a wet spot beside her and a little bit of blood around her sex. Derek's semen was drying on her stomach.

I steadied my phone and started taking pictures.

TWELVE

I had hoped to wake Caitlin in the morning, but when I came in with coffee she was already up. She was sitting in the bed, the blanket wrapped tight around her. Mascara tears lined her face but she wasn't crying anymore. Her eyes had a far-away look even when they met mine.

"Hey sleepyhead," I said, cheerful. "Brought you some coffee. I figure your head's as fuzzy as mine."

She took a deep breath. "Thanks."

As I came closer I pretended to just now notice the streaks of her tears. "Whoa, Caitlin, what's wrong?"

"Nothing."

Her eyes watered and I sat down on the bed. The blanket shifted, revealing her bare shoulder.

"Are you naked under there?" I asked.

She didn't reply. Her face was scrunching pink.

"What the hell is going on?" I asked in my most serious tone.

The levee broke and Caitlin began to ugly cry. Heavy sobs shook her as I took her into my arms. She bawled like that for a while, unable to speak as I patted her head and made soft shushing sounds, telling her it was okay, whatever it was.

"Tell me what happened," I asked. I had been dying for details. "I mean, I thought you just got woozy from the wine and went to bed early."

She came off me and shook her head. "Derek . . ."

I waited for more with my mouth agape.

"I came up here," she said. "With Derek."

"Oh."

She fell silent again, the tears still flowing.

"Was everything okay?" I asked.

"I was so dizzy . . . so tired . . . from the wine, I think." She sniffled. "He was really nice at first . . . then he . . . he . . ."

I feigned anger. "What did he do to you, Caitlin?"

She became hysterical, sniffing and breathing heavily as she spoke.

"I to-told him to stop . . . but he kept . . . kept ta-taking off my clothes . . . He kept . . . forcing me . . ."

"Oh my god."

"I felt all numb . . . I couldn't get him off, Kim . . . he held my wrists. I t-t-told him no . . . but he ke-kept saying . . . kept saying I *wanted* it."

I let silence hang between us, purposely making the moment feel cinematic. Deep, horrible sobs shook Caitlin and her breathing became erratic, strained gasps gusting in her throat.

"You okay?"

She shook her head and pointed to the other room. "My . . . buh-bag . . ."

I got up and went into my room and opened her bag. I grabbed the inhaler and came back to the guest bedroom and placed it in her hands. She took two puffs, slowly calming down.

"Caitlin. This is *very* important. You *have* to tell me—how far did it go?"

She cried into her chest.

"That son of a bitch," I said.

She fell into me now, a shattered mess, and I held her like a sister and just let her sob.

"I'm calling the police," I said.

"Wha . . . ?"

"*The police*. We have to call them."

She pulled away. "Wait a sec."

"We can't wait. This bastard needs to pay for what he did."

"Kim, no, I'm sc-scared."

"You don't have to be. I'm here and I won't let anyone hurt you."

"I have to think."

"Think about what?" I shouted. "For Christ's sake, Caitlin!"

She balled her fists and pounded the mattress. "I don't want anyone to know!"

We both fell silent again and the room thrummed. Caitlin huffed her inhaler once more. I was itching to masturbate.

"Shit," I said. "I guess not. I mean, if your parents find out"— my mentioning them made her curl into her chest—"if everyone at school finds out . . ."

"No, no, *no*."

"You don't want to be known as the girl who got raped," I said. "I sure wouldn't. That label will stick with you forever." I paused. "And Derek could always say you were lying. I mean you did come up here willingly, and you were both drunk. It doesn't look like he hit you or scratched you up either. I mean, what if nobody believes you?"

She buried her face in her hands. "I can't . . . take . . . this."

I put my arms around her, kissed her head. "It's going to be okay. We don't have to tell anybody if you don't want to. We'll find a way to handle this ourselves."

After a shower and some breakfast, Caitlin looked better. There was a funk of depression hovering about her, but it was a gray, subdued sadness, not the screaming hell she'd displayed earlier. I felt confident she would be able to hide her pain when she went home, particularly because she was mortified by the possibility of her parents finding out. If worse came to worse and she did break down, then we could sic the police on Derek. The thought of he and Caitlin being dragged into court, both of them being shamed and tarnished, was amusing, and the possibility that Derek might go to jail was rather exciting. But there would always be time for that if and when I wanted to make it happen.

I knew everyone would believe Caitlin and me over him. He could tell the police about how I'd told him to be rough with her, but nobody would believe that. It would sound like a ridiculous lie, and would make him seem all the guiltier. Seeing Caitlin dragged through the mud and grilled by a defense attorney who would question her sex habits would be delightful, but I was about to set other things in motion. I wanted to be the puppet master of everyone's degradation, not just a spectator.

"Lay low today," I told her. "Tell your mom you're having your period or you don't feel good. Stay in your room as much as you can. Maybe even try to stay home from school tomorrow."

"Okay."

"When you do come back to school, just act like everything's normal. And if you see Derek, just be cool, okay? We just need to take some time and figure things out."

Caitlin nodded and bit her lip. She was fidgeting.

"Caitlin, are you listening to me?"

"Yes. Sorry. I'll be cool, just like you said."

My Caitlin was a good girl.

She stayed home from school. We texted here and there and she told me she was faking a cold and was holding herself together. Mr. Blakley said nothing to me, and neither did Derek for that matter, although he did seem rather up, the lay having done him some good. I wondered how many people he had told. I was certain he would have told Brian the very night it happened, but I wondered now if he would keep his lips tighter than usual because Caitlin's father was one of his teachers, and she a lowly sophomore.

I decided to get the word out myself.

At lunch on Monday I met up with Amy, Brian and Derek in the cafeteria. Dakota arrived shortly after and we all ate together, reliving the highlights of the party. I let them tell their stories before I came to mine.

"Hey, Derek," I said, "you seemed to have a *real* good time."

Brian chuckled. "I'll say."

"Shut up," Derek said.

"Come on," I said, "it's not like we all didn't see you go up with her."

Amy looked at me. "With who?"

"Old Derek was robbing the cradle last night."

Derek looked away, an *aww-shucks* look on his face.

"You smashed with that Caitlin chick?" Amy asked him.

"Come on, you guys."

"Whoa . . ."

"I don't believe it," said Dakota. "She seemed so, like, *innocent.*"

"Just an act, right?" Brian said, nudging his buddy.

Dakota snickered. "Twinkle, twinkle, little whore. Cheaper than the dollar store."

"Hey, come on, now," I said. "She's my friend."

Amy rolled her eyes. "God, it's such typical *sophomore* behavior—always trying to act all mature around us."

"So, Derek," Dakota teased, "you've got yourself a new girlfriend?"

"*Me* date a sophomore? Yeah, right."

I chose my words carefully. "She's a sweet girl, Derek. You'd better not have hurt her."

He gave me a look. "Hey, it was just, you know, a fling. Besides, I was drunk. It's her own damn fault if she thought it was more than that. Now let's drop it. And don't any of you go blabbing this around."

But the blabbing had already begun. Amy was a vicious gossip who loved nothing more than slamming the unpopular. Now she had live ammunition. And Brian always liked to brag about his friends' sexual escapades, as if they made him a stud by association. I wasn't sure about Dakota. She was just cynical enough to spread dirt, but she was just as likely to be indifferent to this sort of thing. But if I gave her a reason to dislike Caitlin, then that could get her to run her mouth. I wouldn't talk about it beyond this group of close friends though, so it wouldn't get back to Caitlin I was talking smack about her.

The week rolled on, Caitlin continued to stay home sick, and the school played the telephone game, talking about Mr. Blakley's slut of a daughter, embellishing and adding their own juicy details. The snowball I had rolled was growing into an avalanche that could crush Caitlin when she dared to return to these halls, and the anticipation of this made me ecstatic. I had the pictures, the rumors, the emotional trust. I knew I could strike now and receive immediate gratification, but I held off, knowing these baby steps of cruelty would cause her deeper and more meaningful suffering. I'm not sure at what point my annihilation of Caitlin ceased to be an effort to inflict further harm on Mr. Blakley, but by now he had nothing to do with it. My torture of Caitlin was for the sake of torturing Caitlin. Any residual suffering this caused her father was merely a bonus. I still wanted to crush him, of course, but hurting Caitlin had become a more thrilling pastime, and hence a greater obsession.

She called me on Wednesday night. I paused the autopsy video I was watching online and picked up.

"How are you feeling?" I asked.

"I don't know. Just kind of numb."

"Only natural, I suppose."

"Maybe."

"When do you think you'll be back to school?"

She sighed, sniffly but not crying. "I don't want to see him."

I gave her my warmest tone of voice. "I know, but you have to come back sometime. And we have to get back to practicing, right?"

She didn't answer.

"Look, you'll feel a lot better if you get back to your everyday life."

"I don't know if I can. I don't know if things will ever go back to the way they were. I'm scared. I feel so—"

"You are *not* alone. I'm always here for you."

Now I heard the tears.

"Oh, Kim. You're my best friend. I love you so much."

My nude body quivered and I ran my fingers over my clit. "I love you too, Caitlin. I love you too."

THIRTEEN

Caitlin was faking being sick, but on Friday morning I felt extremely queasy. I had my head in the toilet at five a.m., dry heaving and wondering what the hell I could have eaten. Lately, I'd been rather strange with my attitude toward food. At times I felt like I needed to avoid it all together; at others I had terrible, bizarre cravings, usually for meat that bordered on raw. One day I was fasting, the next I was a voracious carnivore.

My dermatophagia was getting worse too. I had always been bad about picking at the skin around my nails and toenails and eating it. Blisters and scabs too. Any small bit of my flesh that came off my body went immediately into my mouth, provided no one was looking. But I was picking at myself more now, extra hungry for my own skin. I tried to take it slow, not wanting any of the little tears in my fingertips to draw any attention.

My breasts ached more than ever, which was starting to worry me. I'd had spotting, but my period hadn't come, and now it was late. I told myself not to panic just yet. Part of me wanted to pick up a home pregnancy test, but a bigger part of me felt like that would make it all too real, that it would jinx me somehow if I even acknowledged the possibility there could be a screaming, shitting, little life-wrecker germinating within me like a cancer. But still the fear lingered, haunting me with the threat of black ruin.

Give it a few more days, Kim. It's just hormones. Your period will be here any day.

Still, I wouldn't miss school.

To protest whatever was going on inside of me, I wore tight jeans and made a point of letting my feet fall heavy as I ran down the stairs. I was driving to school when Caitlin texted me. She was coming back today. This news perked me up and when I got to school I was nearly skipping my way down the halls. The smell of her impending heartbreak was like an open sewer.

Amy was by our lockers. "My, you're chipper today."

"*It's Friday, Friday,*" I sang.

"And you *still* have the house to yourself. What do you wanna do?"

I shrugged, thinking: *I want to fuck you with a frozen dog turd.*

"I don't know," I said. "I want to see where today leads."

Dakota came up behind us. "Your little friend is back. You know, Ms. Hot Panties."

"Don't call her that."

"You know I'm just teasing. I will say she looks like shit though."

"How so?"

"She has bags under her eyes like she hasn't been sleeping."

"Well, she's been sick."

Amy smiled. "Must be all that cum she swallows."

"Jesus," I said, genuinely surprised.

"Hey, just teasing, just like Dakota. But I'll bet Caitlin's going to be all over Derek. She'll spread like warm butter on toast."

"Really?" Dakota said.

Amy crossed her arms. "Of course. Isn't it obvious this is all a power play? She figures if she can land a basketball player then a cheerleader position will just, like, fall right into her lap. Somehow I doubt the other cheerleaders will be too happy about her thinking that's how it's done."

And I knew Amy was just the one to tell them. In that moment I was actually glad to have her as a friend. She was proving to be useful. Amy's cruelties were petty and passive-aggressive, but they were pure and unflinching. There was bitter poison hidden within this pretty bouquet.

I knew this was where I, as Caitlin's friend, was supposed to ask Amy and Dakota to lay off of her. But there was a slim chance they actually would; I didn't want to risk it. But saying nothing would look strange too.

"Look," I said, "you guys don't like Caitlin, and she doesn't like you. But you're all my friends, so please, leave her alone."

I watched and waited. Amy's chin went up, her nostrils flaring. Dakota's normally relaxed posture grew rigid.

"*She* doesn't like *us*?" Amy asked.

There was an edge to Dakota's laugh. "Oh, please."

I put my hands on my hips, tilted my head. "Well, she didn't say she didn't like you, exactly."

"Right," said Dakota.

"Don't try and protect her," Amy said. "It's fine if she doesn't like us. I don't care." But she did. She cared a lot. Nobody was allowed to dislike Amy Heidnik. "It's fine. Whatever."

"Whatever," Dakota reiterated.

There was a guarded nature to Dakota now. While not normally vindictive, this change in her demeanor assured me her cruel words about Caitlin would now be out in the open instead of just expressed in our inner circle.

It didn't take long.

Caitlin didn't even make it through the day. Not only did she leave early, so did her father—such was the severity of the situation. From what I'd heard, Caitlin broke down during lunch with heavy, hysterical tears. Some said she'd run off to the principal's office for permission to leave, but most were saying she'd run straight to daddy, which was likely a rumor served to further embarrass her. Word about her sleeping with Derek had spread like a rash, and all around her people snickered and pointed her out to their friends. I had no doubts Amy had spread additional rumors about her too, and she'd been rather creative while doing so. The jocks found it amusing Caitlin was trying to fuck her way into their clique. The cheerleaders resented her for trying to slut her way onto the team. Because popular girls were spitting venom about her, other aspiring high school princesses made crude remarks about her for putting out, as if they didn't hand their bodies over all the time. Boys made sexist jokes, some being brave enough to do it right to her face. And because she was the daughter of a teacher, every attack was that much fiercer.

Dakota was smirking when I came through the hall. The janitor was scrubbing down the locker with acetone. The dean stood beside him, treating the area like they were police at a crime scene, telling students to keep moving.

"What's going on?" I asked.

"Oh," she said, "seems like your friend has quite the reputation."

"What do you mean?"

"She's already the laughing stock of the school, you know, and now this."

She craned her head toward the locker—Caitlin's locker. The janitor had just started his work, and the words were still legible.

"I know what you're thinking," Dakota said. "But it couldn't be Amy or Brian. They wouldn't stoop this low."

I shook my head at what I saw. "Yeah, I doubt they would do this."

I *knew* they hadn't done it. I'd spent last night thinking of the perfect thing to write.

Streaks of black magic marker gleamed on the yellow paint: CAITLIN BLAKLEY SUCKS JOCK.

A quiver went through me when I was called to the dean's office.

Did someone see me do it?

I'd been careful, waiting until the hall was empty, having already scanned for security cameras. I'd been tardy to first period algebra as a result, but because of my perfect attendance record I was not written up for it. I was a model student, after all. Surely they couldn't suspect *me* of such callous vandalism.

I had to wait outside the dean's door for fifteen minutes, picking at my cuticles and the buttons of my blouse. When the door came open, Derek stepped out, his face as red as a fire engine. When he saw me, it grew even redder, and he walked away with his head down, neither of us acknowledging the other.

I heard the dean. "You can come in, Kim."

I walked inside.

"Close the door, please."

I did and came over to the chair in front of his desk and sat down. The dean was writing something and it took him a moment to look up at me. He was a thin black man of about fifty, with a receding hairline and thick glasses. His shirt and tie did not match, so I took him to be unmarried, likely divorced.

"How are you, Kim?"

"Okay, I guess."

"You know why I called you in here, right?"

I paused, then: "I'm guessing it's about Caitlin Blakley."

"That's right." He leaned back in his chair, swiveled. "I'm told the two of you have become close over the past month."

"Yes."

"You've been grooming her for a spot on the cheerleading squad."

He was making statements that were also questions.

"Yes."

"That's very good of you." His face was neutral. I couldn't tell if he meant what he'd just said or if there was a sarcastic glint behind it. A bead of sweat had formed at my spine and was creeping down my back. "A popular girl like you, taking a younger student under your wing; that's very generous."

He formed a temple with his fingers and tapped them against his lips. My fists were so tight at my sides they had turned to fine porcelain.

"Someone hasn't been as kind to her as you have," he said. His voice was softer now, the tone of a friend rather than an authoritarian. Tension began to leave my shoulders. "I was hoping you'd be able to tell me who might want to hurt her the way she's been hurt. These rumors and jokes—and worst of all the writing on her locker. This kind of bullying is not tolerated here at our school. You know that."

"Yes, sir. It's terrible."

He took a deep breath. "I just spoke with Derek Schechter. A lot of the rumors involve him. He told me he and Caitlin had been . . . *intimate* together, but they weren't dating. He admits he told a few of his buddies, but hadn't done any more than that. Do you think he has something against Caitlin, that he would want to hurt her somehow?"

I looked at the floor.

The dean leaned forward. "You can tell me, Kim."

"Well, honestly, Derek is kind of a mean guy when it comes to girls."

"Oh?"

"He brags a lot and tells stories that aren't really true."

"What kind of stories?"

I gave him my bashful face. "About . . . *sex*. He tells people he's slept with certain girls even when he hasn't. And when he does go to bed with one, he brags about it and makes all kinds of dirty comments. He flat out told me he had sex with Cassie Boone in public all the time."

"What else does he do?"

"He treats girls like they're whores," I said, keeping my eyes from blinking so the tears would come. "I know. I used to go out with him."

The dean was silent for a moment, somber.

"Do you think he wrote on her locker?" he asked.

"Maybe."

I didn't want to be too accusatory. I had a nice girl image to uphold that did not allow bursts of anger or snitching.

"Did Caitlin tell you anything about him?" he asked.

"Yeah. She said he was . . ."

The dean waited, then: "He was what?"

"She said he was really forceful with her." I looked up at him quickly. "Please don't tell Caitlin I said that. And *please do not tell Derek*!"

FOURTEEN

I tried calling Caitlin that afternoon but she didn't pick up. I wondered how much she might have told her parents. Had the rape been divulged or had she only admitted to having sex? Or was she playing it all off as nasty rumors and nothing more? Had she told them anything that had happened at the party? If so, I might not be granted the access to her I once had and desperately wanted. Her mother wanted me to help Caitlin achieve her goals, but would likely turn me away if she saw me as a troublemaker. Mr. Blakley might even put two and two together and come after me hard. But I doubted Caitlin would do anything to incriminate me in their eyes. No matter what she told them, I was confident she would leave me out of the picture. To her I was the ideal friend. She would protect that at all costs.

She texted me later that night.

Caitlin: Sorry I can't talk. Things are crazy here. My dad is freaking out.

Me: R U OK? I've been SO worried about you. (Heart emoji)

Caitlin: Everyone was so mean. I don't know why! Everyone knows! Derek told EVERYBODY! They were all making fun of me!

Me: OMG. He's such an asshole. R U OK?

Caitlin: I don't know what to do.

Me: How much do your parents know?

Caitlin: I told them it was all lies. That I never slept with him. I want to go to a new school but they don't want me too. Dad's all mad. He thinks I'm being targeted because he's a teacher and I'm his daughter. Mom doesn't want me to leave school and give up on things.

Me: She's right. You've worked too hard to get where you are. Don't let Derek and a bunch of other assholes break you down and drive you away.

Caitlin: I'm just so scared. Why does everybody hate me now?

Me: Nobody hates you.

Caitlin: Then why are they so mean?

Me: Some people are just bad people. But not everyone at school is like that. Don't let a couple of jerks chase you out of your own school.

Caitlin: I don't think I can go back there.

Me: You can always tell the truth. Let everyone know what he did. They won't make fun of you then.

Caitlin: That'll be even worse! Then they'll make rape jokes instead of sex jokes! I'd rather be the slut than the rape girl.

Me: You're NOT a slut.

Caitlin: Everyone thinks I am.

Me: Not EVERYONE.

Caitlin: It feels like everyone.

Me: This will pass. Derek will get what's coming to him. (Angry face emoji)

Caitlin: You think so?

Me: I know so. Stay strong. We're in this together. I'm right beside you all the way. (Happy face emoji and heart emoji)

Caitlin: (Heart emoji and smiley face blowing a kiss emoji)

Me: Can we get together soon? Do some drills?

Caitlin: K.

Me: Hope so. Don't give up! Cheerleaders never say die!

Caitlin: (smiley face emoji)

Me: LUV U. (heart emoji)

Caitlin: LUV U 2. (various heart emojis and kiss emojis)

Me: Make sure you delete this message thread, just in case.

Caitlin: I will.

Me: Talk to you soon.

Caitlin was not at school the next day and neither was Derek. The rumor mill was on fire, a smoldering inferno that engulfed everyone.

"Did they suspend Derek?" Dakota asked.

"Sort of," said Brian. "He's not in trouble for anything yet, but the whole locker thing is being investigated, so he was told to stay home."

"I'll bet she did it herself," Amy said.

I blinked. "What do you mean?"

"She wanted attention, so she wrote it herself."

"Why on earth would she write *that?*"

"If it looks like Derek's trying to slut-shame her, then he's the bad guy. She's no longer the little tramp."

Brian sneered. "That fuckin' bitch."

"Take it easy," I said to him. "We don't know she did that. Anybody could have written on the locker. You and Derek didn't exactly keep your mouths shut about them sleeping together. Typical guys. *I can't even.*"

It was important to play feminist sometimes.

"Don't blame me," he pointed at the girls, "they blabbed too."

Amy slapped his arm. "Dick."

I noticed how Dakota looked away.

"We barely mentioned it," Amy told me. "Everyone was asking us because we were at the party."

It was a bad lie, but I pretended to swallow it.

"Anyone see Mr. Blakley today?" I asked.

"Yeah, he's back. He seems pissed."

"Of course he's pissed."

Dakota bit her lower lip. "Is Caitlin, like, *okay*, Kim?"

Her humanity surprised me, particularly because it did not seem to be for show.

Guilt is a many splendored thing.

"She's upset, but I know Caitlin. She's going to get back at whoever she thinks did this."

Amy's face pinched, already on the defense. "But she doesn't know who did it—*if* it wasn't her, that is."

"She'll go after anyone she thinks did it, and anyone who was talking shit about her. She can be very vindictive."

"Really?" Brian asked. "She seemed so sweet."

Amy gave him a sideways glance. "She also seemed like a little

virgin, and so much for that. Maybe everything about her is an act."
She looked at me. "Why do you even hang out with her, Kim?"

"I just wanted to help guide someone."

Amy shook her head. "I don't think there's any helping a girl like
her."

I wasn't sure what to expect when I got to life management class,
but felt certain Mr. Blakley would want to have a word with me at
the end of it. He taught only social history today. There was no talk
of sex, for obvious reasons. There was a darkness to the teacher that
was palpable—suppressed rage, embarrassment, even grief. But if
any of these emotions were directed at me he hid it well.

When the class started filing out, he whispered my name, so I
waited.

"I need to talk to you," he said once we were alone.

I stood before his desk. "What's up?"

He seemed saggy, bent. His eyelids were purpled. "Do you know
anything about this?"

"I already talked to the dean."

"Did it happen?"

"Did what happen?"

"Did she sleep with him?"

"I don't know. Who your daughter fucks is none of my business."

He winced. "I know you, Kim. You'd make it your business. Now
did she or not?"

I shrugged.

"I want you to leave her alone."

"Why? What has this to do with me?"

"I'm not sure, but I feel like it might have *a lot* to do with you."

"I'm Caitlin's friend. Just ask her. Ask your wife. You're just
imagining things because of how complicated your relationship is
with me."

He glanced toward the door and shushed me even though I
wasn't being loud.

"We don't *have* a relationship, Kim."

"Oh, yes we do."

"Well, not anymore."

"You don't just get to decide that."

He stood up. "Let me make this very clear. If you think I won't risk *everything* for my daughter, you've got another thing coming." He poked me in my tit for emphasis. "You can fuck with me, but if I find out you're fucking with Caitlin, I will come down on you hard, Kim White. I will fucking crucify you."

I smiled at him. "You'll do anything to protect one of your babies?"

"Damn right."

"Good to know."

FIFTEEN

I was pregnant.

I'd finally sucked up my fears and bought a pregnancy test, and the result was devastating. There was a little fuck-demon in my belly. That was why I'd been having weird cravings and my breasts felt like they'd been beaten with hammers. It turned out the spotting—which I had thought was a sure sign of a coming period—was actually common among expecting mothers, particularly during the first trimester. My head swirled at the sight of the pink dot on the plastic applicator. I tried to breathe steadily to combat the rise of panic.

Get an abortion, my mind screamed.

But I couldn't just charge it to my father's health savings account. Running it through insurance was out of the question because there was a chance he would notice it in the statement. But that was besides the fact. I was under eighteen. The clinic would have to get a parent involved. That was fucking unacceptable.

But what was the alternative? Run off to Mexico for a clandestine abortion? Throw myself down the stairs and hope for a miscarriage? There had to be a way out, there just had to. I needed time to think and do some research. I could use some advice, particularly from someone older, someone who knew about this kind of thing.

One name kept spinning through my head.

I called the house.

"We need to talk," I said.

At first he refused to meet with me, particularly because I wouldn't tell him what it was all about. But once I lied and told him I needed to talk to him about Caitlin, Mr. Blakley agreed to come out. He refused to pick me up, saying the moment I got him alone in a car I would force him into sex. I wasn't sure if he was right about that or not. He didn't want to go to the trails he'd taken me too either. Instead he told me to meet him at the old Cottonwood Plaza, an abandoned strip mall on an economically depressed stretch of road.

When I pulled behind the back of the tomb of the department store I saw his car and parked alongside it. It was full dark now—a particularly black night. There was no moon and no streetlights back here. We got out of our cars. I was wearing a skirt with no pockets, so I held my keys in my hand, fidgeting with them.

"So what is it?" he asked. "This better be important. You know how strange it looks to Simone when I go out this late."

It was nearing ten. I wondered what he'd told her.

"It's not about Caitlin," I said. "It's about us."

He huffed. "Fuck! I knew it!"

"It's not what you think."

"The hell it isn't. Should I just whip it out right now, would that make you happy?"

"No."

He stepped in close. "Well, maybe I'll just whip it out anyway, huh?" he poked me in the chest, harder than before. "Maybe I'll hike that skirt up and jam my cock up your ass."

"Listen to me—"

"No, *you* listen! I've had it with your little games! You're messing with me, my daughter, my family. Maybe it's time I showed you what's what."

He was talking through gritted teeth. A trickle of fear went up my spine and I tried to step back but bumped into my car.

"I have something to tell you," I said. "I need your advice."

That was part of it. Of all the adults I knew, he knew the most about reproduction and everything associated with it, and was the only one I could one hundred percent trust to keep his mouth shut.

But I had additional motivation—I didn't want to suffer this news alone. He had just as much right to vomit with fear over this as I did. And I wanted to see the look on his face when I told him. I wanted to watch him pale as if the life had been snatched from his chest. *He might even cry*, I thought with glee. This pregnancy had certainly not been part of my plan, but it was as sharp a meat cleaver when it came to hacking away at Mr. Blakley. It would be a shame to let such a fine skinning tool go to waste by keeping our little bundle of misery to myself.

"My advice?" he sneered. "What the fuck are you talking about?"

"I need your help, Mr. Blakley."

"Oh yeah? Well now why the hell would I help you when all you've tried to do is ruin my life?"

I laughed. "You think it's been bad so far? It's about to get a whole lot worse."

"Is that a threat?"

"There's no need to make a threat, the damage has already been done. In fact, you did this to yourself."

His mouth fell open slightly. "Did what?"

I smiled and rubbed my tummy with one hand, pretending to cradle it with the other. He backed into his car for support, a cornered animal itching to flee.

"No," he said.

"Yes."

"No!"

"The bun is in the oven."

"You're lying."

"Christ, I wish I was."

"You *can't* be pregnant."

I smirked. "You don't really need me to remind you what happens when you come inside a young, fertile girl, do you?"

He shook his head, fidgeting. "This is a trick. *What do you want from me?*"

"That remains to be seen."

He got off his car, his fury returning. "Get rid of it."

"It's not that easy."

"The hell it isn't. What, you want money? Fine, I'll pay for it."

"I don't want your chump change."

"You *have to* get rid of this, Kim. You must know that."

I had come to ask him if he knew ways to get an abortion in

secrecy. I wanted to talk to him about the possibilities of some sort of purgatives or late-in-the-game morning after pills. In the back of my mind I knew this was all just desperation, and yet I wanted to believe he could help me find a way out of this.

But now, seeing the anguish on Mr. Blakley's face, I simply could not help but have a shift in my priorities, at least for a little while. The news of me being filled with his bastard had terrorized him more than anything else I had done to him so far. The abject horror of it was pure and absolute. This was it. This was the end of his world. He would lose his job, lose his family, go to prison. He was man-filth, a social pariah, and he had made himself that way. This hell of Mr. Blakley's own creation crippled him to his very soul.

"I want to keep it," I said.

I had no intention of having the little fuck-demon, but every intention of making Mr. Blakley think I did. It would elongate his torment, picking at his nerves every second of every day. It would keep him spinning in his bed at night and he would start losing weight. Horror would make a home on his shoulder and whisper in his ears so he could think of nothing but his impending doom.

"No," he said. "You are *not* keeping it."

"It's my decision."

"The hell it is!"

"It's my body," I said, crossing my arms.

"I don't give a shit! This isn't some women's lib issue. This is about wrecking lives. Don't you understand all that I stand to lose here?"

"You should have thought about that before you put your dick inside me."

I saw his jaw shift. "You don't know it's mine."

"I know it and so do you."

Silence hung between us for a moment.

"Look," he said. "You want to have this baby, then I need to know you'll do it without me. Tell people whatever you want about how you got pregnant, but you do not tell them it was me. You leave me out of it—completely, Kim!"

"Come on, Mr. Blakley, I can't do that. Our baby needs a father. And I've seen how good of a father you are. You told me yourself you'd do anything for one of your babies."

I couldn't help it. A small chuckle escaped me. I suppose that's what finally set him off.

When Mr. Blakley moved toward me the look on his face made me dart to one side. I felt a sting in my scalp as my head was jerked back. He'd grabbed me by my hair, and used it now to pull me back and slam me against the car. He pushed my shoulder so my back pressed flat against the door.

I began shaking uncontrollably.

"You little bitch," he said. "My life is just a toy to you, isn't it? Well, I told you not to fuck with me and my family, but you just don't listen do you?"

"You're the one who needs to listen—"

Mr. Blakley's fist went into my stomach, taking away my wind and balance. He caught me with his other hand, slammed me back against the door of my car, and punched me in the stomach again before I could gather enough sense to defend myself. I had never been hit by anyone, let alone a grown man. I'd had scuffles on the playground as a little girl, but that had been little more than slaps, scratches, and hair pulling. This was a heavy, dull pain that rattled me to my core. The world fell away and there was only agony, agony so dominating it even overshadowed fear.

But there was such great fear.

I did not know when he would stop, and I could not fight him. I was in shock, both in body and mind. My limbs were unresponsive. I could not scream for I could barely breathe.

"You're not having this baby," he said, and his fist returned to my stomach.

I tried to cover myself with my arms but he twisted them away. I spun so I could press the front of my body to the car. I was punished for this with blows to my kidneys that made me piss myself.

"I'll beat this fucking baby right out of you," he said.

As he reared back for a more devastating blow, I dropped to my knees and moved just in time for his fist to collide with the car door instead of me. He yelped and grabbed his injured hand and tucked it into him, hissing from the pain.

I had but a moment.

My keys were still in my hands. I doubted I could get into my car and start it up before he got to me, but I knew I could unfold the key knife, the one Father had gotten for me just in case. I slid it out and it clicked in place but Mr. Blakley was too preoccupied to notice it. I was still winded, but forced myself to stand. The blade was only four inches long, with the width of a regular key. It wasn't much, but at the moment Mr. Blakley's back was to me, his head turned to one side, exposing the soft, white neck.

The blade went all the way in.

I aimed for his jugular, figuring I'd miss but would hurt him anyway. But my blade landed true. Dark, heavy blood gushed out of his neck in an instant. It was a good thing too; I'd thought I would be able to pull the blade out and stab him again, but removing it was not as easy as getting it in, especially when he began to thrash. I lost my hold and balance, just barely catching myself on the hood of his car.

Mr. Blakley made no effort to attack me. He was clutching his neck, trying to close the hole to no avail. The rest of the keys on the ring jangled like bells from his throat, and he made wet clucking sounds as more blood filled his esophagus. He was bleeding profusely, the blood steaming in the night. He stumbled about, sprinkling me and spattering his car with blood—writhing, panicking. I didn't know what to do, so I just stood there, watching him die. When he fell to his knees I stepped aside and this got me bouncing on my toes, suddenly unable to stay still. The pain in my belly was still there, but it was duller now, and a pleasant, warm rush filled me with a new comfort. It tingled in my innards and relaxed my core, morphine to my moment of madness.

Mr. Blakley fell against his car with his legs spread. One of his arms dropped to the side. The other hand held onto his neck a moment longer, then it too fell in hopelessness. His life was slipping away and I had a front row ticket. I licked my lips. I knew I should have been terrified of being caught and if I had any sense I would have pulled the keys out of him and driven off as fast as I could. But this was a once in a lifetime sort of experience. Sure, I'd been close to a dead body before, but this was nothing like kissing my mother's ice-cold forehead before they closed the coffin. No. This was a dead body in the making, a death I had orchestrated. A man was bleeding to death with my blade inside him, my fingers having shoved and twisted it in deep enough to destroy him. It was overwhelming, even more intimate than the sex I'd had with him. Murder was the life-changing moment I had hoped for when losing my virginity.

I leaned back against my own car and lifted my skirt.

My clit was pulsing when I touched it, wet with piss and on the verge of frenzy. I rubbed my fingers back and forth, strumming it, and then slid two fingers inside. Mr. Blakley was still twitching and croaking. His eyelids drooped, but a spark of recognition remained behind them as I stepped up. I knew it was risky to get too close, but my desire was ferocious. In that moment I understood why men would follow their dicks into an open grave. My horniness could not be reasoned with, even though Mr. Blakley could grab me at any time. He could pull me to the ground and strangle me, bash my insides again and pound my face unrecognizable. But I doubted he had the strength, and I was willing to take that gamble in order to have my way with him as he died.

Careful of the blood pooling all around him, I squatted and pulled down my soggy panties. I hitched my skirt up further, moved upon him, and straddled his bloody face. I could feel his short, halted breaths on my sex. His face and mouth were slack, but I pushed into him, letting his lips and nose run along my flushed pussy, every ounce of my blood flowing into my vagina. I grinded, clenching his head in my hands, and a bone-rattling shudder ran through me, a tornado having broken loose within, trying to whirl its way out. My toes curled, back arched, bottom lip sucked into my mouth. And then I was coming, coming like I had never come before, coming as Mr. Blakley's dying breath went up inside my body, a simultaneous hello and goodbye to his unborn child.

SIXTEEN

My senses returned, but everything seemed delayed somehow, like a slow-motion scene in a movie.

Get the fuck out of here, you moron.

My hands shook as I reached for my keys. They were still in his neck, lost in the sticky darkness of the gore. I managed to find the ring, slid my finger in, and pulled. The key blade resisted, ripping his flesh before it popped out. Blood ran like a brook over my hands.

Be careful of prints.

I was also cautious not to step in any of the blood as I picked up my panties. I went to my car and opened up my bag, taking out my sweatshirt. I had fallen onto the hood of his sedan, so I used the sweater to wipe it down, then did my best to clean my vaginal discharge off his face.

Make it look like a robbery or something.

I carefully pulled back the flap of his coat and reached into the inside pocket, finding his wallet. Back in my car, I opened my bag to put the wallet inside. I heard a rattle. Looking in, I saw the aspirin bottle, the one I'd bought from Zack, which was filled with the leftovers of the date rape drugs I'd used on Caitlin. I put my sweater on and slid one of the sleeves down over my hand so it covered it like a glove, and then wiped off the bottle. He only had thirty dollars in his wallet. It would have to do. I got out of my car again, opened the bottle of pills, and dumped some of them on the ground around him, putting one in his mouth. I placed a twenty-dollar bill in his hand and then tossed the rest of the cash into the pool of blood before returning to my car and putting the rest of the pills away and tucking the wallet into a small, zippered pocket.

I breathed heavily all the way home, shaking.

The whole thing repeated in my mind as I sat in the bath. I had already used auto wipes on the steering wheel and door handles of the car, and double-checked for blood on the seats but they were clear. I would do another inspection in the morning light. I had also built a fire, where I threw every article of clothing I had been wearing into the flames, including the shoes. The house stank like burnt rubber, but I did not want to take any chances. I used rubbing alcohol to clean the blood out from beneath my nails and cuticles, and I washed and washed but still felt sticky once I was clean. I lay there in the bath for a long time, draining and refilling when the water got cold. When at last I got out of the tub I saw it was two in the morning. I had school in a few hours.

Go to bed, Kim.

But I won't sleep.

Go to bed anyway.

The night was nice and cold so I kept the window open, the extra soft fabric of the sheets soothing me. I thought about the pounding Mr. Blakley had given my belly. I hoped it would cause me to miscarriage, but so far nothing had happened. Maybe it was too early for such a beating to have an effect. My stomach still ached, but I had bigger concerns now, much bigger, much worse.

I stayed in bed until five, not sleeping, and then got up and ready for school.

Today was going to be very interesting.

No one had come knocking on my door, and no one had called during the night. These were good signs. So far, I was not involved. I kept telling myself I never would be. My relationship with Mr. Blakley had been a well-guarded secret on both our parts. I doubted he would have even confided in his closest friend about his affair. It was simply too shameful. No one would suspect his death had anything to do with a mistress, and even if they did, they had no reason to think that mistress was an honor roll student.

I was glad I'd set the scene with pills and cash. He was parked behind an abandoned strip mall; it was easy to make that look shady. It made me snicker when I imagined the cops questioning Simone about her husband's drug habits. But that may not have even happened yet. Surely he'd been reported missing, but that didn't mean his body had been found.

You called his house just before he left.

They would check the phone records and find my number. That was no big deal though. I was a friend of their daughter; of course I called from time to time. I had used the landline to talk to Simone about drills and encourage her to keep Caitlin working, just to pressure both of them.

I wondered if he had cleaned out his car thoroughly after we'd had sex that first time. Would there be semen on the seats? That, combined with the cash and drugs, might even make it seem like he'd had a run-in with a knife-wielding hooker, which was even funnier.

The thought made me laugh as I drove to school.

I was exhausted, but my mood was brightening.

I knew she wouldn't be there, but I couldn't wait to hear from Caitlin.

There were two police cars in the parking lot.

I parked far away from them and hurried to the halls that echoed with hushed chatter, the gossip mill already churning. Somehow even the truth had leaked.

"Mr. Blakley never came home last night," Brian told me as I approached he and Tanner, the first of our squad I came across. "He's missing."

"But why are they here at the school?"

"Talking to the other teachers."

Relief washed over me, drowning my paranoia for the time being. Still, I clutched my books to my chest, as if they could shield me if the gavel fell.

"It's crazy," said Tanner with a mouthful of protein bar. He was a stocky guy, fat in the face but thick in muscle. His scalp always seemed tight beneath his outdated flattop. "I never knew that family was so fucked up."

My phone rang and I excused myself before accepting the call, knowing who it would be. I found a quiet spot outside, unconcerned with tardiness or even the risk of my first detention.

"Hey," I said cheerfully.

Her wet sniffles made static on the line. "Kim . . ."

"Caitlin, are you okay? You sound upset?"

"It's . . . it's my dad. He's missing."

"Oh my god. What do you mean? What happened?"

"He went out last night. Said he needed some books for class. But he never came back. We tried his phone but it just goes to voicemail."

I wondered if the police could track the phone and find the body that way. It seemed possible. But I knew the body would be found one way or another, and soon at that. It wasn't like I'd buried him in a shallow grave in the woods. I'd just left his sorry ass sitting there behind the plaza, and he was likely still there now, the blood still drying, his dead eyes staring at sunny skies.

"I'm sure he's fine," I said. "They say missing persons almost always turn up."

I left out the word *alive*, but deliberately added the *almost*.

"I don't know . . ."

"Maybe his car broke down and his phone died too."

"But the library isn't that far. Maybe he went to Barnes and Noble, but still."

"Well, who knows what happened . . ."

"Mom called the police. They're looking."

"Oh, that must be why there are cops here at school."

Her tone changed. "What? Oh great, everyone must be talking shit about us again. Oh, god."

I stayed silent, confirming her worries even though I had played ignorant a moment ago.

"Oh, no," she said.

"Don't worry. Everything will be okay, you'll see."

But she kept on crying, sugar to my ears. I could hear the puffs of her inhaler.

"Why don't I come over?" I asked.

The thought of missing school made me queasy (or maybe it was morning sickness), but I was willing to make sacrifices to enjoy this time of dread at the Blakley house. Soon enough it would be grief— the deepest, harshest grief. I had to seize the moment before it passed.

Caitlin collected herself with an intake of snot. "Could you come?"

"You bet. I just have to ask if I can go home early. I'll tell the dean I'm having cramps or something. That always works on men."

My joke didn't land. The sniffles continued.

"Thanks, Kim. I can't wait to see you."

There was a single police car in front of the Blakley house when I arrived, along with two other cars I did not recognize. I had decided to play it straight with the dean and tell him Caitlin had asked me over for emotional support, but he was too busy with the police so a general administrator had excused me.

I was such a nice girl, such a caring friend.

The door to the Blakley house was already open. Simone was sitting on the couch next to a man who was holding her hand. She looked ten years older than she was, her face pinched and slicked by tears. Worry filled the room like black fog. I heard other adults talking upstairs in hushed tones. The boy, Dalton, was playing with toys in the corner, not fully aware of the severity of the situation. A policewoman sat in the chair across from Simone, writing in a notebook. The radio at her shoulder buzzed and she said something into it in code. When Simone saw me her face brightened, clearly touched by my presence.

I was such a nice girl, such a caring friend.

Another officer was at the dining room table across from Caitlin. When Caitlin saw me come in she smiled, but it was a sympathy-craving smile, full of gratitude while also being extremely needy. I went to her. She stood, letting me take her in my arms and kiss her on the forehead, as if I gave a flying fuck about her. The officer looked up at me and smiled politely. I smiled back.

I was such a nice girl, such a caring friend.

Comforting the family of the man I had killed was almost as arousing as the killing itself. At one point I had to excuse myself to the bathroom and rub out a quick orgasm just so I could think straight and not show my giddiness. My delight was not merely sexual however. I had not been this happy in a long time, which said a lot, seeing how before all of this had started I would whisper to myself about my own suicide when I was alone, acting like other students the day after my corpse would be found.

Did you hear? Kim White cut her arms open from wrist to elbow.

No way.

Her father found her in the tub. She didn't even leave a fucking note.

But that strange ritual had faded since my involvement with the Blakley family. Joy had come into my heart at last, bringing with it a sense of achievement, of victory earned. The Blakleys were now crippled by the annihilating backhand of my viciousness. I could not remember seeing such worry since my mother had been on her deathbed, and this made me feel warm and bubbly, a little girl with an ice cream cone in one hand and a brand new Barbie in the other. Simone kept sitting then standing, pacing and refilling her wine glass again and again, unashamed even though the police were there. Caitlin was stooped over, rubbing her hands on her legs when she wasn't twisting her ponytail. Now and then she rested her head on my shoulder and I nuzzled her, breathing in her anxiety as if it were the sweetest perfume.

The other man on the couch was Caitlin's uncle, Simone's brother. When they came down I was introduced to the people who had been upstairs—Mr. Blakley's parents. Clearly this was a very close family.

"Nice to meet you, Kim," Mr. Blakley's mother said.

I gave her a genuine smile. I was happy to meet the senior Blakleys and see the concern in their eyes.

I made your son cheat on his wife, then I stabbed him to death.

After the police wrapped up, Caitlin and I went to the backyard for some privacy. It was a bright and breezy afternoon, a false hope to a day that would soon be blacker than any that had fallen upon this house before.

"It's like my whole life is falling apart," Caitlin said.

I'd grown exhausted telling her it would all be all right. Reassuring the hopeless is rather repetitive. "I know. Just hang in there."

"What did I do to deserve all of this?"

"Nothing," I said, which was true.

"Do you think God is punishing me?"

This was a new twist. I didn't know she was religious. "Why would God want to punish you?"

"You know . . . for what happened with Derek."

She was blaming herself for it. Even better.

"Come on, Caitlin, you can't believe that. None of what's happened is your fault."

"I just feel like I'm cursed or something; first Derek, then everything at school, now my dad. I'm so scared they'll never find him, and even more scared they will, that he'll be . . . he'll be . . ."

She couldn't bring herself to say it.

I went to her, put my hands on her shoulders. She felt so little, so fragile.

"Don't jump to conclusions. We don't know what's happened yet."

"I don't even care anymore about Derek or everyone at school. I just want my daddy back."

She started sobbing again so I pulled her into me and held her. We stayed outside for quite a while, sitting on the swings of their jungle gym—two friends bonding in a time of crisis. Simone came out at one point and asked us if we wanted anything to eat. We didn't give her much of an answer, but a few minutes later she came out with turkey sandwiches and chips. I discovered I was ravenous. I ate my sandwich but Caitlin only took one bite of hers and chewed it slowly, sourly.

It was pushing four o'clock when we heard a car pull up and a door close.

Caitlin looked at me but did not move, the tension like a noose around her neck.

All was silent, and then we heard her mother scream.

SEVENTEEN

Two brothers were skateboarding behind the plaza when they'd come across the body. The thirteen-year-old called it in on his phone. The police shared the rest of the information with the adults only, so I couldn't be sure what was divulged. All Caitlin knew was her father had been killed, and that was enough. She was inconsolable. I stayed there, savoring the very instant when grief slammed down upon the family like a hurricane, enjoying the fruits of my malice. It was a bountiful harvest.

But this was a very personal matter. I knew it would look weird if I hung around too long. I also had other things to do, so I excused myself so the Blakley clan could be alone together, a shattered family with a raw, gaping wound they needed to lick. As I went to my car I spotted the policewoman in hers. I hoped it wasn't too early for what I was about to do, and that my sense of urgency would make it seem legitimate. I brought some tears to my eyes for authenticity. When she saw me approaching her window she got out of her car. Her hair was in a tight bun that seemed to pull her face back, aging her clear, black skin.

"Yes?" she asked.

"Um, I'm Kim White. I'm Caitlin's best friend. I thought I should tell you something."

"All right."

"I'm a good friend of the family and I was one of Mr. Blakley's students too. I don't know what all is going on, but something happened the other day and I thought I should tell you about it. I don't know if it matters."

"Any information you can give us is appreciated, Kim."

I paused for a moment, then said: "It's about Derek Schechter."

Just as I had with the dean, I told the officer Derek was very pushy with girls, even forceful. I told her about the party, how Derek had snuck off with Caitlin while nobody was paying attention and when I found her later she was naked and totally passed out. I said I wasn't at all sure, but thought he might have spiked her drink with something based on how things had unfolded. I told her the news of them sleeping together was all over school and everyone was slut-shaming her, and it all had gotten back to Mr. Blakley.

"He knew I was close with Caitlin," I said. "He asked me what had really happened with Derek, so I told him but made him promise he wouldn't punish Caitlin, that it wasn't her fault. He said he would do anything to protect one of his babies, that he would risk everything for Caitlin. He was so mad when he said it. The look on his face really scared me."

The officer took this in. "Thank you for this information, Kim. Is there anything else you want to tell me?"

"Not that I can think of right now. I just thought that, I don't know, maybe something happened between Mr. Blakley and Derek. I mean, maybe not, but I just thought I should speak up."

She nodded. "I may ask you and your parents to come down to the station and make a formal statement."

She asked for my phone number and address and I gave it to her, telling her I wanted to help in any way I could.

As I drove home I rubbed my breasts.

The possibilities swirled through my mind like magic.

I'd hinted at Derek using a date rape drug, the same kind of drug found at the scene of Mr. Blakley's murder. But they didn't know I knew the drugs were there. They'd kept that private from the kids in the house. This, along with what I had quoted Mr. Blakley as saying, would spark an interest in Derek, as would what had been going on with him at school. I didn't even have to lie. Mr. Blakley had said those words about protecting his children, only in relation to me and not Derek. I was also confident that around the house Mr. Blakley had made several comments about how he would like to kill Derek, whether he had banged his daughter or had just made up nasty rumors about her.

The way I'd left his corpse, it could look like there had been a struggle with Derek; that they might have met there to talk about the whole situation. The money could even make it seem like Mr. Blakley might have been paying Derek off to stay away from his daughter. Or, it could look like they'd had a fight and Derek had stolen his money. Maybe the drugs were there because Mr. Blakley had obtained them and wanted to confront Derek with them, threatening to turn them over to the police. Hell, maybe he even intended to drug Derek as he had drugged his daughter, so he could take him deep into the woods, have his violent revenge, and dispose of his body. Or, perhaps Derek had force-fed Mr. Blakley the pills in an effort to make him overdose. There were many scenarios to entertain. I doubted the police would make any of it stick, but that wasn't really the point. Derek being charged with murder wasn't too likely, but he would be brought in for questioning, and the terror this would cause him would be satisfaction enough for me.

But like most of my plans, this too had layers.

EIGHTEEN

Father cut his trip short so he could go with me to the police station to make my statement. He got home late at night, but I waited up for him with stew kept warm on the stovetop. When we went to see the police the next morning, I gave the exact same information I had given to the officer yesterday afternoon. I apologized profusely to Father about having the party, but he was more concerned with everything else that had happened, and was relieved I hadn't been harmed by being caught up in it all. I assured him I was all right, and despite his initial protests he agreed to go back on his business trip. It was an important one after all.

"There's no good reason to let the deal go sour," I told him. "You've worked too hard on this."

"I guess it won't take much longer. Just another couple of weeks. Are you sure you're all right?"

"You know me. I can take care of myself."

He would be gone by six that night.

I decided to finally call Amy.

"Where have you been?" she asked.

"Sorry, things have been crazy."

"I'll say. Mr. Blakley was murdered!"

"Word travels so fast."

"Well, sure, I mean, shit, this is a big deal. You're friends with the family; what's the story?"

She didn't ask how Caitlin was doing. She just wanted the gossip, a pig with her feed.

"Well, you didn't hear this from me, but Caitlin's saying it has something to do with Derek."

Amy gasped. "What?"

"It's crazy. She thinks Derek killed her dad."

"What *the fuck*? No way!"

"I think the stress is messing with her brain. She seems to really believe it. For Derek's sake, I hope the police don't."

"Derek is no killer! He's . . . he's . . . *Derek*!"

"I know. He's a decent guy. I keep telling Caitlin that."

"Ugh, that little . . . why would she throw Derek under the bus?"

"Like I said, I think she's just mixed up. She's hurt and scared."

"Well I think she's still trying to get back at him because he just humped her and dumped her. He's in enough trouble for this bullshit with the locker. They're blaming him for it, you know. He might even get kicked off the basketball team. Caitlin needs to back off of him. This isn't going to help find her dad's real killer, doesn't she get that?"

"I don't know."

She sighed. "Kim, you're her friend. Do you think you could talk some sense into her?"

"I'm trying. You know I don't want to see anything bad happen to Derek."

A few days went by.

Caitlin was a miserable mess. We spoke here and there and while her misery pleased me I tired of being her shoulder to lean on, but still I pressed on with my best friend façade. She stayed out of school, which made it all the easier for me to spread gentle lies about what was going on in the Blakley house. Amy had spread the word about Caitlin's persecution of Derek (while keeping her promise not to reveal who she'd heard it from), so the school was anxious now, half of them rallying behind Derek, the other half wondering if maybe there was a killer inside him after all.

When he came back to school, Derek was quieter than usual. His face had darkened and he kept his eyes on the ground when he walked, though he occasionally looked over his shoulder as if someone was creeping up behind him. People didn't dare ask him what was really going on, and of course Derek didn't say anything about it to me, but he talked to Brian, who talked to Amy, who always talked to me.

"The police have been questioning him," she told me. "This is getting scary."

"What are they asking him about?"

"They were acting like he raped Caitlin or something, and were asking if Mr. Blakley confronted him about it."

"What? He didn't *rape* her!" Even if it somehow got back to Caitlin I had said this, I could claim I had done so to protect her secret. "I mean, we were all there that night."

"Right? She was totally all over him. Trash."

"What else did he say?"

"He said he couldn't talk much about it. But it's clear Caitlin's been crying like a baby bitch to the cops."

It was all coming together. "We need to do something to help clear his name, to rally behind him."

"Damn right." Defending Derek would turn more people against Caitlin, so of course Amy was on board with that. "What do you think?"

I pretended to give it some thought, as if I hadn't already mapped all of this out.

"I know," I said. "Let's start with making a Facebook group. We'll invite everyone in school to join so we can all show our support for him, remind everyone what a great guy he is."

She beamed. "That's a great idea!"

"Would you mind putting one together? You're more active on social media than I am."

It was true. I lurked on Facebook just to stalk people, but never left comments or posted much myself. Amy, however, was a social media champion, with an army of followers on every imaginable platform.

"I'll make it right away," she said.

That afternoon, the *Save Derek Schechter* Facebook group was formed, and in just two days Amy and I got it up to almost one thousand members, mostly fellow students from all grades. Derek himself had joined, perhaps not even realizing the implication that in order for him to be saved he would have to be in trouble. He was just happy to see so many people posting pictures of themselves with him, sharing stories about how cool he was, and uploading video highlights of him scoring during basketball games. I'd been counting on his narcissism, and he had not disappointed me.

I scrolled through our members to make sure of one thing.

Caitlin had not joined the group, and likely knew nothing of it.

The hate toward her ran free of objection.

I went to the library to do it.

It's called *catfishing*. First you create a new email under a fake name. Then use that email to start a new Facebook account under an alias. I chose the random name Billy Hawkins. I searched Google images for a picture of a boy my age, taking my time to find a face that was fat and pimply, not in any way attractive (this would be important for what I would imply he'd done). I created the account and then sent a request to join the *Save Derek* group. Amy approved it almost immediately. She would approve anyone who asked, unless it was Caitlin.

I posted in the group, posing as Billy. I claimed I knew Caitlin and she was a total lying bitch, that there was no way anyone could rape a slut like her, that she would give it willingly to any guy who asked for it. The comment started getting likes right away. Other guys backed up this statement, as if they'd fucked her too, which of course they hadn't. It was easy to get guys rolling this way, especially behind the shield of social media, but I was surprised by how many girls chimed in, all of them calling Caitlin just as bad of names as the boys. Not one of them criticized me/Billy for my harsh words or came to Caitlin's defense, and no one would. Derek was popular. Defending him increased their chances to be popular. Bashing Caitlin would help them fit in, whereas defending her in any way would ostracize them and invite some of the bullying to be redirected their way. It was far better for everyone to just put down Caitlin. It was what all the cool kids were doing.

I would always use the library to log in as Billy Hawkins. I would never use the account on any of my personal devices, because I had plans for Billy that went beyond nasty comments.

Later that same day I went to a cell phone store and paid cash for a disposable phone with limited minutes, one of the untraceable ones drug dealers used. When I got home I plugged my regular phone into my computer, as well as a thumb drive.

I waited until the day of the funeral.

The family decided to keep it small and private. I was disappointed to not be invited, as I had been looking forward to seeing them bawl over a lowering coffin. I was especially interested in seeing Caitlin's brother, who would now be fully aware of his father's death. I just knew seeing a boy that little feeling a pain that large would give me incredible orgasms.

"I wish you could be there," Caitlin told me over the phone.

She still hadn't gone back to school, and it seemed nobody had told her about the vicious things being said about her online. I was friends with her on Facebook, and while she wasn't on there much to begin with, now she had not been posting anything at all, which was not surprising given all that was going on.

"I'll be there in spirit," I told her, "and in your heart."

I was laying down a thick layer of sap but she was slurping it up.

"Thanks, Kim. I hope we can see each other soon."

I could sense she was holding something back, so I pressed.

"Has anything happened with the investigation?"

"I don't know. Not really, I guess."

"Well, I hate to bring it up, but word is Derek's been in some trouble over this."

She swallowed so hard I could hear it. "They asked me."

"About Derek?"

"Yeah, about that night."

All my hairs stood on end. "What did you tell them?"

"I had to tell them something. I couldn't totally deny it and flat-out lie to the cops. So I told him we slept together. God, my mom was *right there* when I said it. She started crying."

"You didn't tell them he raped you?"

"No! I couldn't do that. I still don't want anyone to know, especially not Mom."

"Why did his name even come up?"

"They thought . . . thought maybe Derek and Dad had got into an argument over it."

"Had they?"

"No! I mean, I don't know, but no. No way."

I couldn't be sure if the police had told anyone in her family what I had told them. Caitlin didn't bring it up, so I figured at least she was in the dark about it.

"So what happens now?" I asked.

"I don't know. I just want to get through the . . . the funeral."

The word pained her and I pinched my nipple.

"Well," I said, "just know that I love you."

"I love you too, Kim."

"After today you should come back to school. It'll be good for you."

After our conversation, I went to the library.

I uploaded all the photos I had taken of Caitlin to a computer. I had cropped each of them so the room could not be identified. Some of them were as I had found her, naked on the bed after having been raped by a drunken, oblivious Derek. But she'd been so knocked out by the pills I had been able to manipulate her body, so I had put her in different poses so it would appear she was touching herself. I'd used the flash, so in many of the pictures you could see the wet spot on the bed and Derek's semen on her body.

I logged into Facebook as Billy Hawkins and went to the group. Now there were more anti-Caitlin posts than pro-Derek ones. I made sure no one was near my desk and posted the dirty pictures of Caitlin and wrote: *My buddies and I fucked the shit out of this cum-dumpster and she loved every minute of it.* I signed off before anyone could happen to walk by and see what I was doing. Facebook had a rule about not posting pornographic photos, but in order for them to see the pictures, someone would have to report them to Facebook. The people in the *Save Derek* group were not likely to do that at all, and even if someone did, by the time the pictures would come down a good chunk of people at our school would have already seen them. And Facebook would suspend Billy Hawkins, not me. I could create as many other Billys as I needed.

NINETEEN

"Jesus," I said. "I'm not online much. I never saw them."

"Stay awake, Kim," Brian said. "Everyone else has seen them. They were on the Facebook group page for a full day before they got pulled."

I put my hand to my face. "Oh my God."

We were all at lunch, barely eating, too energized by the scandal.

Amy dangled her diet soda between two fingers. "That's why you don't take naked pictures of yourself. You never know where they'll end up."

"Does anyone even know that Billy guy?" Dakota asked.

"Yeah," Brian said, "a couple of people have told me they remember when he used to go to school here."

"He's an ugly bastard."

"Yeah, he could scare the crap out of a toilet."

"Think she really fucked him?"

"Hey, you saw the pictures," Amy said. She turned to me. "Have you told her yet?"

"God, no. How do you tell someone everyone at school has seen them naked?"

"Not *just* naked. She'd clearly just been—"

"I know, I know."

Dakota was staring at me again. "She's bound to find out

eventually. A lot of people even saved the image, and they've been showing it to the people who didn't see it on Facebook."

"Jesus Christ!"

"Hey," Amy said. "I told you not to get emotionally involved with her. The girl is screwed up. You need to cancel that bitch. I mean, what is it going to take for you to cut her loose?"

I didn't answer her. Instead I looked to Derek, the only one eating so he wouldn't have to talk. I'd done my best to crop out anything that revealed it was my guest bedroom—all you could see were sheets—but he was the only one who had seen her that way that night. He'd been drunk, but he might have remembered just enough. He sensed me looking at him and glanced my way before going back to his food.

"Man," Dakota said. "I sure wouldn't want to be Caitlin right now."

"Or *ever*," said Amy.

"You know when she comes back to school, people are going to torture her with this."

"So she gets chirped. Serves her right."

Brian turned to me. "When is she coming back anyway?"

"Tomorrow," I told them, as Caitlin had told me.

When we finished eating we went out to the commons area for the rest of our break, and when the bell rang I headed toward my next class, Derek tailing along behind me even as everyone else went their separate ways.

Once we were alone he tapped me on the shoulder.

"Hey," he said.

I turned around to see his twitchy face. "Yeah, what?"

"Those pictures . . ."

Shit.

"What about them?"

"They're from . . ."

I opened my mouth in shock. "Oh my god . . . *you* took them?"

"What? No!"

"Jesus, Derek, they're from when you fucked her, aren't they?"

"No! I mean . . . I thought that . . ."

"You thought what? What did you do, pass them out to your buddies, huh? Give them to your friend Billy to post?"

"No! I don't know him! I didn't know there were any pictures."

"Hell, is Billy even *real*? Or was that actually *you* posing as somebody else?"

"Keep your voice down."

"Fuck you!"

I stormed off and he did not follow me.

That takes care of that, I thought.

After school, Summer Scott, one of the cheerleaders who had been at the party that night, came up to me before practice. We'd been issued new team gym bags and I was shifting my things around when she approached.

"So what is going on with that girl?" she asked.

"I have no idea."

"I mean, is her whole family crazy or something?"

"How do I know? I was just trying to give her a leg up because I felt sorry for her. I had no idea she was . . ."

I let Summer fill it in. "A freak?"

I sighed and bowed my head.

Summer put her hand on my shoulder. "It's not your fault, Kim. Nobody blames you for this. We all know you had the best of intentions."

After practice I went home and got on the computer, logging on to Facebook using my own account, not Billy's. People had banded together in some sort of protest for Facebook banning Billy for telling the truth. There were all sorts of hashtags:

#punishcaitlin

#exposetheslut

#brosbeforehoes

#caitlinsucksjock

I exited out of the group page and visited Caitlin's personal page. I hoped her wall wasn't filled with comments from other people calling her a lying bitch, a whore, and more colorful names that were even worse. If she hadn't seen it herself, one of her friends (though she seemed to have few good ones) would have let her know. But the page was clean. I kept my fingers crossed she wouldn't find out about the group yet. I didn't want anything to be spoiled for tomorrow.

Shutting down my computer, I went to the manila folder on my desk and opened it up again. I just couldn't get tired of looking at the pictures. The photo quality of Father's printer was as crisp and clear as Kodak. I hadn't found these pictures erotic before, but now that they were bringing out the very worst in the people I knew, they were incredibly arousing and intoxicating. I had created an army of assassins, and these photos would be their sharpest swords. Spreading the photos out across the desk, I leaned on it with one hand while touching myself with the other. When I was done I cleaned myself up in the bathroom. Tossing the tissue in the wastebasket, I frowned at the remains of the second positive pregnancy test I had taken. I was several weeks pregnant now. It was in my health's best interest to see a doctor, but I still hadn't figured out how I was going to handle all of this. I'd been far too busy hatching my plot to destroy Caitlin. But I had to do something. In another eight weeks or so I would have a baby bump.

Christ, I thought. *Why does everything bad have to happen to me?*

TWENTY

I told Caitlin to text me as soon as she got to school. She needed emotional support and was grateful I was offering it. When her nightmare started, I wanted to see it firsthand. Part of me wanted to drive her to school, so I could be sure not to miss the first slung insult as she stepped onto school grounds, but for the sake of my popularity I could no longer risk being seen with her in my car. But if we were seen together in the school, I could claim she was pathetically clinging to me and I was simply too nice a person to push her away.

We met in the commons area. She looked hollowed out. Her face was puffy and her nose was a damp, red nubbin. She was fingering the cross around her neck, her arms tucked into her body like a cripple. Bloodshot eyes told me she had been crying and I cursed under my breath, worried I might have missed the first thrown stone.

"Are you okay?"

"It's kind of hard to be here."

"Did something happen?"

She glanced back and forth. "Everyone keeps giving me dirty looks. I think some girls were whispering about me too."

"Oh, you're just on edge. It's understandable. You've been through so much. Come on, we'd better get to class."

We entered the halls. Caitlin was right; *everyone* was staring at her.

Even some of the teachers watched her from the corners of their eyes. I stepped away from Caitlin a little and moved faster.

"Wait for me," she said, jogging until she caught up.

I noticed then just how bad she really looked. Her hair was greasy and unwashed, tucked back in a childishly lazy ponytail. She wore sweatpants and an ill-fitting flannel shirt; I recognized it as one of her dad's.

"Why are they all staring at me?" she whispered.

I didn't reply.

That's when the group of boys approached. They were sophomores, willing to do anything for a high five from a senior. They saw their opportunity to go another rung higher on the social ladder and they weren't going to let someone else swoop in and take it from them.

One of the boys had a tablet in his arms. When he got close he opened its case, revealing the picture of Caitlin where she was sprawled out with legs spread, the semen on her belly shining white. A shriek escaped Caitlin's chest, and the head boy spun from side to side to show the onlookers the picture. The boys with him started cracking up, and each of them flipped on their phones, revealing the other pictures of her with her fingers in her mouth, on her breast and over her pussy. One picture was a close-up where I had dipped my finger in the semen and then smeared the drops on her face.

Laughter spread through the crowded hall.

Caitlin's jaw dropped and she began shaking. Her face took on that pink, strained look a baby's gets in the seconds before it starts to scream bloody murder. She looked at me for help but I offered nothing.

"Fucking bitch!" someone yelled from the safety of the crowd.

"Yeah," came another voice without a face. "That's what you get for lying about Derek!"

Caitlin shook so hard I could hear her teeth chattering. Her face was slack with shock but tears burst from her eyes. Most of the gathered crowd pulled out their phones to record the scene. Caitlin screamed and her hands went to the sides of her head, surprising all of us as she began pulling clumps of her hair out by the roots. The crowd was growing now, others having been drawn in by the commotion. I spotted Amy and Dakota amongst this sea of barking vultures. Dakota's face bore the look of a prankster who just realized they'd gone too far, but there was a small, sideways smile curling

Amy's lips, a cruelty in the soft pearls of her perfect teeth.

"Caitlin sucks jock!" the boy with the tablet yelled, and his cronies began to chant it.

"Stop it!" I told them, wishing I could kiss them. I still wanted Caitlin to think I was on her side and for the school to think I was a good girl. "Get out of here!"

Caitlin fell to her knees, breathing strangely.

"She's hyperventilating!" Dakota said, coming closer.

People crowded around her now, not meaning to rob her of air but doing it anyway. Caitlin fumbled with her gym bag for her inhaler. I knew what she was going for, and I didn't help her. Instead I stood there in faux shock and forced some tears to my eyes.

"Get out of the way!" an adult voice said.

My algebra teacher, Ms. Newman, pushed her slender body through the crowd and dropped to Caitlin's side. She saw Caitlin's hand halfway in the bag, so she opened it up and got the inhaler for her and put it to her lips. Caitlin tried to puff but her breathing was too erratic. Her face was purpling. I was right there, so the teacher looked to me.

"Call an ambulance," she said.

I really had no choice, so I took out my phone and dialed 911.

Everyone else stood there and watched, some of them still smiling, still recording.

Much of the school fell somber afterwards. It seemed many of my classmates had a heart after all. Making fun of a girl behind her back was one thing, but bullying her into a nervous breakdown that sent her to the hospital . . . well, that sent them into a brief spell of shallow guilt. Not that anyone was going to reach out to her. No one would dare be the first to buy a card to pass around the school for everyone to sign, sending generic well wishes. They could feel bad, but they couldn't let anyone *know* they felt bad for the school's pariah. So while this somber mood was a group thing, the group dealt with it as individual mutes.

There were still those vicious internet troll types who found this amusing—the teenage sadists, the lipstick mean girls and the bullies smirking with lowered sunglasses. Though she hid it better than others, I knew Amy well, and could smell the ripe stench of her self-satisfaction, exuded from the glands of her inner poison. The evil in her was admirable, irresistible. It made me want to fuck her.

"I'm sorry," she said, not sorry, "but she brought this on herself."

"They're going to murder those boys," Brian said, finishing the last of his lunch. "I'll bet they get expelled."

"All four of them? No way."

"What about Derek?" Dakota asked.

He was absent from lunch. We all knew he'd been called to the dean's office.

"Betcha they're blaming him for the pictures," Brian said.

Amy shook her head as if it were a shame. "He's been through so much already."

"Yeah," I said. "Poor guy."

I went straight home after school and signed on to Facebook. The *Save Derek* page had been deleted. I knew this was not Amy's doing. Guilt must have made people report it as a hate group, and Facebook shut it down. That was okay by me. It had served its purpose, and I still had the prints and the files stored on the thumb drive. There was also my plan for the disposable cell phone, which had been made all the easier now.

I'd been planning to pull all the numbers out of Caitlin's phone at some point when she wasn't looking, maybe when she would be showering after our drills. But the opportunity had not arisen because we had not been practicing. But when she was rushed off to the hospital, I had taken her bag for her. Her phone was inside. I copied the phone numbers of every single contact she had in it: family, friends, coaches and more. I entered them all into my disposable phone and put hers back in her bag.

I wanted to let some time pass before I went to the hospital, to let Simone and the family deal with the latest tragedy before having any visitors. To pass the time I browsed online for shock and horror porn, finding some bestiality videos that only made me laugh, some (probably fake) incest ones that grossed me out, and then a wonderful series of abuse movies where people were being shit on. While disgusting, the degradation gave me an enjoyable quiver. They were still too gross for me to masturbate to, but the humiliation passed the time nicely, even though Caitlin never left my thoughts.

When I recalled her fit of hair-tearing and her shaking on the floor, warmth radiated through my body and tickled my guts. This elation got me out of my seat, humming, and I started to sway, letting the hot rush course through my blood. I began to dance, performing the old ballet routines right there in the office, the memory of Caitlin's screams serving as my music. At first I felt my weight on my straining toes, but then the warmth lifted me up and I was floating, spinning, twinkling like New Year's Eve. My movements were smooth and without hesitation, the images of Caitlin's shameful photos flickering across my mind's eye in a rapid-fire slideshow. I imagined this was what hard drugs must be like, only better—purer, more natural, maybe even stronger.

At dusk I drove to the grocery store, picked out an expensive bouquet and card, and even sprung for a Snoopy *Get Better Soon* balloon. I bought a Slim Jim, wishing I had time for some rare meat, and got to the hospital by six-thirty. The woman at the check-in counter confirmed Caitlin was out of the emergency room but was still in the hospital. I had lucked out by making it in time to see her in a bed, hopefully hooked up to wires. I took the elevator to the floor she was staying on and carried my gifts and Caitlin's bag down the hall until I found her room. The door was half open, so I knocked on the wall beside it. Caitlin's grandmother came out, her face gray as her long hair, her eyes like slate behind her glasses. The lines in her skin were deeper than canyons. For a moment I was afraid she was angry with me, that the whole family was, that Caitlin had told them about my failure to act. But a pained smile assured me the grandmother was just beaten down by all she and her loved ones had recently endured.

"Hi, Kim," she said. "Come on in."

The room smelled like all hospital rooms smell—vitamins, urine, death. Simone was by Caitlin's bedside, a husk of sorrow and body fat. The little boy was not present, probably being watched by his uncle. Caitlin's grandfather sat on the other side of the room with his arms crossed over his paunch and his eyes closed. He looked asleep. Only one light was on, but it was a harsh fluorescent that made everyone look like they were in the early stages of rot. Simone looked at me with her anguished face. She tried to smile but it turned to silent tears. Caitlin's head was turned away from me. At first I thought she was ignoring me, but as I got closer I realized she was only half conscious, some sedative lulling her into la-la land. There were bruises and cuts along her arms and neck.

"They gave her something to calm her," the grandmother explained. "She was hysterical . . . hurting herself."

"I'm so, so sorry," I said to the family. "I just went into shock. I didn't know what to do, I just froze up."

The grandmother's hand was warm on my back. "It's okay, honey. I don't think any of us were prepared for this."

I put the bouquet and card down on an end table and the bag on the floor.

"I brought this for her."

Approaching Caitlin's bed, I tied the end of the balloon to it. Simone's hand was on the railing and I placed mine over hers. It was surprisingly cold. Her other hand came up and covered mine, patted it. She started to say something but choked on the words.

The grandmother spoke for her. "We appreciate you coming by, Kim."

"Caitlin's okay, right?" I asked. "She's breathing all right now?"

"Yes, she is. But she's not well."

Simone took a fresh tissue from the box in her lap. "It's all too much for her. It's too much for any fifteen-year-old girl to bear."

"Will she be able to come home soon?" I asked.

Simone didn't answer.

"Not yet," the grandmother said, "but she won't be staying here. She's going to go to a different hospital."

Simone gagged on tears again, her body curling inward like a dying insect.

"What kind of hospital?" I asked.

But I already knew.

Simone admitted her daughter to a behavioral health center, a hospital for the mentally ill. Caitlin was admitted voluntarily but she ended up being held there for mandatory observation after being labeled a high suicide risk. I desperately wanted to see her in there (picturing it in my mind made me feel breathlessly giddy), but she was not allowed to have any visitors other than her immediate family. I did my best to keep in touch with Simone, fishing for updates, but while she was polite and appreciative of my concern she had become withdrawn and rarely answered her phone.

Derek had been suspended and was kicked off the basketball team indefinitely. It seemed he had been unable to deny the pictures were from that night. He was a bad liar. He insisted he had not taken or shared the photos, but he did not try to blame it on me. Even if he thought I had something to do with it (and by now he should have), he knew no one else would believe it. Along with him, the group of boys that had come at us with the tablet were each suspended for a full month. This sent out a stern warning—anyone imposing any further harm on Caitlin Blakley would be drawn and quartered. Students were afraid to even say her name around faculty, so I only heard bits and pieces of hushed conversations in the halls. Those who had not seen the meltdown in person had seen the videos other people had taken. Someone had anonymously posted one to YouTube and it already had nine hundred views.

Days went by and Caitlin didn't come home. I wondered if she ever would and the thought of her growing old in a madhouse pleased me, even if it made my disposable phone and print photo plans obsolete. But while this would be a satisfying conclusion to the game, I still wanted to play. There are many things a girl my age can achieve to become powerful. There is the power of being beautiful, so you can be lusted after and fawned over by boys, thereby becoming the envy of all other girls. There is the power of intellect, so you can manipulate and conquer others. There's the power of your sexuality, your popularity, your wealth and privilege. But there is no power as thrilling as being able to completely decimate another human being, to demoralize and deconstruct their very soul until all that's left of their fragile sanity is frenzied, blurry tatters. It makes a girl feel like a goddess.

I finally got through to Simone.

"The doctors tell me she's doing better," she said, "but I'm not seeing it. When I visit her . . . she just seems so *broken* . . . it's like she's not even my Caitlin, but someone else . . . someone lost and hopeless."

Getting her to be honest like this was another victory. The veil between adult and teenager had been lifted between us. I was *her* friend now, not just her daughter's.

"I wish I could see her," I said.

"Don't worry. She's coming home soon."

"Really?"

"They can't keep her there forever. I don't think she's well, but I suppose she has to come home sometime. I've set her up with a psychiatrist. Honestly, I don't think we'll be staying here much longer."

Something sank inside of me. "You're moving?"

"Nothing's official yet, but I think that would be best. My parents live in Colorado. We'll probably stay with them for a while and then try to . . . start over."

Colorado was on the other side of the country. Caitlin would escape.

"It's such a shame," I said. "She was a shoo-in for head cheerleader next year."

But I knew this wouldn't be enough.

"Well," Simone said, "there's cheerleading in Colorado too. You know how much I appreciate what you've done for her. Maybe you can come visit us sometime and see her on the field."

"I'd like that."

There's no time to waste now, I thought. *She's coming home. You need to go full brutal.*

TWENTY-ONE

As I drove through the Blakleys' neighborhood, I read off the addresses, my phone recording my voice. When I got home I typed them up on my computer, adding *Our Neighbor* at the top of each one because I didn't know the residents' names. I also typed up return address labels with Caitlin's name and address appearing at the top. I wore gloves as I taped the addresses to the envelopes, forty in all. I filled them, sealed them, and mailed them from three separate post offices, two different towns over from my own, so the postage marks wouldn't be from my local office.

There had still been no arrests in the case of Mr. Blakley's mysterious death. No one had called me in for further questioning, and Derek Schechter—if he suspected me of involvement with the photos or anything else—had not come to anyone with my name. There was still a lot of tension at school, but a small amount of time seems much bigger to the young, and as the weeks rolled on, pushing us into early May, the name Caitlin Blakley fell lower on the list of hot topics. She was a dramatic headline whose ink had faded.

Father came home and his presence brought back a staggering reality, one I had been avoiding.

I was now nine weeks pregnant.

I had been doing my best to ignore it, as if denying it would make it go away. But denying it was getting harder and harder. I was throwing up a lot and my breasts had swelled and become extremely sensitive. It seemed like all I did was pee, but taking a dump was painfully difficult. After reading up on this, I started taking fiber supplements and ate Raisin Bran twice a day. My friends were annoyed by the fact I never wanted to hang out much (when I wasn't at school, all I wanted to do was nap in front of the TV while watching gory movies), and my grades were slipping a little.

I had to get rid of the little fuck-demon inside of me. I'd been so preoccupied with the systematic ruination of the Blakleys I had been neglecting this massive problem. I was on the verge of nuclear meltdown but had busied myself with fireworks. Caitlin was home but Simone didn't want her having visitors just yet, the mail had been sent out, and I was saving the phone numbers for later. It was time to address my own health before further sabotaging Caitlin's.

All my research on miscarriages was disheartening. Most miscarriages are caused by chromosomal abnormalities or other uncontrollable issues—incompetent cervixes, immunologic disorders, polycystic ovary syndrome. These were ailments I doubted I was lucky enough to have. I was young and healthy, the perfect housing for a bouncing brat.

But there was some hope.

I could poison the little fuck-demon.

Hard alcohol was my best bet. I didn't want to mess with street dope, but I could score some prescription pills from Zack if need be. I would just have to research which ones not to take when you were pregnant, which I was sure would be *most* of them, and then take them. I really did not want to take up smoking, but I was desperate. If burning through butts would put a noose around the fetus's still-forming neck, then I would do it, but only in private so it wouldn't hurt my image, and with caution not to get addicted.

I could also cause trauma.

Women with high physical and emotional stress are far more likely to have miscarriages. Riding horses came to mind, as did hardcore weightlifting. I could get into more intense gymnastics without raising any eyebrows. I briefly thought I had struck oil when I thought of taking up boxing, but dismissed the idea when I remembered the danger it would pose to my pretty face.

I never thought I would have craved abdominal pain and discharge so badly, but here I was, up the duff and jolly well fucked.

There was another Blakley in my life now, and it too would have to be destroyed.

It made me nervous when the police were called in.

The dirty pictures of Caitlin had reached everyone in her neighborhood. Simone was nearly as hysterical as her daughter had been on her last day of school. She called me about it, raging as she asked me questions about Derek and his relationship with Caitlin. I told her what she already knew and apologized for not having more information. The woman was furious—in my mind's eye she was foaming and gnashing like the dog in *Cujo*—and coming at me hard, digging for any information I might have held up until this point.

"You have to tell me the truth, Kim. And I mean all of it. I know about the party."

I knew Caitlin hadn't confessed willingly. Everyone knew about the party by now. It was bound to get back to Simone.

"I'm sorry. It was just a party. I wanted to introduce her to some cheerleaders. I didn't even notice when she and Derek snuck off together."

"That's not your fault. She should have told me it was a party instead of telling me it was just a sleepover. Had I known boys would be there . . . I mean, she's just a girl, she doesn't know how to deal with boys like Derek. But why on earth did she *sleep* with him?"

"I think she was just taken in. He's older, good looking, a jock. He knows how to charm girls to, you know, get what he wants."

"But if he got what he wanted, then why is he doing all of this awful stuff to her?"

"I don't know. Maybe he wants more than she'll give. I know Caitlin regretted going to bed with him."

"Do you . . ." she hesitated. "Do you think he forced himself on her?"

I waited to reply, letting her hear my deep breath. "I do."

Wet sniffles filled the line. "That son of a . . ."

"Caitlin swears he didn't, but I think she's just too ashamed to admit what happened. I tried to get her to tell you." I made crying sounds of my own, reminding her I too was *just a girl*. "I really did, honest."

"This isn't your fault, honey. I'm not mad at you, okay?"

"Okay."

"But you do think it's him that's doing all this, right?"

"I don't know. Those pictures . . . they got all over school."

"But he was the one who took them and shared them to begin with. I *know* it was him. My little girl made a mistake and slept with him, but I know she hasn't slept with anyone else. So it had to be Derek who took the pictures, and I'll bet it's him sending them to everyone we know. He's a son of a bitch and I'm gonna get him for this. Mark my words. He's dead meat!"

I knew post offices had surveillance cameras, but would it really be possible to notice who was sending these particular packages? It seemed unlikely. I'd been careful not to get any prints on them, wearing gloves even though the weather was mild. I'd paid in cash. I had also worn a different jacket in each post office, and a knit cap to hide my hair, making me harder to identify if they did go back to the tapes. It was not like me to go through with anything without thinking about every possible outcome, every remote danger.

"I hope they catch whoever did this," I said, "whether it's Derek or not."

When we finished the call I hung up and got the disposable, untraceable phone from my dresser. The photos were already uploaded to it, so I put them into a mass text that went out to every single contact that had been in Caitlin's phone. Along with the pictures I wrote a message:

I want every one of you to cum in my mouth.

I took the phone to the garage and crushed it with the vice grip on my father's workbench. It was garbage night, so I hauled out the bin and looked around. The street was empty. I walked over to one of my neighbor's trashcans and put half of the bits in it, and the other half in the can belonging to my neighbor on the other side. Once I was back in my room, I laughed until my sides hurt and hoped the pain would damage the little fucker in my belly.

TWENTY-TWO

I wasn't surprised when the police asked Father and I to come in for questioning again. I had expected to be nervous when this finally happened, but instead an eerie calm had come over me. I felt like I was floating around in an impenetrable sphere that not only protected me from harm, but also suspicion. When I pictured this sphere, I imagined it completely filled with blood that was not my own, warm and smelling of wet pennies. There was no doubt in my mind the police didn't want to learn about me, but rather about Derek Schechter, and I was right.

So I told them.

Derek is always aggressive with girls. He forced himself on me once in an Applebee's parking lot, but I fought him off so that he could not enter me. He had never pursued a sophomore before, so I didn't watch him and Caitlin as closely as I should have. I admit we all had been drinking a little. By the time I noticed they were gone it was too late. Derek came stumbling downstairs, fumbling with his pants. He had his phone in his hand; I didn't think anything of it at the time, but now I think he used it to take those pictures. He told me he had just had sex with Caitlin and she had fought him a little, but he insisted she liked it, that with girls like her no *means* yes. *I found Caitlin passed out naked in the guest bedroom, and I mean* really *passed out. I couldn't wake her. At the time, I thought she'd just drank too much, so I just covered her with the blanket and closed the door.*

The next day she was so distraught. She said she felt like she had been drugged because she wasn't able to move much when Derek got on top of her. I tried and tried to convince her to tell her parents and report the rape, but she was just so scared. She made me promise to let her handle it her way. Now I wish I hadn't, but you just don't understand how upset she was. She didn't want anyone to know what had happened.

Of course Derek blabbed it all over school. He didn't admit to raping her, he just told everyone what an easy lay she was, probably so everyone would think she was a slut, so if she did report the rape no one would believe her. I think that's why he took those pictures too, and made sure everyone saw them. He figures if she's a slut, then he walks away.

I'm sorry I didn't come out with this sooner. Caitlin wouldn't admit to it no matter what happened, and with all of the pain and embarrassment she'd been through with her dad dying and the pictures getting around school, I just didn't want her to have to deal with this rape stuff. She wanted to let it alone, so I did.

I was afraid of what would happen to Caitlin if she did accuse him, and afraid of what might happen to me too. We're both afraid of Derek. Very afraid.

"I think you should stay home from school for a while," Father said.

He swirled the mushrooms on his plate before lifting one to his mouth.

"I can't do that," I said. "I have perfect attendance, except for that one approved half day."

"It's just I worry about you with all of this craziness going on."

I sipped my cabernet. "I'm fine. Really. I don't want to fall behind on my classes or miss any games."

"And I don't want you to have to worry about seeing that Derek kid."

"I won't. He's been suspended."

"But you run in the same circles. Amy's boyfriend is friends with him, right?"

"Yeah, but Derek's kind of on house arrest, if you know what I mean."

"Somehow I don't think that'll stop him. He's bad news."

I shrugged, smiled. "Don't worry. I always have my key knife. I know how to protect myself with it. Trust me."

"He'll wish he'd only had to face a key knife if I get a hold of him."

"Now, Father, let the police handle it."

His jaw tightened around his food. "I hope they arrest him soon."

They did.

On Mother's Day, Derek Schechter was charged with aggravated sexual assault. Simone had pressed charges. The police picked him up at his house while his family was handing out gifts to his mom. Seeing her firstborn son hauled away in cuffs must have been one memorable present. His parents sprung him out on bail as soon as they could, and he was ordered not to leave town.

Amy gave me this news in a hyperactive monologue as we shopped for new wardrobes for the coming summer. We were in a dressing room together and she was complaining about needing to lose five pounds so I would tell her how skinny she looked, which I did. All of the sundresses looked very nice on her, but Amy Heidnik could make a shit-stained burlap sack look good, and she knew it, which was even worse.

"What about mailing the pictures and all of that?" I asked.

"I don't think they can pin that on him. But Brian said Derek's more worried about the death of Mr. Blakley, like *super-worried* about it. They found a date rape drug at the scene that night, and they think Derek used that kind of thing on Caitlin. They're connecting all sorts of dots like that. It's nuts!"

"Jesus. Are they going to charge him with the murder too?"

"I don't know. But the Schechters hired a lawyer. Things don't look good, Kim. They don't look good at all." She spun around in the mirror. "But how do *I* look in this green dress?"

Derek's trouble with the law was a great comedy, but it gave me the jitters when I thought about him cracking and telling them I had encouraged him to be rough with Caitlin. I could swear otherwise, and would, but it made me a little uneasy to know my questioning by the police probably wasn't over. But they hadn't called on me yet. Either Derek had kept his mouth shut, or he'd blabbed but no one had believed him.

The school was electric with the news—it bubbled and steamed with acidic gossip, Caitlin Blakley on everyone's lips again, fear of punishment be damned. We were in the midst of a movie-quality drama and it jazzed everyone whether they would admit it or not, including teachers and parents. Despite Father's wishes, I kept on going to school. I wasn't going to miss a minute of this sweet madhouse, although there were days where the little fuck-demon seemed determined to make me puke up my own colon. I'd been smoking as much as I could stomach (it was absolutely revolting), but I was worried about how the stink clung to me. I'd joined a CrossFit gym and was pushing my body to the limit with medicine balls, chains and all sorts of bizarre workouts. I was faithful to my drinking though, knocking back whiskey and scotch every night before bed, sending myself into a delirium that left me sluggish the next day.

When Simone called and told me Caitlin could see visitors, I was so happy I skipped along the driveway toward the car. It was Sunday, and Father never went anywhere on his day off, so it was all mine. On the ride over I listened to my favorite driving soundtrack—the dead static at the end of the AM spectrum, turned all the way up.

Simone greeted me at the door, looking like she'd just had a massive stroke. Every inch of her was in a grayed state of decay. Inside, the Blakley house was all shadows and despair, the foul odor of an overflowing trash bin and the used dishes scattered about revealing long days of despondency. The family had surrendered themselves to the heartache of their new world. Their home was not the only thing in ruins.

"Bob's mother comes by to help me keep up," Simone said, "but I just don't have it in me to do it on my own."

"I understand."

"Dalton is staying with his grandparents for now. I have my hands full with Caitlin."

"How is she?"

Simone's stare was distant. Her chin trembled. "I don't know if she's ever coming back."

I took her in my arms and hugged her. It paid off briefly with Simone crying into my shoulder, and it took everything I had not to slide my hand between her legs and grab her snatch. I wanted to chew her lips off and paint the walls with her brains.

When Simone gathered herself, she guided me upstairs.

"I think seeing you will get her spirits up," she said. "I appreciate this, Kim. I'll warn you now it won't be easy for you to see her like this."

It feels like I've waited all my life to see her like this—my little cum-splat of sorrow, the human demolition derby of Caitlin Fucking Blakley. She was my masterpiece, a one-on-one terrorist attack on the soul, conducted by strategic infiltration and the most savage of betrayals. I wished I could live forever in this moment.

She opened the door and as we went into the room I saw the dresser first and recalled with fondness how Mr. Blakley had fucked me up against it while calling out his daughter's name at my command. Knowing I'd had sex with someone who was now dead was a pleasure all to itself. The shades were drawn and only a pale, gray light seeped through. Bits of dust and dead skin danced in it like gnats. There was a stale smell here, like dirty laundry and used tissues.

Caitlin lay in bed with a comforter on even though it was very warm and stuffy inside her room. Her arms and neck were covered in bruises and cuts where she had hurt herself. Her hair was frizzy and greasy and I wondered when the last time she had washed. It made me picture her mother trying to force her into the tub as she thrashed and clawed and screamed like she was being stabbed in her cunt. The table beside the bed had one of those pill containers old farts use, the ones that list off the days of the week, and greeting cards were tacked over the headboard like a pre-mature memorial.

"Hi, Caitlin."

She turned to me. Her features were slack but her eyes grew wet at the sight of me. A hand emerged from under the blanket and reached out. The knuckles were raw, fresh scabs not fully closed. I took the hand in mine, resisting the urge to peel her scabs back and eat them. She felt like snow and was just as white, a derailed train of a girl. When she spoke, it was like she was gargling rusty nails, and I wondered just how she had made herself so hoarse.

Screaming all night?

The thought tickled me.

"Kim, you came."

"Of course I did."

She sat up. "I was worried . . . you were mad at me."

"Why on earth would I be mad at you?"

She sniffled and I sat down on the bed with her and tucked a strand of hair behind her ear. A sad smile made dumplings of her cheeks. She looked so much like a child then, so weak, so small.

Simone walked backwards toward the doorway, taking the pill container with her. "I'll leave you two alone."

She left but kept the door open a crack.

"I had to tell Mom," Caitlin said. "About Derek. She knew I wouldn't have just slept with some guy. She knew something was wrong with it."

"Are you going to testify against him?"

Her face pinched. "I don't know. I don't think I can."

"You'll have to, though. You'll have to talk about it in court, in front of everybody."

The tears were falling already, making my nipples harden into pebbles.

"What's in that pill container?"

"Stuff to calm me down and make me sleep."

"You don't look calm."

"How could I be with all of this happening? You know, I went onto Facebook the other day, and I had all of these messages from people all telling me to kill myself!"

Excellent.

"Oh, Caitlin. I'm so sorry. That's awful."

"How can I be calm after that?"

"Well, are you sure you're taking enough pills?"

She blinked away the wetness in her eyes. "I take them the way the doctor told me. They don't help much."

"That's because you're not taking enough."

She looked at me, confused.

"Take them as needed," I said. "Doctors have to tell you to limit your pills just because so many people get addicted to painkillers and all that. If they're not working you should take more. Take as many as you want."

The thought of her overdosing was a nice enough finale. She seemed to think about what I'd said and then shook her head. "No, I don't even want them."

Rats.

"You know . . ." I said. "I probably shouldn't tell you this, but I think you have a right to know."

I let that hang for a moment. Caitlin stirred.

"What?" she asked.

"They . . . they think Derek killed your dad."

Her face contorted into a horrible, pink mess.

"What? Oh god." She covered her face with her hands. "No. No!"

"They think there was a confrontation and Derek stabbed him. There were drugs everywhere too. Date rape drugs, like what he must have used on you. They think it has something to do with it. Maybe your Dad knew—"

"It's my fault!" she cried. "It *really is* all my fault."

"How is it your fault?"

"Dad was so mad when word got around school. He kept saying he was going to *kill* Derek. We didn't think he really meant it. God, he must have threatened him or done something that made Derek kill him. My dad's dead *because of me!*"

She was sobbing now so I pulled her in close to feel the texture of her suffering.

"It's going to be okay," I said.

"No it isn't! Nothing is *ever* going to be okay!"

Caitlin mewled and the door came all the way open. Simone came in carrying a glass of water. Her other hand was closed.

"I don't want any pills!" Caitlin barked.

"Honey, this is one of the strong ones. It'll calm you down."

Simone bent over and Caitlin reared back and slapped the glass from her mother's hand. It crashed into the table, shattering in a mist, and Caitlin banshee-shrieked, veins bulging out of her head. I got up off the bed to watch and Simone tried to take her daughter in her arms but Caitlin struggled, screaming like a girl possessed. When Simone put her weight on her, Caitlin spun and reached for a big shard of the broken glass.

I didn't blink for fear of missing a single second.

Caitlin writhed free of her mother's grip and turned the shard upside down and sent it into the underside of her forearm. She pulled the shard upward, digging deeper and opening the upper part of her arm before Simone could wrench away the shard. The room seemed to explode then—limbs flailing, bed shaking, the lamp falling over, mother and daughter wrestling as Caitlin's blood soused the sheets.

"Hold down her legs!" Simone cried.

I moved onto the bed and grabbed at Caitlin's kicking feet, in love with the idea of holding her down because it was so much like bondage. The blankets came off in a flurry as Simone tried to use them to stop the bleeding. Caitlin wore only a long t-shirt (her dad's, no doubt) and panties. I worked my way between her bare legs, savoring the feel of their soft, child-like flesh on my arms. I could smell the fresh copper of the blood and a squall of desire blurred my vision until I blinked myself back to the present. With both of us on top of her, Caitlin stopped screaming and broke down into terrible sobs that contracted her stomach. Her breaths were loud and halted. She was hyperventilating.

Overwhelmed, Simone screamed in frustration. She took the inhaler from the nightstand, trying to force it into Caitlin's mouth while at the same time putting pressure on the wound. The sheets were slicked red and the headboard and walls were streaked with bloody handprints and smears. Caitlin was shaking like she was in an electric chair. When Simone put the inhaler into Caitlin's mouth, she bit it so hard it cracked and splintered. Her eyes rolled.

"Call the paramedics!" Simone said.

I took out my phone and left the room. I didn't want to miss the show, but I also didn't want the ambulance to get there in time. Listening to Simone's anguish, I stayed in the hall, waiting before calling 911.

"Caitlin!" Simone wept. "Breathe, honey! Breathe!"

If I stayed in the hall too long she would know I was stalling, so after a few crucial minutes I called 911 and asked them to send out an ambulance, then ran back into the room to watch Caitlin die.

PART TWO

EATING FOR TWO

TWENTY-THREE

It was a beautiful, sunny day, and while that kind of weather normally displeases me, the insensitive juxtaposition of it being the day of Caitlin's funeral held a certain charm.

By the time the paramedics had arrived, Caitlin had stopped breathing all together. She had also lost a great deal of blood, so much that her mother came off the bed looking like she'd been attacked with a chainsaw. C.P.R. brought no results, so they took out the defibrillator and zapped her tiny body, making her heave as her mother cried out in horror. Despite their best efforts, the paramedics failed to resuscitate Caitlin. She was dead before they loaded her into the ambulance.

Simone was an incredible sight. Her disintegration was immediate and all consuming, a glorious implosion, better than anything I could have imagined. A fresh hell closed its flames around her and dragged her down, down, down—grinding her into a black abyss from which she would never return. And I watched it all with numb euphoria, doing my best to keep up my act of shock and sorrow while being totally at ease with the world. The gray hull of the Blakley house seemed to slip away in that moment, and my body relaxed as that invisible sphere came around me once again, warming my soul with its bloody embrace, pumping my heart with darkness and bliss, the spoils of a job well done. Tears filled my eyes. No one had to know they were tears of joy.

Standing there now, looking down upon the coffin, those same tears returned. Caitlin's family surrounded me in their heavy grief, making my pussy froth in reply. I couldn't wait to get home and fuck myself, even though I had been masturbating so much since Caitlin's death I had made myself sore. As the priest droned on about Jesus and heaven and all that shit, I pictured Caitlin's corpse on a mortician's cart with hoses pumping her full of formaldehyde. I wondered if the mortician had fucked her dead body. I know I would have. Just thinking about her chilled carcass made me tingle. She would be nude and bloodless, clean in a way only the newly dead could be. There was such poetry to young corpses, such art. Their youth intensified the sense of loss, and I wanted to rub that loss across my flesh until I passed out from the force of my orgasm. The priest rambled on, and I wondered how hard it would be to sneak back into the graveyard by night and exhume the body, maybe take it home as a fuck-trophy, Ed Gein style. This was a ridiculous idea, but it kept me entertained while I endured the monologue.

Caitlin's death kicked the whole town right in the nuts. The school shut down for a full day. People were treating it like it was their own personal soap opera. The very kids who had taunted her, bashed her online, and spread her pornographic photos like an S.T.D were now all talking about what a sweet girl she was. Cheerleaders Mandy Clark and Summer Scott told everyone who would listen about how much potential she'd had, and how they'd been planning to help me get her on the team next year. Even Amy made a point to let everyone know how much she had liked Caitlin, not even hesitating to do so when Brian, Dakota and I were around, as if she just stepped out of an alternate reality where she hadn't been shitting all over the girl with every breath.

And Derek?

Well, the school had a new magnet for their anger.

Derek was now a goddamned son of a bitch. He had raped and tormented an innocent young girl, driving her to suicide (everyone kept referring to it as a suicide, despite the facts). Add to this the suspicion that engulfed him pertaining to Mr. Blakley's murder, and Derek was a far bigger pariah than Caitlin had ever come close to being. The shift was stunning in its briskness and intensity. It sure made me laugh. Our school—our town—had become a Shakespearian tragedy, and the drama was still peaking.

Father had to go to Atlanta on business. I had been to Atlanta before, so I did not envy him, especially seeing how this was going to be an extended trip. He asked me again and again if I would be all right alone, which irked me. Normally he would never ask that sort of thing—it was almost insulting—but with all the death going on he was hesitant to leave. Still, he did, giving me the house and car back to do with whatever I wished. This made it easier to smoke and drink. I had also researched over-the-counter medications one is not supposed to take while pregnant, and now I was taking high risk castor oil every day, some Pepto-Bismol here and there, and was randomly popping ibuprofen, naproxen, and congestion medicine. I was brewing an abortion cocktail, or so I hoped.

It was almost June. I was going on three months pregnant now. Even if I could find some way around the parental guardian aspect, it was too late to legally have an abortion.

Fuck!

My nightmare was unfolding like a soiled napkin. The little fuck-demon was having its way with my insides. I was ravenous much of the time and weirdly craving nothing but rare meat. At one point I had even dug into a package of fresh ground chuck and devoured it raw while standing in the kitchen in the dead of night. The fetus was changing me. Soon I would even be able to feel the beast within writhing around like a burrowing snake. It sickened me to think of it.

Did you hear? Kim White killed herself . . . and she was pregnant!

I shook the thought out of my head as I stared at my naked body in the mirror. I felt a little pudgy, but I did not have a noticeable baby bump yet. From what I'd read, I could expect one very soon. I could cloak myself in baggy sweaters for a while, but that was just putting off the inevitable reveal. I had to push this fucking thing out of me while it would still kill it to leave my body. Imagining the gory mess belching out of my vagina filled me with wishful thinking, but that hope seemed so distant, sometimes even unreachable. But it was a goal, and I never gave up on my goals.

The ringing doorbell woke me.

The clock read three-thirty in the morning. I groaned, wondering if I had just dreamt the sound. As I stirred the bell rang again, several times in a row. I looked out the window, surprised by who I saw waiting below.

He can't be this stupid.

It was possible Derek knew Father was out of town. Amy, Dakota and Brian knew. They'd already come over to hang out. It was also possible he was too crazed to consider this. Maybe he even wanted Father to be there, so he could try to talk to him about what had really happened and convince him to make his daughter . . . what? Confess?

I was only wearing a t-shirt and panties, but I charged down the stairs. Whatever was about to happen would look bad on Derek's part. He was coming to a witness's house in the middle of the night. I would body-slam him with this. Before answering the door I went to the security box on the wall and made sure the silent camera overlooking the porch was on. The screen revealed Derek standing there alone, shifting from one foot to another in his anxiousness. The bell rang and rang as I went into the kitchen and took the longest butcher knife from the block.

When I opened the door I brandished it and Derek flinched and put up his hands.

"I just want to talk to you," he said. He gulped and stress-tics blemished his face. "Just talk, that's all."

"Hands on your head."

He did as he was told and I walked over to him and touched his chest to make sure he wasn't wearing some kind of wire. I patted him down for weapons or recording devices, and he was clean.

"I came on my own," he said. "Nobody knows I'm doing this. It's just between you and me."

"Talk if you want to talk," I said.

"It was you, wasn't it? You did it on purpose, didn't you?"

"Did what?"

"That night. The party. *You* told me she liked it rough. *You* got me drunk enough to believe it. You have to tell the cops I didn't rape Caitlin."

"You *did* rape her."

"No, I didn't. You told me she liked it rough."

"And you believed it because you wanted to believe it."

"I believed it because of what happened with you and me, that night in my car."

"It doesn't fucking matter what you believed, asshole. What matters is you held her down and fucked her while she begged you not to."

"It wasn't like that!"

"The only reason she didn't fight harder was because she was drugged."

His eyes narrowed. "What do you know about that?"

I smirked.

"You bitch," he said.

"Easy, tiger."

"*You* slipped something to her, didn't you? You wanted me to rape her for your own sick reasons. Jesus, why would you do that?"

I shrugged. "Boredom? Laughs? I must say I never expected it to have results quite this satisfying."

Derek's mouth hung open as he took a step back. "You're fucked up, Kim."

"I'm not the one suspected of murder."

"Shut your mouth. I had nothing to do with that!"

"Well, I don't see any other suspects being rounded up, do you?"

"The cops already cleared me of that." He tried to wave this away. "You have to tell them I didn't rape Caitlin! This whole town has turned on me since she died. I don't want to go to prison."

"Then you should listen to your lawyer, you moron. I'm sure he told you not to talk to anybody about this."

"I had to try and talk some sense into you. What you've done isn't fair, Kim. It isn't right! We don't have to tell them what you did, but you could at least tell them Caitlin was totally willing."

I snickered. "Why should I lie for you? What do I gain from that?"

"Okay. What do you want?"

I mulled it over.

"How did you get here?" I asked.

"I had to sneak out, so I walked."

Derek only lived about two miles away. He could walk that in less than half an hour. My only concern was he may have been seen, but I knew the route. It was all neighborhoods, no main roads, and it was very late.

"Come inside," I said.

"I'd better not."

"You can't even do that much?"

"Why do you want me to go in there?"

"Because."

"Because what?"

He was annoying me. Either we were going to do this or not.

"I want you to come inside so I can tie you up."

Derek's eyes went wide. "What?"

"I want to play bondage. I tie you up, smack you around, humiliate you."

He couldn't even reply for a moment. The shock was too strong.

"Yes or no?" I asked.

"You're insane."

"Who's to say what's sane anymore?"

He took another step back. It was a cool night but he was sweating.

"I'm not going to do that," he said.

"Then you're going to rot in prison."

"Damn it! I'm not stupid. If I go in there you're just going to try and make it look like I attacked you or something."

"No, *you'll* be the one tied up, Derek."

"Even if I did go in, what guarantee are you giving me you'll clear my name?"

I laughed. "*Guarantee*? Shit, Derek, I can *guarantee* you anything you want."

"Oh, I get it. Your word isn't worth shit."

"But you'll just have to take me on it, won't you? Maybe I'll help you, maybe I won't. It all depends on how good a boy you are. Good boys get treats, bad boys get the whip."

Derek's whole body tensed. "You're insane."

"You said that already, dipshit. Now stop farting around. Either get inside so I can have my fun or get the hell off my property."

Derek deflated. He looked at the ground with his head bowed, a child forced to finish his cold dinner.

"Well?" I asked.

Amazingly, he moved toward the door.

"Push me," I said.

"What for?"

"You know I like it rough. Push your way through and take my knife away. Then drag me in behind you."

He rolled his eyes. It was a lame performance, but he did as he was told, wanting those treats so bad.

TWENTY-FOUR

Watching degradation porn didn't do the real thing justice. Derek, bathed in my urine and spit, sat naked in the chair I'd brought into the garage. I had roped his ankles to the legs of it using the knots I'd learned as a Girl Scout. His hands were tied around the back of the chair and I had my fist in his hair, tilting his head back, savoring the look of disgust on his face as he blew drops of piss from his lips.

"I thought you'd be happy," I said, flicking his limp dick with my fingernail. "You're finally seeing me naked."

I had tossed my shirt and panties on the concrete floor. It was cool in the garage and it made my flesh pimple.

"I didn't know you were gonna *piss* on me!" he said.

"I'm full of surprises, Derek. You should know that by now."

"Are we done?" he asked.

"Not even close."

"Haven't you humiliated me enough?"

"Oh, please," I said, batting his arm playfully. "We're not done until I reach orgasm."

"No fucking way!" he shouted. "There's *no way* we're having sex! You'll say I raped you. You'll give them samples or whatever, samples of your—"

I snapped at him. "What makes you think your puny little pecker is what will get me there? Forget about sex, Derek. That's for the lamewads. I'll leave that to you Axe Body Spray Romeos and your selfie-obsessed sluts. There's more pleasure to get out of these bodies, you know."

He just looked at me. This wonderful situation had me at full tilt, a revving motorcycle of hot flesh and clicking bones. I was floating again, adrift in the black tango of my sadism, my heart pumping acid, my sex boiling plutonium. The only part of me that wasn't ecstatic was my stomach, which pinched as it made the guttural, bubbling sounds of hunger.

The little fuck-demon was awake. I felt it swish like diarrhea and cursed it for being such a mosquito. Not even born and it was already trying to ruin my good time.

"You've had your fun," Derek said.

"Just a taste."

"Well, a taste is enough."

"Says the man with a mouthful of piss!" I laughed. "I'll tell you when I've had enough, and for that matter I'll tell you when *you've* had enough."

"Untie me," he said, teeth bared. "Let me out of this chair."

"You haven't earned your help from me yet."

"I don't give a shit. You're never gonna do anything to help me! This is just another one of your twisted games. You've gone crazy, Kim! You need help!"

I smacked him. I wasn't mad really, just trying to keep my buzz going.

"Untie these fucking knots!" he yelled.

"No."

"The deal is off!"

"There never was any deal."

"What the fuck do you want from me?" he asked, his voice going up an octave as the fear nestled in his heart.

I took the duct tape and balled-up sock off the workbench where I'd placed them.

"I want what every girl wants," I said, "for my pleasure to be just as important as any boy's."

He turned his head away when I tried to stuff the sock into his mouth, and started shaking the chair, making it dance and clatter.

"Help!" he cried.

It was late and the garage doors were closed, but I didn't want to risk my neighbors hearing.

"Shut up."

"Help!" he yelled, louder this time.

I tried to get the sock into his mouth but he shook and writhed, making it impossible. He kept screaming and screaming, and my heart began to race, my tongue turning to sandpaper as I reached for the butcher knife I had put on the workbench. Things were going too quickly for me to process. I was just going to threaten him with it, but then he lunged at me. In that moment, I forgot he was bound and could do nothing but scream, or at least I wanted to forget. I had entered a fuchsia zone where all I could feel was cruel desire and the grinding pain of the fuck-demon forming in my guts. My sweet sphere tore, and the blade gleamed before our eyes like a silver wing, catching the light of the bulb overhead as I shoved it into Derek's throat. The momentum sent me into his lap and we fell backwards together. The concrete met us like a fist, Derek taking most of the blow but my elbows receiving some punishment. He was gasping for air, the knife wiggling as his throat moved against it. It reminded me of how Mr. Blakley had looked in his death throes, a happy memory I frequently masturbated to. But I had not severed a vein, nor had I sunk the blade in very deep. Derek's neck was too tough and muscular. Once he caught his breath, he opened his mouth to scream again, so I sat on him, took the knife from his neck, and brought it down into his abdomen. A quick intake of air and his eyes went wide. I twisted the blade, imagining his innards coiling around it like serpentine belts. My sex was just below where I had stabbed him, his flaccid cock pressing against my anus, and as the knife exited the wound his stomach heaved, pushing out dark, crimson bloats of blood. It rolled down his sides and pooled in the crease of my pussy.

I quivered in mad estrus.

Before he could scream I sent the blade back into him, driving it down by putting my bodyweight into it. My every muscle flexed as I turned the blade, and a foul, fecal stench rose from his new holes. I had punctured something important, but it wasn't enough. I wanted more. I wanted every last fucking bit. The thunder of demons shuddered through me, making my body feel like a mere pod of skin and sinew, as if my consciousness had exited the confines of my body and had become its own ethereal being. My violence was frenzied—it had to be—and yet I savored every second, every slash and hack, every piercing thrust and bile-producing pop.

Derek's obliteration filled my heart with heavenly light.

One more thrust and I left the blade inside him, and then started punching him in the face. He was still alive, but fading, and he made no effort to resist my fists. I beat him and beat him until my knuckles hurt, and then took his flaccid cock and squished it up into my blood-slicked pussy, climaxing as he died still inside of me.

Fuck.

It all happened so fast. I'd been a bitch in heat, not as calculating as usual. My desire had gotten the better of me and the situation had spun out of my control.

Derek Schechter was dead in my garage.

Blood was all over the goddamned place. I was sopping in his bodily syrup.

My whole body shook like winter and my every instinct told me to run, but there was nowhere to go, no safe space from what I had done.

Fuck.

I tried to wrangle my spinning thoughts.

My first one was of the security camera. It had no audio, which was good in this case, and the angle of it over the porch would show Derek shoving his way in and grabbing me by my shirt collar, as I had asked him to do. I had planned to use this footage to further incriminate him, to accuse him of trying to bully me out of testifying against him. Sure, I also entertained the idea of using it to accuse him of attempted rape, but I didn't want my image to be tainted by having people picture me being sexually assaulted by Derek. But could I now use it to make it look like he was going to rape and kill me?

We were naked and he had been inside of me. I could take the ropes off him and put them on me, but wouldn't they leave faint marks on his wrists and ankles? Maybe I could say he tied himself to me for some weird sexual kink. I could certainly say he was having his way with me and was threatening to kill me, that he'd been bragging about the rush he'd felt while killing Mr. Blakley, and it thrilled him to know that by raping Caitlin he'd helped put her in the ground. Basically, I could accuse him of having all of the feelings I hid from the world.

He attacked me, and I managed to get the knife and fight him.

I would have to cut and beat myself up.

To hell with that, I don't want bruises and scars. I want to stay pretty.

I had also stabbed him so many times. It was a ferocious murder. Would the police believe it was panic that caused me to rip him apart?

I decided it didn't matter.

I wasn't going to call them.

Looking down at Derek's mutilated corpse, I knew I couldn't go through with it. Even if the cops believed my story, I simply could not have this. Being part of Caitlin's drama was one thing. That was an attractive tragedy the whole town was enthralled by. Being a major player in our local weepy movie gave me character. It added to the image I had honed, one of innocence and yet strength. Being a victim, on the other hand, was no fun at all. I didn't want that hanging over me as I walked down the halls, receiving pity to my face and whispers and jokes behind my back. I was not going to be a rape victim for the same reasons Caitlin didn't want to be one. It would leave too big a stain.

And being a murderer was even worse, even if I had become one out of self-defense. Adding violence to the picture—brutal, fatal violence at that—was social cyanide. I would become a trauma case, receiving perfect grades by default rather than through hard work. I would miss school, and when I returned I would be a freak, worse off than the lowliest freshman maggot who sits picking his nose while reading fucking *Spider-Man* comics. My friends would evaporate, and my teachers would tiptoe around me, never looking me in the eyes. I may as well be tracking Derek's blood through the halls with every step I took. Everything would be so different I would simply have to start over somewhere new.

Well, fuck that.

I'd worked too hard and achieved too much to have my life disintegrate over this.

But I had to do something, and fast.

Dawn would be breaking soon.

Come on, girl. You've gotten away with so much already. You can pull off a little more.

First I untied Derek, and then rolled him onto the tarp I had laid out.

There was enough blood on the concrete as it was. It took a lot of mopping and bleaching to get it up, but it was fresh enough it hadn't stained. When that was done I returned to the body.

"You asshole," I said to him—to *it*.

Sure, this mess was my own fault, but none of this would have happened if he hadn't come knocking. Now I had a big, mutilated corpse on my hands. This was going to be a lot of messy work.

But my god, how I had loved killing him.

The rush I'd experienced while murdering Mr. Blakley was kid's shit compared to the wild, animal ecstasy of ripping Derek Schechter apart. For so long now my daydreams had been caked in blood. Gore dominated my sexual fantasies as a relentless obsession. Whenever I was close to someone—to *anyone*—I thought of slaughtering them and playing with their entrails. Pregnant or not, it was only a matter of time before I killed again.

Thinking of my pregnancy made the little fuck-demon roll against my uterus. My sexual desire had been satiated, but still the burning hunger made me ache inside, making me feel hollow and sick. It wasn't just *my* appetite; the beast within was ravenous, and looking down at Derek's carcass I felt a sudden pinch in my belly, and then a jerk and a tear. The pain was like passing a stone and I bent over, nearly tripping over Derek. I felt like it was I who had been stabbed now.

Time seemed to stop and there was nothing but pain.

It's eating you.

It's eating you from the inside.

I went toward the door so I could go to the kitchen for something to eat, but with each step I took the pain intensified.

Is this it? Am I having a miscarriage?

The prospect made me flutter with excitement. As if in response to this joy, my stomach wrenched again, filling with sewing needles and acid rain. When I spun in place, I opened my eyes to see Derek's corpse, and the pain quickly subsided.

"What?" I asked the fuck-demon.

It grumbled in reply and Derek's open stomach seemed to hiss a warm welcome. It was not pain I felt now, but a harrowing hunger, and a thirst that turned my tongue to sand. I was overpowered by a terrible need.

"No," I said, nearly laughing at the thought.

My rejection caused the agony to return worse than ever. I

dropped to my knees, gasping and shaking as the lining of my womb was clawed and mangled, pointed stars of agony raking its walls. I fell all the way, putting my hands out to catch myself, and I slipped on the bloody tarp. With Derek just inches from me now, the grumbling in my belly grew to a deafening roar inside my head, one that made it impossible for me to think. It was like a combination of an oncoming train and television static turned all the way up. My suffering was a dull thud now, allowing my own hunger to shine through, and it was braying like a horse in a burning barn.

Raw ground chuck would no longer do.

I lowered my head to one of his many wounds.

What are you doing?

I stuck out my tongue and lapped at the bloody cut, and my body vibrated with relief. The salty flavor tickled my taste buds and raced down my throat to feed the beast. There was a moment of calm, then the fuck-demon started thudding. It needed more.

I punched my fist through the hole I'd made in Derek's stomach, then opened my fingers, feeling the sticky viscera wiggle through them. I took a fistful, expunged it, and smelled the reek on its steam. It had a rancid yet sweet smell, like rotting yams, and while I wanted it, I was not yet ready to cross this threshold. I'd done so much I could not return from, but this . . . this . . .

The fuck-demon shrieked in that way only babies can and it made my breasts ache, as if I could already give milk. It was sending me a very clear message, one that was half bargaining, half threat.

You or them.

Suddenly it dawned on me that despite how I did not want to be a mother, a mother was what I was. I had a biological need to satisfy my cub. If I did not, nature itself would turn against me, this time in the form of a cannibal fetus. I lowered my head again, breathing whispered nothings, telling myself it was all going to be okay in just a few moments, that I just had to power through. I put the innards to one side. I took the knife and sawed at the loose skin around his abdomen and peeled away a layer of flesh on the side of his belly where there was no hair.

Come on, you love eating your own skin.

The flesh was still warm, still dripping.

To my surprise, it was delicious.

TWENTY-FIVE

It took some time, but the table saw took care of things. Thankfully it was Saturday and I didn't have to leave the dismemberment until after school. I wanted to just get it done and have it be over with already. There was a good deal of splatter, and I had to do yet another round of mopping and then some wiping down with paper towels and 409. I used a power sander on his fingertips and the bottoms of his toes until there was no flesh left, and then I went through the arduous task of pulling all the teeth out of his head with pliers. I wanted there to be no way to easily identify him. This proved difficult, so the ones that wouldn't come out I bashed with a hammer until they were chipped, jagged messes. I put plastic wrap on the limbs and severed head, then a layer of tin foil over that, and then double-bagged them in lawn garbage bags. I fully eviscerated his torso with the butcher knife and a saw, working my way around the remains of his intestines and removing the kidneys (separating them from the bladder), the spleen, liver, and pancreas. These organs I placed into individual Tupperware containers, along with several slabs of skin and connective tissue. I castrated him and put his shriveled cock in a sandwich bag. These all went into the refrigerator and freezer.

I went outside. No one was around. Even if someone came by, all they would see was trash bags, so I carried the limbs to the car and put them in the trunk. I went back inside and destroyed the bloody chair. It was made of wood and the pieces would burn easily in the fireplace. I would tell Father I had broken it accidentally.

This still left me with the torso. It was big—tough meat and strong bone.

It took some time to come up with a plan. I thought about the true crime shows and movies I'd seen. When I finally had an idea I liked, I put down another tarp, rolled the torso onto it, and then tied the tarp up with rope, careful to tuck in the edges, which I sealed with duct tape. I tied another rope around the center of the lump, and then hauled it into the house and dragged it down the hallway. I had done a good job sealing the tarp. No blood had seeped through by the time I got it to the downstairs bathroom. It was not easy for me to get this remainder of Derek into the tub, but I managed. All of my cheerleading, CrossFit and gymnastics made me strong for a girl my size. Unwrapping the tarp, I laid the torso down flat and turned on the faucet to fill the tub.

I took the bottle of peroxide from the cabinet in the hall, and the remainder of the bleach from the garage. Then I poured it all over the torso, letting it mix with the water where I would let it soak. Then, later, I could break up the bones more easily—or at least this was my plan for now. I was tired from all this work, and Derek had kept me up most of the night. It was near noon.

I went upstairs, showered the blood off, erased the security footage, and while I was still damp I ran a bath and soaked in it to relax. It gave me a sense of calm knowing Derek and I were both soaking at the same time. I thought about the events of the morning, but the stress and panic I'd felt earlier had left me, as had the pain in my belly. The little fuck-demon was satiated, as was his mommy. Cannibalizing Derek had been good for both of us, and despite my previous hesitation, I now had no reservations about feasting on the remains in the fridge. The meat cuts from his body had kept the fetus from chewing apart my womb and had soothed my upset stomach like a glass of warm milk. When the terrible hunger hit, I would have leftovers to fill me up and keep my cub from mauling me. It only made sense.

But I had other plans for Derek's dick.

After a little nap, I did my hair and makeup, put on a blouse, blue jeans, and a new pair of cream-colored slip-on shoes, and went out to the car. Driving through town, I thought about the French class paper I needed to finish. It was due on Monday, and I was still having some trouble with the language. I entered the new housing community where all the lawns were stacked with incomplete homes. Dumpsters lined the sidewalks like freight cars. Being a weekend, the construction teams were not out, and looking at the Amazon boxes and other refuse, I could tell that I wasn't the only one using the dumpsters for personal use.

I drove all through the surrounding neighborhoods, seeing no one as I tossed parts of Derek into different dumpsters. On the way back, I stopped at a CVS and picked up more bleach and peroxide, as well as some jerky to snack on. Meat was all I wanted to eat anymore.

Amy called as I got into the car.

"What's up?"

"Not much," I said, starting the engine.

"Sounds like you're driving."

"Yeah."

She was hoping I would elaborate on what I was doing, but I didn't.

"Want to do something tonight?" she asked.

I almost rejected her just out of habit, but reconsidered. It would be good for me to do something asinine, just to clear my head. I could always work on my report all day Sunday.

"Sure. Did you have anything in mind?"

The cheer in her voice made me wince. "Awesome! You still have the house to yourself, right?"

Not all *too myself*, I thought with an inner chuckle, thinking of Derek sizzling in the bathroom.

"Yeah," I said. "I'll be on my own for a while."

"We should have another party. Not tonight, but still, we should have another one."

"I don't know . . ."

"We can talk about it later. How about I come over tonight and we'll do pizza and movies?"

I pictured Amy excusing herself to the bathroom, the stink of bleach and gore hitting her just before she saw what was left of her boyfriend's best buddy. I fantasized about her having time to shriek just once before I cracked her skull open with a hatchet.

"I'd rather do something fresh," I said. "I've been all cooped up, you know?"

"Sure, okay."

"We should get the squad together."

"Well then, we should have a party."

I changed the subject. "What's your bae Ashton been up to?"

"Being amazing."

"Are you gonna sleep with him or what?"

She gasped, but jokingly. "Kim White! How dare you! I am a lady!"

"You're a slut," I said, sounding like I was kidding, the way people do when they want to deliver an insult without consequences.

"I haven't done anything with Ashton."

"Why not?"

There was a pause on the line before she said: "Are you being serious right now?"

"Yeah."

"And what about Brian?"

"Cancel."

She laughed. "Cancel? He's my boyfriend!"

"You know you like Ashton better."

"Well, I love Brian. Besides, Ashton would never go for me."

"Are you kidding? You're movie-star hot. He'd be lucky to get you to bed."

"Oh, stop. You're so bad, Kim."

"Tell you what," I said, actually getting interested. "Why don't we have a very small party, and you invite Ashton but *not* Brian."

"Oh my god, you're not serious."

"Why not? We could just see what happens."

It was a small game compared to the horror and pain I'd caused lately, but there was something about getting Amy to ruin her relationship with Brian that sparked my interest. I guess it was the idea of hurting two friends at once. Amy's meanness showed so much potential. I was curious to see just how much I could hone that mean streak into something more exciting, something sharp and lava-hot.

"Whomever else we invite will talk," Amy said. "You know that."

"That's why we keep it small. Ashton for you and somebody new for me."

"Oooooh, now I see."

"What?"

"You've got some new guy you want to have over, but you don't want to have him over alone."

"Actually no. I was hoping Ashton could bring a friend."

"You little whore!" she laughed.

"Hey, remember *I'm* the virgin. I didn't say I was going to do anything with him. I'm just trying to get you your dream guy."

"Don't be so sure. Ashton has some cute friends."

Whatever. "So have him bring one over tonight."

Amy was silent for a moment, the gears turning in her mind.

"This is so bad," she said.

I had her.

I didn't want to get Amy raped. Not because she was my friend, but because I'd already done that with Caitlin. My lust demanded new adventures, new debaucheries and destructions. Besides, Ashton wouldn't have to rape Amy. She would jump on his cock like a bull rider the moment he popped it out of his jeans. What I wanted was to start Amy down a path of sex, lies and betrayal, to get her to hurt others and hopefully herself. It would be good to play a simpler sport for a while. I'd had so many explosive experiences of late. Something more low-key would keep me entertained without being so consuming I would forget about my little fuck-demon problem.

Father called that afternoon while I was dousing Derek's torso in the additional bleach. I'd Googled using lye, which I learned was what Mexican cartels used to liquefy their victims. Apparently it took care of things in just a few hours. It was cheap enough online, so I ordered some, but even with the fastest shipping it wouldn't be here until tomorrow.

"Just want to make sure you're okay," he said.

"Yeah. I'm good."

"That Derek boy giving you any trouble?"

The torso fizzed in the tub, the flesh bubbling away.

"No trouble at all."

An hour later Amy called to tell me Ashton was on board and would be bringing his friend Keith, who was a college freshman. She made a way bigger deal about this than was necessary, building Keith up even though she didn't know him.

"I can't believe we're doing this," she said.

"Why not? It'll be cool. I'm going to make my famous lasagna so it can be a fancy dinner date. Then, well . . . who knows what might happen?"

As we spoke, I arranged Father's digital video camera in the guest bedroom, situating it between two pictures on the dresser so it wouldn't be seen unless someone got close and looked behind them. *Should have thought of this on the night of the party*, I thought. But my goal back then was to just get Caitlin raped. With Amy, no rape would be involved, so humiliation would have to take a different course. This sabotage was just a way for me to pass the time until the next big exploit, but I felt it could very well spiral into it somehow. The future of my enterprises remained vague and nebulous, a world still forming in a blank, dead universe.

"I love your lasagna," Amy said. "It's *soooo* good."

When we got off the phone I went to the kitchen and took out everything I would need—noodles, tomato sauce, spices. I preheated the oven and filled the dish with ground beef, onion and garlic. In place of the usual cooked sausage, I chopped up Derek's kidneys and connective arteries and rolled the pieces in Italian herbs. When the oven beeped I put the dish of saucy meat inside. I still had plenty of time to freshen up, tidy up, set the table, and close off the downstairs bathroom.

I was ready when the doorbell rang. I was in the mood for something erotic, so I dressed in my tight, red cocktail dress and black, ankle-strap heels. My push-up bra showcased my girls like two snow globes, and I had misted them with the hundred-and-fifty-dollar Juliette Has a Gun's Not a Perfume (it always amused me that whale vomit could smell so pleasant and cost so much). My hair was all volume and curls—black ribbons that shimmered in the dim light like ravens. Opening the door, I saw Amy was also dressed to the nines—a blue cocktail dress she was poured into, the pale flesh of her exposed shoulders looking soft and succulent, framed by her natural blondness. She was jittery with anticipation that made her flutter about the house like a moth.

"This is gonna be way live," she said. She saw the dining room and the perfectly set table with the fresh candles and flowers. "Oh my god, Kim, you're a goddess. This looks magical."

"Fairy tales can come true."

"And look at you! You are on point! Keith is going to faint when he sees you."

"You're not so bad yourself."

We gushed, each of us silently wishing we had something the other did and hating one another a little for it.

Amy had brought a small suitcase so she would have everything she needed to stay the night, and two six packs of local beers for the boys, bought by her older cousin. She brought them to the fridge and moved a piece of Tupperware containing Derek's spleen and then closed the door.

"I'm glad we have a few minutes," she said. "I want to check my hair and makeup."

She started toward the downstairs bathroom, and I almost let her go in just to see the look on her face when she saw the bubbling mess of the very asshole she'd tried so hard to pair me up with. Well, he and I were together at last. There were bits of him still in my belly. I doubted Derek or Amy had ever imagined one day he would be turned into my feces. Even I hadn't dreamt of such a thing. It was a comical thought. Still, I was not ready to kill Amy to protect my secret, at least not yet. Murdering her was an entertaining idea, but two friends of mine disappearing at the same time would raise a lot of eyebrows, and I was tired of talking to the police.

But then I thought: *maybe it would be good if they both vanished at the same time*. It could look like they'd run off together, like they'd been screwing behind Brian's back and she couldn't bear the thought of Derek going off to jail. Hell, Amy had even packed a bag!

"Use my bathroom," I said. "The downstairs one is being remodeled and the water's turned off."

I had placed a rope across the downstairs one's door, with a taped piece of paper reading *Out of Order*, but that was it.

As Amy went upstairs, I weighed the pros and cons of killing her. I certainly wanted to see her dead. More than anything, I wanted to see the look on her face as I killed her. I also wondered if women would taste different than men. Something about her milky white skin and the way she took care of it made me believe she would have a much better flavor than sweaty, hairy Derek. Ashton and Keith were on their way over, so murdering her right now was out of the question, but if I wanted to stage it so it looked like Derek had jumped bail and taken her with him, I would have to do it soon. But it would be best to kill her somewhere other than in the house. Derek had been a goof, a spontaneous clusterfuck. I wanted to keep the slayings away from my home. Mixing them felt too much like mixing business with pleasure. All of this gave me something to think about.

When the doorbell rang again Amy galloped down the stairs like a kid on Christmas morning.

"Jeez, you have no chill," I said. "Don't be so eager when I let him in."

"I won't, I won't."

She straightened her dress and bit her lip. I imagined biting her face and ripping her cheek off in a single pull, exposing bloody teeth beneath, and I realized just how badly I wanted to have sex with her.

Ashton came in and Keith followed behind him. Keith smiled like a goon when he saw me. He'd hit the jackpot. I was not particularly impressed with him but, to be fair, I was never particularly impressed with any boys my age. He had a farm boy grin I wanted to smack and a tall but wiry body. Dark hair and eyes made him look brooding even when a shit-eating grin was on his face.

We all made small talk and then gravitated to the kitchen, where all parties congregate for some reason. We talked college, majors, local sports and other banalities, so it took some time before the conversation got remotely interesting to me.

"You guys hear anything from your friend?" Ashton asked.

Amy was all smiles no matter what he said. "Which friend?"

"That Derek guy."

My ears perked. "What about him?"

"They say he jumped bail," Keith said.

"Who says?"

"My little brother dates Emily Schechter, Derek's sister. He told me she said Derek wasn't in his room when they all woke up this morning. They're worried he skipped town because of that whole rape charge thing."

"Whoa," Amy said. "He bolted? Is he crazy? That'll just make him look guilty."

"He *is* guilty," I said, peeved.

Now that Ashton and Keith had seen Amy here and the word was already out about Derek, it might be harder to make it look like they'd run off together, unless I could make it look like she had run off to meet him somewhere after he'd already left.

Ashton looked at me. "Yeah, that's right. I heard it happened here. The night of that party, right?"

I nodded.

"Man," he said. "For real? Right under our noses? Fuckin' creep."

"That Caitlin girl," Keith said to me, "you were, like, friends, right?"

"Sort of."

"That's crazy. Sorry about what happened."

Playing the nice guy gets you nowhere, asswipe.

"Thanks," I said.

Amy gave me the winks that meant *no* in our private code, because she didn't want this to be the topic of conversation any longer. She quickly changed the subject to Ashton's potential football career, and we went into the dining room and I served everyone their alcohol of choice, then brought the lasagna to the table where it steamed with gooey goodness.

"Smells amazing," Keith said.

I gave larger portions to the boys, but made sure I gave Amy a segment stuffed with Derek's organs. I was curious to try it myself, hoping the texture wouldn't be too jarring now that I'd cooked it in a sea of tomato sauce. Everyone dug in. Ashton was rather voracious.

"This is delicious," Keith said.

I certainly was enjoying it. I felt so much better now whenever I devoured human remains. It was what had been missing. The kidney bits were chewy, but not as tough as I had worried they might be. I tensed as Amy's brow furrowed.

"Did you add something new?" she asked.

"Yes, but it's my own secret recipe."

"It's really good," she said, relieving me, "whatever it is."

"Thanks. I put a lot of work into it. Everything's super fresh."

After dinner we went into the den with more drinks and I put on the latest album by Drake. It didn't take long for Amy to get Ashton dancing, and even less time for her to get him dancing close, his arms around her waist, hers decorating his neck like garland. Keith and I sat on the couch with an empty space between us. He was boring me, but I smiled when I saw Ashton lean down to be kissed by Amy. It took so little to get the selfish bitch to betray Brian.

"So what kind of movies are you into?" Keith asked.

"Horror."

"Oh. Really? You like that stuff?"

"Love it."

"I haven't met a lot of girls who are into scary movies."

"Well, you've met one now."

"Do you have a favorite?"

"They fluctuate. Right now I'm into *Cannibal Holocaust*."

He rubbed his chin. "Hmm. Never heard of that one."

"You heathen. It's a classic."

"Cannibal movies kind of gross me out."

I couldn't help but laugh.

"What?" Keith asked.

Amy and Ashton were making out in the corner, still standing up. His hands were on her buttocks now. Their lips had not yet unlocked.

"Let's give them some privacy," I said.

Keith and I got off the sofa and walked down the hall to the living room. When we got there he held back a burp and put his hand on his stomach.

"Something wrong?" I asked.

"No, um, I'm good."

Clearly the food had upset his stomach a bit, but he was too polite to say so. He didn't want to blow his chances with me by insinuating the meal I'd prepared was making him a little sick.

"If you need to use the bathroom, use one of the ones upstairs."

He nodded, embarrassed.

We sat down on the sectional, Keith sitting rather close, trying to build up his nerve. I would have loved to take him upstairs and fuck him, but only if I could cut him up with Father's straight razor while doing it. I doubted he would be on board with that, and having non-violent sex with Keith was about as exciting to me as vacuuming.

I heard footsteps going up the staircase, and a moment later the door to the guest bedroom closed.

"I think your friend really likes Ashton," Keith joked.

I ignored this. "Tell me about Derek's sister."

He blinked. "Huh?"

"Your brother's dating her. What else did he have to say?"

"About what?"

"Jeez, *about Derek*, what else?"

"I dunno."

"Is she upset?" I asked. I needed something, some taste of the misery I had caused. "Is the family freaked out?"

"Pretty much, I guess."

God, Keith, you are a special kind of useless.

It would look strange if I pressed him too much on this, and besides, he didn't seem to have much to offer anyway. I was getting listless. The pleasure I'd experienced while feeding my guests Derek's organs still lingered, but now the night was dragging. I was sure Amy was having a good time, and I looked forward to watching the video, but my night was fizzling out like . . .

Like Derek's torso.

"Excuse me a moment," I said.

I went down the hall, lifted the rope, and went into the bathroom. The bleach smell was strong, but I'd left the fan on and cracked the window, so it wasn't overpowering. The water was brown and murky, the meaty lump of Derek festering within. I reached down and tugged at his skin with my fingernails. The top layers slid off like slow-cooked chicken from the bone. The process was taking some time, but it was working. Still, I was glad to have the lye on the way. I pulled the shower curtain closed to hide the torso and then slid out of my panties and tucked them behind the toilet.

I opened the door and called for Keith.

"Yeah?" he asked when he got there.

I grabbed his shirt and pulled him inside, putting a spark in his eyes now. I got up onto the sink counter and spread my legs. I pulled up my dress slowly, giving him a teasing show. When he saw my bare pussy—neatly trimmed just that afternoon—that farm boy grin of his stretched across his face like an accordion. He didn't even mention the stench in the room. He didn't even care.

"Eat me," I said.

He crouched and started performing sloppy cunnilingus. If it weren't for the fact a dead body was hidden only inches away from us, I wouldn't have enjoyed it much, but the conditions made blood rush to my sex. After a few minutes Keith stood up and began undoing his pants.

I was firm with him. "No! You get your face back in there, bitch!"

His disappointment amused me, but despite that disappointment he dove back in with his tongue, still hopeful, a beggar willing to work for what I was never going to give him. I closed my eyes and thought of the knife going in and out of Derek, of Caitlin convulsing on her death bed, of Mr. Blakley shooting his load all over his daughter's cutesy little panties. I grabbed the back of Keith's head and fucked his mouth, smacking him on the back of his skull to push him into me. His grunts brought me to climax.

Keith stood and took out his inflamed penis. It curled toward me like a pink banana.

"Not tonight," I said, pushing him away. "I don't know you well enough."

"But . . ."

"But what?"

"What about . . . ?"

I waited, but he didn't have the balls to ask me, therefore he didn't deserve it. Not that I would have given him a blowjob (or any other satisfaction) anyway. Knowing I would only give him blue balls had been crucial to my enjoyment of our interlude, as had the proximity of the corpse.

"Hey," I said. "Keep this between us. Maybe you'll get luckier if there's a next time."

TWENTY-SIX

The next morning, Amy could not have been more annoying if she was a smoke detector on the fritz.

"He's an incredible lover," she said. "I mean, like, I didn't know if I was going to go all the way with him last night, but he is just *soooo* hot. I *had* to have him, you know? It was so good. Way better than Brian. I mean, Brian's good, but Ashton is like, super, *mad* good." Her face was upturned, eyes bright. She kept reaching out and touching my arm as she spoke. "I can't believe we actually did it! I know, I know—I've got *no chill*. But *oh my God*, right?"

I sipped my coffee. "So what happens now?"

"That's the thing. I mean, he really likes me, right?"

"If he didn't before, I'm sure he does now."

She batted my arm. "Come on, he's into me, don't you think? I mean, I think if I break things off with Brian, Ashton and I can be a serious item."

"Break things off with Brian?"

Amy seemed to have it all figured out. That put a damper on my plans to create the trifecta of her emotional Armageddon. I was hoping she would be torn up over what she'd done. I'd underestimated her cold heart.

"Brian and I had our good times together," she said. "He'll always be special. But you were right all along, Kim. Ashton is the guy for me. I just needed some convincing I could actually get him." She kissed me on the cheek and my bowels churned. "Thanks for giving me that nudge."

I smiled and winced at the same time. Painful daylight was coming through the window. Amy had opened the blinds, embracing the day like she was Snow-Fucking-White. I almost expected little birds to land on her arms and whistle.

"So," she asked. "Did you and Keith hit it off?"

"He's a toad."

"A what?"

"We didn't hit it off."

"Well, if he's not your type, then he's not your type. It's too bad though. I love double-dating with you." She went to the fridge and opened it up. "I'm starved."

"There's some lasagna left over," I said.

She came up from the fridge with a container in her hands. She shook it and a brownish, rubbery mass crawled down one side.

"What's this?"

"A liver."

"Yuck! I hate liver! When I was a kid, my grandfather used to make this crap. Does your dad eat it?"

"Actually that's for me."

"Nasty!"

"I'm going to cook it with onions. They say that brings out the flavor."

"You going to have it with some fava beans and a nice chianti?" she joked.

I was surprised Amy knew a line from *The Silence of the Lambs*, that she knew of *any* movie made before she was born. I laughed, but not at the joke as much as her obliviousness.

The doorbell rang and I got to it just in time to see the UPS man getting back into his truck. I took the two packages from my doorstep and brought them in.

"Anything good?" she asked.

"Just some stuff I ordered."

"I love ordering stuff online. It's like presents you mail to yourself. What did you buy?"

"Some lye."

"What's that?"

"It's a cleaner. For the bathroom."

"Oh. That's not very fun, is it?"

"We'll see."

Amy left after breakfast. She was amped up over Ashton and had a lot of thinking to do. I was glad to have her gone. Her inane girl-chatter had become enraged hornets in my brain.

The night before I had turned the water heater's temperature all the way up, so when I drained and refilled Derek's tub the water was scalding. After coating the torso with lye I covered the tub with the tarp to seal it in, weighing down the sides with various tools from the garage. Turning the thermostat's heat all the way up, I went into the kitchen to satiate the growls of the little fuck-demon before it could start gnawing my interior walls. Derek's flesh was trimmed down and I fried it up like bacon, making a BLT on pumpernickel. Taking it upstairs, I put it by the computer. I got the video camera from the guest bedroom and hooked it up to the computer and watched Amy suck Ashton's cock before he fucked her in the missionary position, then doggy style, and came on her ass. She'd let him ride bareback. The camera was equipped with night vision, but they'd left the bedside lamp on, so the picture quality was excellent. You could see everything. Ashton was a fine specimen of male virility, but Amy was what really drew me in. She was even more gorgeous naked, more than I could have imagined. It was then I knew I had to break her. Not out of jealousy of her beauty, but out of a deep, boiling need to cripple and destroy all the world most cherished—youth, beauty, vitality, life and the love of life.

I opened the second box that had been delivered—the one from the sex toy warehouse—and placed it on the desk. Opening it, I took out the clear, hollow dildo and uncapped the seal on its end. Unzipping the plastic bag beside it, I inserted Derek's severed cock into the latex tube of the dildo, packed it in tight with gauze, and resealed it. When I restarted the video, I fucked myself with my new toy, coming quickly. My sexual desire spent, I saved the video file and pulled up the most popular porn site I visited, the one that came up first when you typed *free porn* into Google. I went to the amateur's section and uploaded the video, calling it *Blonde Teen Amy Cheats on Her Boyfriend*, knowing the words *blonde* and *teen* would help get it views. I had to make a submitter's name, so I called myself Dirty Ashton.

In between working on my paper, I read about famous cases of cannibalism and vorarephilia, a sexual deviation characterized by the erotic desire to be consumed by another person. I read of murderous cannibals like Alfred Packer and the revolutionary United Front in Western Africa; of cannibalism as a means of survival, as in the case of the Stella Maris College Rugby Team who, after their plane crashed, had to eat their fallen teammates to stay alive; of different cultures who ate human flesh based on superstition, vengeance and ritual, such as the Maori People and the Carib West Indian Tribes. In a way, I felt connected to each of them, as I consumed people out of my own lust as well as a means to keep myself alive by warding off the fangs of the fuck-demon, and had made my meals ritualistic, or at least routine.

But the case that interested me the most was that of the Mauerovas, a family from the Czech Republic who, just sixteen years ago, tortured, abused and skinned two young boys from their own family. The boys' own mother and aunts kept them chained in the basement in their own filth, beating them and even making them cut themselves with knives. The family was part of a cannibal cult, and was directed by a man known only as "The Doctor," who instructed them on how to torture the boys via text message. The mother skinned her sons while they were still alive and the family devoured their flesh. She also used a video baby monitor so she could watch the boys suffer from the comfort of her living room. This led to her arrest when a neighbor bought the same monitor to watch their own child and the receivers transferred images from the Mauerovas basement, causing the neighbors to call the police. Even though the boys had been skinned and tortured, they had survived the ordeal.

This was of particular interest to me because of the family ties. A mother eating her own children was a like a topsy-turvy variation of my own situation. My fetus was eating me when I didn't feed it what it desired. When my water finally broke, would I push the fuck-demon out the natural way, or would it shred its way out of my belly with gnashing, shark-like teeth? Was there a bond of cannibalism in certain families, something hidden deep in the blood? Was it a genetic mutation, or something all of humankind was made for but had just shied away from?

When I finished my paper I went downstairs to check on Derek. He was now just a pile of spindly bones in fetid, shit-colored murk.

I put on dishwashing gloves and drained the tub and collected the remaining chunks caught in the drain. I went to work on gathering the bones, wondering if there was a way I could grind them up to use them as flour. It seemed wasteful to just dispose of them, but I wanted all of this to be over with now, and for my house to be clean and orderly. In the end, I decided to just bag them up and put them in a tote in my garage, for now.

TWENTY-SEVEN

Caitlin had been weak and vulnerable, two things Amy was not. My best friend trusted me, but probably not as much as Caitlin had. There was an innocence and gullibility to Caitlin, two traits Amy did not possess. She was conniving and sadistic in her own right. It was easy for her to detect manipulation and sabotage, for she had become an expert in these black arts. I was prepared for her to pose more of a challenge.

A few days passed and I heard nothing about Derek, which assured me he really hadn't told anyone he was coming to see me. I also didn't hear anything about Amy's online porno. I thought about bringing back my Facebook alter ego Billy, but decided against it, reminding myself I didn't want to just do a remake of my assault on Caitlin. The video had been up for perverts everywhere to jack off to; that was awesome all by itself. If anyone we knew happened to see it, that was a nice bonus, but I wasn't going to work at making the video go viral. I had Amy's porno for my future use. It could prove to come in handy somehow, but it was a mere tool in my arsenal, one to be brought out when the time was right.

I did however decide to take the video down from the site, but only because it had been shot inside my house. Amy and Ashton would both know this, so if they learned about the video they would come to me for answers, and hard. Amy would be livid. Also, everyone knew Caitlin's nude photos had been taken in my house. I didn't want to be painted as some sort of voyeuristic pervert if word got out about the filming location of the video. And while losing Amy as a friend was not a problem for me, it would put a damper on my efforts to destroy her. I needed to keep her close if I was going to put the knife in her back.

The video had already gotten over two thousand views.

That's a lot of jizz, I thought.

Amy licked at her chocolate ice cream, trying to keep it from running down the cone and onto her arm. The boardwalk was filled with excited children and their roaming parents, who looked exhausted as they carried paper trays of fried food, their only source of enjoyment here. The sound of the rollercoasters roared overhead and beeps and dings echoed from the dark cavern of the arcade. Beyond the walkway, the Atlantic Ocean glimmered, hordes of half-dressed young people playing volleyball in the warm sun of Memorial Day weekend. All of this exposed flesh made me hungry for something other than my milkshake. Beside me, Dakota licked her cone, looking suggestive in her black bikini. Her big, pillowy breasts were out and already tan even though summer was just beginning.

Amy had dumped Brian and now she and Ashton were indeed an item. The ease with which she'd made this happen was infuriating. I had so wanted chaos and emotional pain, at least from one side if not both.

But there were no boys with us today. This was girl time, and we wanted to be looked at and flirted with by fresh faces. While my friends wore only bathing suits and skirts, I decided to wear a beach dress to hide the slow ballooning of my belly. My big, dark sunglasses created a comforting filter from the real world.

"So," Amy said to me, "a real party, or what?"

"I'm not sure, not after what happened at the last one. I don't want people coming and gawking at the room where Derek raped Caitlin."

"Nobody is going to do that."

"Caitlin's old news anyway," Dakota said. "Derek's disappearance is all anyone wants to talk about. It's straight fire."

He'd been missing for over a week. The police had talked to

everyone.

"Well, it's interesting," I said. "I mean he left no trace. No note or phone calls. He didn't even take a car."

Amy shook her head. "I don't think he just decided to skurt. I think something happened to him."

"Such as?"

"Like, something to do with the Blakleys."

"What do you mean? Like, somebody kidnapped him?"

"Or worse. Keith's brother told him that Derek's sister said the cops weren't ruling out foul play."

"Whoa," Dakota said.

I put down my milkshake. "You mean they're looking into Caitlin's family on this?"

"I don't know, but it makes sense to, right? I mean, you know they're all salty over Derek."

"More than salty," Dakota said.

"Exactly. They must want his head, right?"

"I know her mom," I said. "There's no way she could have done anything to Derek."

"Who says she had to be the one to do it?"

I thought about this, and the bones that were in a tote in my garage.

The police could have been monitoring the Blakley house. A stakeout seemed unlikely, but I didn't want to take any unnecessary risks, so I drove down the street behind their house. It was late, pitch dark. I wore black jeans and a matching turtleneck sweater, and brought along Father's ski mask, the one he always took with him on his winter trips to New Hampshire. The shovel was in the trunk, along with the garbage bag of bones.

There was an empty house on this block with a *for rent* sign on top of the mailbox. I passed by it, checking for any signs of life in the neighborhood, and then turned around and parked in the driveway so my car wouldn't draw attention by being in the street. There were no lights on over the driveway, keeping me in the shadows. I was nervous, but also excited. Even the fuck-demon was wiggling with anticipation. I took the bag and shovel from the trunk as quickly as I could and ducked around the side of the house the streetlamps did not touch, trotting toward the tree line of the woods that separated this lawn from the ones on the Blakley family's street. I slid into the ski mask, the cloth growing moist from my breath.

I entered the woods, wincing at every snapping twig and shuffle of dirt. There was a terrifying silence here. My asshole closed tight and my scalp went taut. The heavy clothes were making me sweat. I stopped before breaking through to the backyards. The Blakley house was three houses down from the one I was looking at, so I retreated into the woods, keeping my slight sounds far from any listening ears, and made my way down the block. When I got close to the backyard where Caitlin and I had spent so many afternoons practicing for something she would never get to do, I stayed in the woods just outside the property line, as close to the yard as I could get without being in the open. I put down the bag, opened it, and shoveled.

<hr />

Amy had understated what was going on, but she also didn't know the full story. Derek's sister had probably been in the dark too. There was more to this than the police having not ruled out foul play; they had been actively investigating Simone Blakley in the disappearance of Derek Schechter.

Two days after I'd buried his remains on the edge of the Blakley property, she was arrested, and three days after that Amy had gotten the story through the usual grapevine that led back to Derek's sister. My hand clenched the phone so tight my arm shook. I was living in such a wonderful world.

"You have got to be kidding me," I said.

"No way. I'm being totally honest. Hundo P."

"They think he's *dead?*"

"Well, the emails seem to imply that."

"This is so crazy."

And it really was. It had not been the shallow grave I'd dug that had sent Simone into the slammer. She had actually been up to some grim business of her own. After Derek was released on bail, Simone started looking to hire someone for a special job, the type that AC/DC likes to call a *dirty deed*. She scoured online want ads in our area, even delving into fetish groups who shared short stories about their murder fantasies. Eventually, she started a dialogue with a man who claimed to be a hit man for hire. They began sending private emails, detailing the method of murder and the cost of the job.

It was not clear to us whether Simone had called off the hit after Derek had gone missing, or if the hit man had been an undercover officer. No one else had been arrested in association with the crime. Amy had no information about how exactly law enforcement first started to tie Simone to Derek's disappearance. I wondered if she'd been clumsy, looking for a hired thug in seedy bars, letting the word get out in a drunken stupor as she tried in vain to drown her sorrows. I was pleasantly surprised by the intensity of Simone's wrath. With her husband and daughter taken from her, she had mentally disintegrated, devolving from suburban mom to revenge-obsessed madwoman. The Blakleys had dark hearts they'd hid from the world, perhaps even from themselves. Mr. Blakley had beaten a teenage girl he'd impregnated, and his wife had taken out a hit on a boy of seventeen. They were hardly the old sitcom family they tried to paint themselves as. I had peeled back that paint, layer by layer, exposing the rotted wood beneath.

"I can't even," Amy said. "I mean, he was our friend, you know? It's like something out of a gangster movie."

"Man, could he really be dead?"

"He really could. It's so surreal. I've been thinking about Brian a lot. He's already had to deal with losing the love of his life, now he's lost his best friend too."

Her vanity was mind-blowing.

"Have you talked to him?"

"No. That'd be too awkward."

"You worried Ashton won't like it?"

"That's not what I meant."

"Well, I don't think he would mind, under the circumstances."

There was a pause on the line.

"You think I should?" she asked.

"Yeah." I was hoping to stir up the mixed emotions I'd been shooting for when I'd first pushed her into Ashton's arms. "It'd be, like, super sweet of you. Everyone would know that."

Feeding Amy's narcissism was a surefire way to get her to do something.

"You're right. It *would* be big of me, to be brave enough to reach out to my ex in his time of need."

I could sense her looking in the mirror.

"For sure," I said. "You're a great person, Amy."

———————◆———————

I'd left the front door unlocked, and Dakota came into the house, already wearing her pajamas, a huge purse slung over her shoulder.

"Whud up, fam?" she said as she came into the kitchen.

Amy, Brittany and I were drinking wine and snacking. A slumber party may have seemed immature, but a slumber party with booze and no parental supervision was another story. Amy had on pajamas, and Brittany wore gym shorts and a green top that complemented her dyed red hair.

I poured Dakota a glass of wine. I was in my silk pajamas and she looked me up and down, blushing a little when I caught her doing it.

"Big news," she said.

A gossip whore, Amy turned her way. "What's going on?"

Dakota reached into her purse and pulled out something rolled up in a clear bag.

Brittany chuckled. "Is that an actual newspaper?"

"Yeah," Dakota said. "My dad still gets them. This is the local one."

"I didn't think they even made those anymore."

Dakota slid it out of the bag, unfurled it, and spun it around so we could read the headline.

"Holy shit," Amy said.

I dropped my jaw so as not to smile in front of them.

The headline stretched overtop of a picture of low woodland closed off by police tape where men in HAZMAT suits stood over a small mound of dirt. A German Shepherd by their side was wearing a black K-9 vest, standing on the edge of a hole.

Human Remains Found at Home of Local Woman Accused of Murdering Teen.

My fingertips tingled and though I curled my toes I could not feel them. The floor and earth seemed to drift away on an unseen current, and I was hovering again, washed in the blood I could smell and taste but could not see. I moaned without thinking about it.

"Yeah," Dakota said. "Our town has, like, turned into *Game of Thrones.*"

Amy took the paper in her hands, holding it closer as if she expected the headline was a prank.

"This is it," she said. "He's really, really dead."

I was surprised by the look of sadness in her eyes until I realized it was for show. *Saint Amy—a heart of gold-plated feces.*

"He was such a cool guy," Brittany said, hugging herself.

"One of us," said Amy.

And just like that, everything spun back around for Derek Schechter. It was amazing. While you're alive, people will shit all over you and break you down till you're crying on your knees, but then the moment you croak they act like the two of you were best fucking friends. They leeched off your death, hijacking the one drama that really should be all about you.

"He didn't deserve this," I said.

But he did. They all did.

I poured myself another glass of wine in silent celebration. With the exception of the monster festering in my womb, this had been the greatest year of my life, and there were still six months to go. Everything had been going my way, and just when I'd felt I'd hit a snag, somehow I'd been able to turn one problem into a solution for another, victorious every time, coasting on intelligence, ruthlessness and luck.

"To Derek," Dakota said, raising her glass.

We clinked them all together and toasted him.

To Derek, I thought, *more useful in death than in life.*

Amy lowered her glass. "Think they'll cancel school again? If they do, we should all do a road trip or something."

Not only were they pinning Derek's murder on Simone, they were charging her in the death of her husband. It was all in the paper. From all of the books I'd read on murder, I knew you're more likely to be killed by a loved one you live with than by anyone else. The paper didn't specify the reason why the police were attaching her to the crime yet. I figured now they believed she was a killer, or at least contracted killers, then it only stood to reason she was behind her husband's murder. Caitlin had been home with Simone on the night of her husband's death, but Caitlin couldn't offer her testimony now, could she? Simone could deny her involvement in the killings till she was blue in the face. With her internet history, no one would believe her. She had a clear motive to murder Derek, and there is always an endless list of motives for one spouse to kill the other. Maybe Simone had found Mr. Blakley in the arms of another woman; perhaps she wanted to collect insurance money; maybe he had asked for a divorce she did not want; or maybe she was just sick of the sound of football games emanating from her living room. It was a sordid mess Simone was now in, one that was bound to obliterate what little was left of her sanity. I couldn't have been happier if I had killed her myself.

Well, maybe *a little* happier.

I had run out of pieces of Derek to eat.

TWENTY-EIGHT

The warm summer breeze rushed around my body as I tumbled through the air, flipping and spinning before coming back down into the arms of Summer Scott and Mandy Clark, who were serving as my bases, and another cheerleader named Connie serving as my back spot. School was back on after shutting down in honor of Derek's death, but in two weeks school would be out for the season. That didn't keep us off the field. We needed to be in prime shape for tournaments. Our coach, Mrs. Morrell, blew her whistle to call forth the next group, who started on raising their flyer into a split lift. The gusty day made our hair pull loose from our ponytails and braids. Mrs. Morrell's dirty blond hair was an outdated feathered cut and it rolled like an ebbing tide as she squinted against a brilliant sun.

Mandy and I took our Powerades from the bleachers and sat down, the cool touch of the metal on our thighs making us sigh with relief.

"We'll be level six next year," she said, her eyes looking dreamy, sparkly, a postcard of a girl. "We'll be the seniors of the team."

"International Open Large Co-Ed is a long way from cheerleader camp."

"I'll say. I'm thinking of doing camp again this summer, though. I want to be sharp for next year, with the NHSCC and all."

"Yeah, that's probably smart. Mrs. Morrell has already scheduled us for a lot of practices at the park. I just don't want to be in the cheerleading grind all summer."

And you're pregnant.

"You have other plans?" Mandy asked.

"Oh, I'm sure I'll get into something."

Normally I would have had some academia or other activities lined up for the summer months to prepare for my future, but it had been a hectic spring to say the least. There was still more I had to do—the mean, black things that made me feel alive. I could feel them lingering on the edge of every dawn, creeping toward my life like cockroaches. They filled my mind with brown noise and drenched my dreams in blood, giving me nightmares involving mutant versions of my parents being tortured in playgrounds of fire. Their bodies were warped from elephantiasis, bulging grotesqueries smoldering and oozing pus, my mother hung by the neck from the swing set and Father crucified on the jungle gym.

And there was the hunger, terrible and deep, the parasite working on me like a cancer.

Mandy held her shoulders high. "Guess it's been a pretty crazy year, huh?"

I shot up in bed from the pain.

It knifed through me, a hot poker curling my innards, inflaming my intestines from gullet to asshole. My womb twitched and I dry heaved and curled onto my side in case vomit came. I was sweating, shaking as if in fever. My vagina kept expelling air. My blood pulsed in my ears. Even my teeth hurt.

The fuck-demon was screaming inside of me, both of us in withdrawals.

I struggled to sit up and tried to step out of bed but a bullet of agony crippled me and I tumbled to the floor.

I'm glad Father isn't home for this.

When I tried to get up, my stomach groaned and sent me back down, so I crawled on my hands and knees toward the bathroom, hoping I would make it before something shot out of one of my holes. Once inside, I managed to slide out of my clothes and climb into the tub. I ran hot water over my head and whimpered. While it soothed me, there was still an ache in my belly that grumbled with the threat of worse pain to come.

You have to feed it.

I'd been doing my best to satiate it with raw steaks and eggs, but that was just a cork in a hole of a dam continuing to crack.

"I need time," I told the fuck-demon.

My guts seemed to explode. I thrashed, kicking shampoo and body wash off the shelf of the tub.

You have to feed it.

You have to feed it now.

I gnawed at the skin around my fingernails, taking little nips of my flesh and swallowing them. The pain began to fade, but I knew this wouldn't be enough, not nearly. The bottoms of my big toes were coarse and hard from cheerleading, so I picked at them, peeling away bits of hard, dry skin. They were bigger than my cuticles and gave me more to chew on. I let these settle in my belly—in the fuck-demon's belly—and sat back, hoping this appetizer would hold it off. But the pain rose up again like a gas bubble. It rose slowly but steadily and I twisted my body in an effort to escape it, splashing in the water as my screams echoed off the walls of the tub. As the pain reached its blinding crescendo, something cracked inside of me, and in my panic I reached for my lady shaver on the edge of the tub. I worked my thumbnails beneath the plastic tip, then pulled the piece apart and released the blade.

Not wanting to show scars, I cut into my inner thigh, barely feeling the sting of the razor, my stomach pain drowning it out. Still, my hand shook and I had to lock the wrist with my other hand to keep the lines straight. Once I had made a two-by-three square, I sent the edge of the blade under one corner and began to slice, back and forth, separating the flesh from the meat below. Blood flowed, making it hard to see the lines, so I repositioned myself under the faucet to keep the cuts clean and clear. I sawed from one side to another, then dug my fingernails into the gap and pulled, slowly at first to test the accuracy of the cut. There was still some connective tissue, so I had to burrow my fingers deeper and tug from the bottom up. Blood splattered against the tub walls and swirled down the drain. There was a stinging sensation, but otherwise I felt numb to the fresh wound, even as the flap of skin came free from my body with a sound like wet Velcro.

I looked at it for a moment. It seemed like an alien curio, like it had never been a part of me. I was a self-producing meat farm, and it is a natural thing for a mother to feed her cub from her own body.

The skin was supple and slippery.

It tasted much better than Derek's.

———————————————————⬤————————————————————

Girls had better flavor. I knew that as a fact now.

I hated the mark I'd put on my perfect body, but god, I had been delicious. And it would heal. I hadn't gone too deep and had cleaned it out with alcohol and covered it with gauze, and my bathroom closet was packed with expensive skin creams that could prevent scarring. Even if it left a mark, it was in a very private place most people would never see. Besides, there was always plastic surgery.

It wasn't like I'd had any other option. When the beast was roaring, there was no other way to calm it down. Feeding it a small chunk of my epidermis was better than having it rip and tear its way out of me. But I couldn't just go on skinning myself like a deer. Autosarcophagy was literally a dead end. I needed human flesh, and lots of it. It's always best to stock up on things. I'd been too wasteful with Derek, tossing out and boiling down valuable meat (although, some of him had been easier to eat than others, and some parts were too tough and gristly and had to be tossed). Now I was paying for it. The little bit of skin I'd fed the fuck-demon would not satisfy it for very long. I needed to think this through. I needed a plan.

I thought about killing a homeless person because no one would miss them, but I worried they would be too dirty and ripe with diseases. I felt the same way about hiring a hooker off Craigslist. Just because I needed to eat people didn't mean I had to risk getting AIDS or come into contact with bloodborne pathogens. If I were going to prepare a human being for slaughter, they would have to be relatively young. They would be leaner and cleaner, having had less time to become tainted.

Luckily, I knew a lot of people who fit this description. There was a whole school full of flesh for me to browse. There were lots of steaks and chops on the jocks, but the tender bodies of the girls called to me. Somehow I felt there would be less waste, that they would be leaner, their bodies more yielding to blades and teeth.

It would be easy enough for me to pick random prey. Almost any girl in school would love to hang out with me, and Caitlin had been a perfect example of how awestruck younger girls became in my presence. I could take a freshman into the woods for slaughter without them asking a single question. They would be too blissed out to sense danger. Their bodies were petite and soft, still transforming out of childhood. Gutting them would be a breeze compared to Derek's hulking corpse.

But there was a problem with this plan.

Any girl who was suddenly asked to hang out by an A-list girl like me would tell the goddamned world about it. She would brag to every one of her friends. Everyone would know whom she had been with when she disappeared. It was a better idea to go with someone who knew me and was used to being around me, someone who would be easygoing about hanging out.

But which of my friends was ripe for the plucking?

TWENTY-NINE

Dakota and I didn't hang out one-on-one all that much, but it didn't seem weird for me to ask her to. On the rare occasions we did, she always jumped at the chance because it made her feel more important than she was. She was usually just an add-on, an accessory to whatever Amy and I were doing. Showing an interest in her outside of a group setting brought her up a rank, and that was all the motivation she needed.

"Hell yeah," she said. "I can come over."

"Awesome. The house will be all ours."

"Your dad has been gone for, like, a crazy long time, huh?"

"Well, he sealed the deal but now they're scouting locations for the new buildings."

The last class of the day had ended and we were taking the only books we would need from our lockers. I had waited until the end of the day to ask her. It gave her no time to tell anyone else what she would be doing or who she would be doing it with. Dakota usually took the bus and was glad to get a ride with me instead, but she wanted to stop at home to drop off her books. She was a latchkey kid, which was one of the reasons I had selected her for slaughter. She came and went as she pleased, never having to check in with her mother. Dakota's mom worked long hours and had a five-year-old daughter to handle, a child from a second husband who had up and left just like Dakota's father had. I'd met her on a few occasions. She was one of those common American women who retained some of the good looks of their younger days but had still grown haggard, prematurely aged by stress and one too many disappointments. Dakota's mother considered her eldest daughter old enough to take care of herself and, being a teenager, Dakota was happy with her freedom, even smug about it.

"Is anyone at your house?" I asked her.

"No. Mom worked this morning but she texted to tell me she would be working a few extra hours this afternoon. And Mara is at daycare. A friend of ours runs one out of her house, so she can pick her up whenever."

She didn't ask why I had asked. She was aloof, in love with the arrival of summer as she stretched her arm out the window and played with the wind. Her low-cut V-neck shirt revealed ample cleavage that assured the world she was still ripening and would soon be an even more buxom knockout than she already was, if only she lived that long. Looking at those huge tits, I imagined cooking one in a crock-pot until the meat would fall apart like a sopping tenderloin.

I had been plotting to take her out somewhere instead of going to my house. I didn't want any more murders in my home and would rather ditch a body than go through the trouble of getting rid of it piece by piece. But I had not come up with much of a plan. The best I could think of was to tell her I'd found a secluded creek out in the woods I wanted to show her. But nature wasn't Dakota's thing. I would have to spin it somehow, tell her it would be a good place to have a bonfire party or something. Then I could take her deep into the forests around the mountain, well off the trails, and kill her and make off with a duffle bag full of remains. This was a shitty plan, but what else could I do? I would have loved to find an abandoned barn where I could hang her by her ankles and cut her from her cunt down to her breastbone, butchering her like a doe. But this option had not presented itself. An empty house or strip mall was an option, but Dakota was not the type to break and enter, and she would be surprised and confused if I suggested such a thing. So when she asked if we could stop by her house so she could drop off her backpack and change clothes after the hot, sweaty day, I spotted the opportunity immediately. Now that she had confirmed the house was empty and would be staying that way for at least a few hours, I had a plan that was perfect in its simplicity. Killing her in her own home was ideal because I could just leave her there. I could make it look like a home invasion gone wrong, like a robbery or rape attempt that had turned ultraviolent. However, there were still some concerns. It was daylight and would stay that way well past seven o'clock. There was a risk of being seen going in and out of the house. When the news broke, someone might remember my car being in the driveway and give a description of it that could lead back to me. No one at school had taken much notice of us leaving in it together—or at least not that I'd seen—but someone could be walking their dog or checking their mailbox when we arrived. I would have to play things cautiously and be aware of my surroundings. I would be taking more risks here than I liked to, but I was out of time. The fuck-demon would not wait any longer, and I could not bear the pain I'd receive as punishment for failing to deliver the goods. I had to roll the dice.

When we arrived at her house Dakota led me to her room at the end of the hall. I told her I wanted to change too, so she didn't think anything of me carrying the gym bag into the house, the one I had prepared that morning, lining it with plastic bags. It was not my new team gym bag, nor my old one, but a cheap one I had bought just for this purpose, one I could easily dispose of. I'd been in her house before and knew the layout; it would be easy to find knives in the kitchen or tools in the garage. I wouldn't have to use my own. When we got to her room, she tossed her book bag onto her unmade bed and put her phone down on the dresser. She opened the top drawer and took out a bra and panties, then went to the closet for shorts and a top.

"I'll be right back," she said as she left for the bathroom across the hall.

The moment she was gone I picked up her phone and checked her recent text messages. She hadn't texted anyone about being with me. She was permanently logged into her social media accounts, so I checked her Facebook, Twitter and Instagram pages for any mention of whom she was going to be with or what she was going to be doing. The pages were clear. It was more like Dakota to post while she was doing something rather than announce it beforehand, which would take away the impact of posting pictures later and risk fewer "likes."

I put the phone down. Now I was thinking about her in the

bathroom, peeling off her sweat-drenched panties. I imagined her plump, juicy body writhing beneath me, breasts pressed to breasts, tongues darting. I wondered what her pussy would feel like pressed against my own.

I slipped out of my sneakers and walked down the hall.

The bathroom door was ajar and I pushed it open slowly, catching her in nothing but her bra. The cups of it struggled to contain her tits.

"Hey!" she said, covering her crotch. But she said it with a laugh. She wasn't outraged by the intrusion. "I'm still changing, Kim."

I smiled and looked her up and down. She had a marvelous, shapely body that made my vagina flush and tingle.

"You're so hot," I said.

Now she was the one to smile. She blushed a little, her eyes looking around the room but finding nowhere to land. She still held one hand over her trim sliver of bush, but her other hand ran curiously through her hair.

"Um, thanks," she said.

"Do you think I'm hot?"

She just looked at me, saying nothing, so I pulled my shirt over my head. She still didn't say anything, but now her eyes had fallen on a particular spot. I unsnapped my bra to give her a better look. It fell to the floor, clacking as the snaps hit the tile.

Dakota quivered. "Um, what are you doing?"

"You've thought about it, haven't you?"

"Um . . ."

I wasn't hearing a *no*, and I'd seen the way she often looked at me. I kicked out of my jean shorts. We were both near nude now in the tight bathroom. Together we had on one set of women's undergarments.

"I've never done anything with a girl before," I said. "Have you?"

Her voice was uncommonly quiet. "Um, no."

"Are you curious?"

I slid my hand between my legs and caressed myself through my panties.

Dakota was doing a lot of blinking. "What happened to your leg?"

I had a bandage over it, but the white had pink dots speckled through it.

"Hurt myself cheerleading," I said.

I came closer.

"This isn't a prank, is it?" she asked. "Are you punking me?"

Reaching out slowly, I took the hand she'd been covering her pussy with and placed it on one of my breasts.

"Just touch me," I said. "Let's see how it feels."

Her hand didn't move at first, but she also didn't recoil. I put my hand on her side and rubbed her hip. She was baby soft. She obviously properly moisturized to keep her tan from toughening her skin. Her hand moved, gentle on my breast, fingertips gliding across the nipple like feathers. I moved closer and kissed her cheek in various spots and nuzzled her neck. She gave in, locking her lips to mine. The taste of her made my stomach grumble loudly. We both ignored it.

"I'm not really gay," she whispered. "I just want to, you know, experience . . ."

I shut her up by kissing her. Her mouth tasted faintly of the Tic-Tacs she'd been eating earlier. Her tongue was dancing in my mouth, warm and wet and wiggly, pulsing with breakthrough passion. I wanted to crawl into her through that hot little mouth and lick her from the inside out and emerge from her pussy like an oversized newborn, shredding her vaginal canal, shattering the bones of her pelvis and dislocating her hips. My stomach groaned again at the flavor of human meat. My womb began to burn.

Pulling the bra off her chest, I ran my fingernails across the shudder and flow of her mighty breasts and she moaned with her tongue still in my mouth. The feel of her yielding flesh, the smell of her pheromones, and the flavor of her gums made the fuck-demon croak with excitement. I grew impetuous in my fever and lust. My teeth closed gently around her darting tongue and I sucked it in deeper, then bit down with all the strength of my jaw.

Dakota's scream was deafening in its volume and closeness. I already tasted blood, the thick, salty flavor making my heart quake. She tried to push me away and I bear-hugged her, pinning her arms to her sides. She was heavier than I was, but I was a gymnast and cheerleader, whereas Dakota rarely worked out. When she tried to pull her head away I bit down harder and she squealed and shook, her blood dribbling down our chins. Dakota sent a knee into my groin and I stumbled back as pain hollowed me. Tears ran down her burning pink face and she gargled a scream as she went for the door. I grabbed a fistful of hair, snapping her head back on her neck, and hauled her back into the bathroom. She slipped on the bloody tiles and fell into me. I kept my balance, but Dakota fell heavily and barely caught herself before her head could hit the toilet. I lifted the seat and put both hands on her head and slammed it into the rim of the bowl. The bathroom palpitated. Dakota kicked and clawed at me, her fingernails lifting thin layers of skin from my forearms. On the third slam of her head into the rim a gout of red exited Dakota's forehead, spattering the bowl and putting ripples in the water. She found strength in her panic and rose up, arms windmilling, and pushed me backward. I hit the wall hard enough to dent the drywall, and my back crackled from the shifting vertebrae. Blood from the dent in her head was dribbling into her eyes, blinding her as she reached out for the door, more bubbling from her mouth like crimson beer foam. She got to the door just as I stood up.

There was a toothbrush holder by the sink, which also held a hairbrush and a stainless steel pair of barber scissors. I snatched them, holding them underhanded so the blades pointed down out of my clenched fist. Making sure the blades were just slightly parted, I lunged at Dakota as she swung the door open. The blades sunk into her right shoulder and stuck there as she fell into the side of the door. It shuddered from the impact and as she fell again she grabbed for the doorknob, which slipped away from her blood-slick hands. I turned to the toilet, adrenaline driving me into a frenzy, and lifted the tank cover and swung it at the top of her skull. It made a sound like a walnut being opened and Dakota completely collapsed under me. Her limbs twitched and she garbled words I could not understand. Trying to push herself up, she only managed to spin and fall onto her back. I lifted the heavy tank lid over my head, my arms fully extending so the end of the lid was near the bottom of my shoulder blades, and then I swung it over my head and sent it crashing down upon her pretty face.

The blow was devastating. Her nose was crushed to one side, the cartilage obliterated, releasing a wad of bloody snot. Her screaming stopped and her eyes rolled, the lids fluttering like moths. I cracked her again and again, the fuck-demon giggling with applause as Dakota's face was reduced to a heap of gory pulp and fragmented bone. I found this even more erotic than fucking her. I was destroying something of such loveliness and purity, annihilating beauty and youth, stealing the life from this teenage girl and taking her as my own, forever. There was a different kind of beauty to her now. She was the art of the broken, a Picasso burning in a dumpster. I bashed her and bashed her and fucking bashed her, her teeth being forced through the face. Her cheekbones were pulverized and one eye popped from the socket, the forehead bowing and collapsing until I could see spongy gray beneath the bone.

I lost myself in her.

Dakota now had the look of an uliginous monstrosity. Dropping the tank lid, I bent over and stuck my tongue into the jagged hole I'd made in her forehead so I could lap at the bit of exposed brain. The pit gave way as a loose piece of skull separated, and I was able to French kiss her forehead. The brain within was surprisingly mushy and salty. I kissed the red ruin of her face and sucked on her dislodged eye, the force of my sucking stretching the optic nerves. Then I reached her lips. They were wide open, the jaw dislocated and slack. It took some time for me to chew through her bottom lip. While it was silky to the touch, the inner tissue was resistant and strong and I had to nibble it loose, then slurp it back into my molars to gnaw it into a gruel I could swallow.

I had to use both hands and all of my upper body strength to expunge the scissors from her shoulder, the force jiggling the grisly jigsaw of her face. I knew I should get better tools, cut and gather parts of her, and get the fuck out of there as soon as possible, but the hunger was upon me now, unwilling to listen to reason. Every inch of me ached with a terrible urge. I could not leave the bathroom until I had had my fix.

The scissors were strong and sharp. Cutting into the tenderized face, I picked bits and pieces away, barely chewing as I rushed to get them into my belly. I snipped the eye from the optic nerve and held it with one hand as I ruptured it and split it in two with the blades. Then I swallowed each half whole. I ate her remaining lip and one cheek and rolled blood on my tongue like a whore with cum. Saving the best for last, I closed the scissors and stabbed them straight through the hole in her skull, puncturing the brain. I forced the scissors open and twisted them around and around, then pushed the blades upward at a slant. They came up glistening with gray matter.

There was no hesitation now, no reluctance or doubt. I did not question what I was doing anymore. I went with my most primal instincts—killing to satiate, to survive. The hunger chased out all other thoughts from my mind, putting it on a single track.

The scissor blades went into my mouth and when they left they came out sparkling clean.

That's when I heard the front door open.

THIRTY

"**D**akota?" a voice called out. "Come help me with the groceries."

My car was in the driveway. Dakota's mother knew her daughter was home—home with someone else. I had not expected her to come home so soon. Had she left work earlier than expected? How long had I been in the bathroom?

My body locked up despite my burning impulse to run. I was still straddling the fresh corpse of her dead daughter in a crimson pool, caked in her gore and chewing on a piece of her brain like it was taffy. The world came to a sudden halt.

I heard bags being placed on the counter, keys jingling.

"Dakota, come help me unload the groceries. I still need to pick up your sister."

At least the kid wasn't with her. The thought of devouring flesh that young and supple was an exciting one, but it was going to be enough trouble to handle this without some screeching brat scampering about. I began whispering to myself, my mouth unable to keep up with the garrulous nature of my thoughts. There was no time to plan. There could only be action.

I stood and opened the door slowly, listening to the sounds of rustling plastic bags. She was in the kitchen. It was far enough away from the bathroom, but it gave a clear view down the hall. If she happened to be looking up, she would see me as I ran into Dakota's room, where I could jump out the window if needed. There was no time to wash up. I looked down at my clothes on the floor. They had a minimal amount of splatter on them, considering, so I threw on my shirt and stepped into my shorts as quickly as I could, stuffing my bra into my back pocket so not to leave a clue. But looking at the walls, cabinet and toilet, I realized my bloody fingerprints were everywhere.

Dark images of what could happen blazed through my mind.

Fuck.

I couldn't leave the scene like this.

Clenching the scissors, I put my back against the wall and steadied my breathing to lessen the trembling of my limbs. Then I bolted across the hall, seeing Dakota's mother look up from the groceries as I ducked into Dakota's room.

"Who's that?" she asked.

She'd seen something, but the hall was shadowy. She was coming now. I could hear her shuffling down the hallway. I clutched the bloody scissors. The bathroom came before the bedroom on Dakota's mother's trip down the hall, and the light was still on, the door wide open. The sound of horror that came from the woman was like nothing I'd ever heard before. It was the kind of scream that tells a tale worse than death. It echoed through the hallway as I stepped into it on the tips of my toes, dripping with blood, the scissors held above my shoulder, a ballerina about to draw a final curtain.

When I came up behind her she was kneeling on the floor, lightly patting her dead daughter, as if she could stroke the reality of it all away. Her frantic breathing reminded me of Caitlin at her moment of dying, and that keyed me up, turning my fear into a hormonal rush, my flight turning to fight. I came in close, smelling the sweat of panic in her hair and tasting it at the back of my throat. I turned, lowering my arm so I could stab the scissors into her side, underhanded.

She turned just as I was crouching, and screamed.

It startled me and I took a defensive step back instead of stabbing her like I should have. She stood up, all tears and misery and fear. I tried to imitate her, forcing tears to my eyes and allowing myself to shake now. I was nearly as bloody as Dakota was. There was no way to know it wasn't my blood, at least not at first glance. I didn't need the ruse to last. It wouldn't. I just needed enough time to get Dakota's mother to let her guard down, so I could administer the deathblow.

"K-K-Kim?" she asked, convulsing.

"Help . . ." I whispered. "I think . . . he's . . . still here."

I expected her to go into the mode of protective adult, but she was too far-gone, too crippled by the freshness of her grief. She only looked at me for a moment, then turned back to her daughter and fell to her knees into the blood puddle, sobbing, shaking and screaming. This was Caitlin's fit tenfold. Her eyes were more hopeless than my victims' had been at their moment of dying. If there really had been a madman after me, Dakota's mother would have been useless. She hadn't even gathered enough sense to call 911.

I took a moment to savor what I had accomplished. They say the greatest tragedy is when a mother outlives her child. I had delivered this tragedy, and had underlined it with ghastly brutality. It was painful enough for a mother to lose their daughter to cancer or a car accident, but to find them on the bathroom floor with a gory cavity where their face had been was beyond the stuff of nightmares. By killing Dakota, I had not just committed murder; I had shattered someone else's entire world. I had driven a woman to complete madness in a matter of seconds. In this wonderful moment of enlightenment, I could have set a nursery ablaze, so great was the feeling of taking a child from its mother.

Bliss put me back into my sphere of detachment, and once again I was floating, dancing, scissor blades gleaming in the light of the bathroom, reflecting all that glorious red. They opened just slightly, to better slide in, and as Dakota's mother bent over her child, I sent the blades into her kidneys so she could join her daughter.

A fist hit the side of my head like a baseball bat. Stars burst through my eyes as my brain shook against the walls of my skull. I struggled to stay on my feet. Dakota's mother was lashing out at me, knowing now what had happened to her daughter. There would be no phone calls, no police. Vengeance was hers, and her fury gave her a strength I never would have expected from the woman. She was meaty, like her daughter, but she'd always seemed so exhausted. Now the woman was on fire.

She took another swing at me but slipped in the blood, and I brought the scissors down toward her back but they bounced off the toughness of her ribs, ripping her shirt but doing minor bodily harm. She lunged, fists flailing without any thought behind them, and I was knocked into the cabinet, sending all sorts of pill bottles, tweezers and floss picks tumbling down. I was hurting now. Dakota's mother put her hand on the sink to help herself up, and I came down on it with the scissors, piercing the top of her hand and going through to the palm. Her scream hurt my ears but made my nipples hard. The violence was so salacious, the danger making me feel carnal and alive. I was a primitive carnivore and I fucking loved it. She pulled away, taking the scissors with her as she tumbled. With her good hand she grabbed the shower curtain for support and, ring-by-ring, it pulled free and she fell into the tub. A manic laugh came out of me. I was on the verge of hysteria.

I took the tank lid from the floor. Every inch of it was slippery with blood and I struggled to find a good grip. Dakota's mother was still screaming as she tried to pull the scissors out of her hand, every vein in her neck and arms bulging as she strained. I roared as I came at her. The lid hit her in the mouth, costing her some teeth and splitting her lip. She tried to get up but slid on the slick walls of the shower. She put her arms up as the lid came crashing down again, but one of her hands was useless, so the best she could do was try to shield herself rather than attempt to take the lid away. I clobbered her arms until they dropped and then cracked her head open. She fell unconscious, and I pulled the scissors out of her hand and slashed her throat, laughing and laughing, gone.

Bathrooms were becoming incredible places for me.

When Dakota's mother was dead, I sat there on the floor, catching my breath in a meditative state. My movements in the blood sounded peaceful, like footfalls on rainy pavement. Time was slowing down. I had to remind myself not to sit there for too long. There'd been a lot of screaming; luckily, it was a hot day. Everyone's windows were closed and their air conditioners were running. Plus it was the afternoon, which meant music and televisions and other drowning noise. This bathroom didn't even have a window, so the sounds we had made were as muffled as they could be. Someone still could have heard something, though, considering how these two bitches had squawked. But I would just have to risk staying. There was still so much to do. I would just have to hope if someone had called the police I would be able to stab myself a few times before they got to the bathroom, so I could pretend I was the lone survivor of a vicious attack.

I got naked. I went into the kitchen, grabbed a sponge and put on dishwashing gloves, and then went into the garage for the other things I needed. I came back to the bathroom and wiped down all the prints I could see.

The handsaw didn't cut as cleanly as I would have liked. It ripped at Dakota's breast meat, tearing the fat and sinew like the teeth of an animal. I went to work on the rest of her good parts, using the axe on the big joints and skull, and then sawing away at whatever connective tissue remained. I was short on time, so I wasn't as deft as I'd been with Derek.

Dismembering someone is not as easy as the horror movies make it look. I've seen many slasher films where the masked maniac swings a chainsaw and a young victim's leg goes flying. That is Hollywood bullshit. If you've ever taken down a tree limb with a chain saw, you know you have to hold it steady and wait for it to saw through. Bone is even tougher than wood. It gives eventually, but not easily.

I crushed her ribcage with the axe and sawed at the concavity to get to the viscera below, not being picky as I tossed them into the freezer bags I had put into my disposable duffle bag earlier that day. The only thing I was picky about was her vagina, which I mutilated, placing the bits into a small sandwich bag. Once the duffle bag was stuffed full, I looked down at the disaster of what remained of Dakota's carcass, amazed at how different someone could look in the course of a single day, given the right treatment.

While older, Dakota's mother was still in good shape. She had a hard body from harder work. There would be a lot of lean muscle on her, lots of steaks. I could have diced some of her up and used the grocery bags to carry her out. But no, I wanted to get into the car and go with a minimum of fuss, and I needed to do it *now*. There wasn't even time for me to have sex with her corpse, which was a real shame. I didn't want her to be a complete waste though, so I placed her good hand on the edge of the tub, using it as a chopping block as I took two of her fingers off with the axe. I placed one of them in the sandwich bag with her daughter's mangled genitals.

I walked down the hall to the master bedroom. There was a second shower attached, so I rinsed myself off, wishing I could stay under the hot, cleansing water forever. After drying off, I put my bloody clothing into the duffle bag and went to Dakota's room and slipped into one of her summer dresses. It was a little baggy on me, but it would do.

Before leaving, I went into the kitchen and opened the door that led to the side of the house, which faced into the woods. Making sure no one was around, I put on oven mitts so not to leave prints and whacked the doorknob with the butt of the axe until it fell apart and then bashed the wood to make it look like someone had broken in. Then I went back to the bathroom and tossed the axe in the tub.

Outside I was shocked to find dusk settling in. I'd been working in there for a long time. The neighborhood was quiet but for a pair of boys riding their bikes in circles at the end of the cul-de-sac. I put the bag on the passenger seat, and it was a relief to set it down. Body parts are heavier than you'd expect. The bag must have weighed seventy pounds.

I started the car and drove into the growing cover of night.

It was late and I still had to make dinner.

THIRTY-ONE

After packing the food into the fridge and freezer, I drew a bath and nursed my wounds. I had scratches on my arms from Dakota's fingernails, but most of them had not drawn blood. I had bruises on my back from when I'd hit the wall. While my head ached from the punch Dakota's mother had connected, she'd hit the side of my head, so my hair would cover any bruising there. I was sore in spots, but I'd made it out relatively unscathed. The scratches were the only thing I had to cover up, and I had thin summer sweaters that would do the trick.

Despite the dull aches of my body, I was still incredibly aroused by all that had happened, so I played with the hollowed out dildo as I soaked. I'd removed the gauze and added the pieces of Dakota's vagina and her mother's finger to Derek's decaying cock. They were my sweet mementos of flesh and they felt so right inside of me, as if they belonged, as if they should always be a part of me. I made myself come twice before I got out of the bath and went downstairs to check on Dakota's tit, which was in the oven in a small baking pan with onions, carrots and more butter than I would care to admit.

My phone rang and I saw it was Father. He'd called after hearing the news about Derek's bones being found in the Blakley's yard, but I'd assured him I was doing fine and there was no need to come home. Now he was checking in more regularly.

"Things are good," I said. "I was just hanging out with a friend, now I'm making a breast."

"I love your chicken. Boy, I sure miss having home-cooked meals. The hotel has a five star restaurant, and it's good, but it's just not the same."

I basted the tit. "When do you think you'll be back?"

"It won't be long now." That could mean a month or days. "Now that it's summer, I was thinking we could take a vacation. Maybe go to the Bahamas. In between whatever else you have going on, of course."

The whole county was in panic, if not the state.

To my hometown's citizens, our ever-growing tragedy had played out like their own little movie, but this . . . this was a *horror* movie. Americans have come to believe serial killers are the stuff of TV dramas and are no longer stalking our streets. They aren't in the news much anymore. We have new monsters; mass shooters and suicide bombers have replaced the Ted Bundys and Richard Ramirezes who had once made us lock our doors at night. But they're still out there, and now our community had one of its very own, and a barbaric one at that. Because of the ghastly nature of the crime, all the news networks had come out. It was in all the papers and on every local evening news program. Of course, many people were saying not to call it the work of a serial killer, seeing how these two victims were taken at the same time and no other murders had been connected to it. Nonetheless, the extreme brutality of the killings, and the fact body parts had gone missing, made most people consider this the work of a lust/rage murderer who would strike again.

The daycare owner had brought Dakota's sister home after calling Dakota's mother several times without getting through. The child was with her when she'd discovered the bodies. The case was being treated as a break-in slaying, which implied randomness, but the police were questioning everyone that knew the family, and that included Dakota's circle of friends. Instead of seeming suspicious that I was back in their station again, the police were actually apologetic, treating me with empathy considering all I had been through. The questions were similar to the ones they'd asked about Derek, very basic ones about who Dakota might have been dating, if she had any enemies or jilted lovers, if we'd noticed any suspicious behavior, and so on. But, for the most part, they seemed to be putting more focus on her mother. I kept tears in my eyes and my answers short and unhelpful. I wasn't the only youth that kept getting questioned. Brian, Amy, Brittany and Tanner had also been questioned in the disappearance of Derek as well as the murder of Dakota and her mother. The police were seeing a lot of our group, and they weren't the only ones to take notice of it.

"Do you think someone's targeting us?" Amy asked. "Targeting our squad?"

"No way," I said. "These were separate incidents."

The summer night had cooled and Amy slipped into her long sleeve shirt. She appeared spectral in the light of my swimming pool, the ghost of a girl who had died under suspicious circumstances. The night was speckled with stars, the crickets serenading us as we sipped our wine. We would have gone swimming, but I didn't want my cuts and bruises to show, so I told her I was on my period. God, how I wished that were true.

"A lot of people are saying they aren't separate incidents," Amy said, "that Simone Blakley was framed by Derek's real killer, and this same guy killed Dakota and her mom and is still at large."

"But the police haven't said that."

"Well, duh, they don't want to create a panic." Tears came to Amy's eyes and I was surprised to realize they were genuine. "Christ, Kim. Parts of her body are missing. And they never found *all* of Derek."

"Mrs. Blakley did a poor job of burying him. He's probably scattered all over those woods."

Amy dabbed at her eyes with her cuffs. "I'm fucking scared, Kim."

I touched her shoulder. "Hey, it's okay, really. You'll be fine."

"I'm scared for all of us. I mean, who knows who this sicko will target next? Even if Mrs. Blakley really was the one to kill Derek, whoever killed Dakota is still out there. That's *terrifying*. This wasn't just some break-in-gone-wrong. This is a fucking maniac."

It wasn't until that moment I realized just how separated I had become from my fellow human beings. They saw what I did as the depraved actions of the lowest form of human life. To them, this was the aberrant behavior of a psychopath. Certainly I understood the killings would be seen as criminal, but it had not occurred to me what I'd been doing was in any way deranged. Butchering my friends was exciting, but it seemed no crazier to me than partying with them. Was I totally detached? I had immersed myself in my obsessions, spending greater amounts of time alone, reading about murder and cannibalism and watching torture porn. Had my understanding of the human condition been warped? I saw what I was doing as a matter of necessity. The fuck-demon had to feed, and so did I, and it wasn't like I could buy human meat at McDonald's. I had no choice but to hunt and butcher. The fact I had grown to enjoy it so much was irrelevant.

"He's probably a drifter," I said. "Skips from town to town."

"You're awfully optimistic seeing how we'll be burying another one of our friends in a few days."

I hadn't gone to Derek's funeral. I thought it would look strange for me to do so, given my whole Caitlin story. But Amy had attended, always wanting to be at the center of any drama.

"Let's change the subject, okay?"

Teenagers are resilient. Even with big events going on, it doesn't take much to get them back to their own personal issues. Amy nodded and we moved on.

"How are things with you and Ashton?"

She hesitated before saying: "Okay."

"Just okay?"

"I've been meaning to talk to you about this. I have to tell someone, and you're my best friend."

I sat up in the lawn chair to face her. "What's going on, Amy?"

Her knees were bouncing and she started twirling her hair in her hands. "Well, you know how we talked about me reaching out to Brian, because of what happened to Derek?"

"Yeah."

"Well, that whole thing was, like, way intense, right? He and I were both real emotional about it all. I went to his house that night and . . . well . . . we sorta slept together. It wasn't a hook-up though, it was like, making love, you know?"

"So you cheated on Ashton."

"I didn't mean for it to happen, it just did. But it brought up all these old feelings I had for Brian. I started thinking I was wrong to curve him, that I'd made this huge mistake."

"So are you going to dump Ashton?"

"That's just it. Ashton is so cool, right? I mean, he's *Gucci*. I don't want to give that up, but at the same time I have all these mad emotions when it comes to Brian. So I've been seeing them both, with Brian on the down low."

"Whoa. You've been having sex with *two* guys at once?"

"I know, I know. Don't say it. But it's not just a sex thing. It's about the things *I need*, Kim. Some of what I need I get from Ashton, some from Brian."

She was just that self-centered. I was proud of her.

"But doesn't Brian want you all to himself again?"

"Well, yeah, he was *begging* to have me back. But for now he's willing to take what he can get."

"What about Ashton?"

"What about him?"

"What do you mean *what about him*? Are you gonna tell him what's been going on, or what?"

"Are you kidding me? No, of course not. That would ruin everything. Ashton would dump me in the time it takes to flick a light switch."

Amy didn't even tell me to keep this a secret. It didn't just go without saying; there was a concrete trust between us, at least on her end. I knew she wouldn't tell anyone else, and that made this confession very special. I wondered how I could use this information. It was heavy and dirty. There were so many ways to hurt her with it, not to mention Ashton and Brian. Destroying my best friend was still a point of focus for me. The fuck-demon and its demands were the dominating factors of my life now, but that didn't mean I couldn't partake in the joy of sadism. Sabotaging people romantically might seem timid compared to crushing their skulls with toilet tank lids, but hurting people is an art, and I enjoyed it in all its many forms.

Life can really be a kick to the cunt sometimes.

The poisoning of the bastard in my belly had not gone well. All the smoking and drinking and power-lifting and everything else I'd done in an attempt to rid myself of this curse had failed to produce the desired result. Was it possible the fuck-demon was indestructible, that it truly was a *demon*? After all, it did demand human flesh. It did torture me. When it finally came out of me would I find *666* burned onto its cranium? Hell spawn or not, it was coming. With each day I felt more bloated and sick, and I was noticing the slightest hint of a baby bump. I was full of worry and out of ideas. Barring some miracle, I would be a mommy in six months.

Thoughts of suicide returned. This was not out of self-pity, but out of total unwillingness to face what was to come—humiliation followed by the complete demolition of my life. It was naive to think I could hide my pregnancy for very long. Even if I hibernated all summer, I would return to school at the end of August with a beach ball for a belly. And then there was Father. As often as he was away, I doubted business would keep him out of the state for six more months. Suicide was becoming more and more attractive, an old solution that always returned with huge fists. I suppose I should have looked at killing myself as just another way for me to be embarrassed; after all, it would destroy the image I had created. But the shame of suicide is nothing compared to the shame of teenage pregnancy. Killing yourself is profound. It's the ultimate *fuck you* to the world. But getting knocked up in a sloppy fashion when you're too young to vote, with no baby-daddy to call your own . . . well, that is just plain trashy. Suicide is a New York City art major, teen pregnancy is a Jacksonville, Florida strip club waitress.

I'd always taken offense to the negative view many have of killing one's self, that it's some sort of defeat or the ultimate sin. I admire people with the strength and determination to check out of this burning sewer. There are hotlines and medications and support groups all designed to keep people from committing suicide because people put such value in human life, mostly because they themselves are human. Meanwhile overpopulation is a bigger problem than it has ever been. Human life has hit record numbers. Why should we value something we have more of than we need? I think a lot of suicide prevention efforts are not so much to save someone from killing themselves, but rather an attempt to keep anyone who knew them from having to accept blame or live with pain. Everyone is a contender when it comes to losing someone they love to suicide, and nobody wants to be stuck with that pain and stigma the rest of their lives. People keep others from jumping off the ledge because they don't want to have to scoop brains off their front porch.

While I still heavily romanticized suicide, it was not as easy to consider now I had found a reason to go on living. I was enjoying my life now I had embraced the side of myself I'd kept hidden for so long. Torturing, degrading and butchering people who were close to me not only gave me intense pleasure, but it also gave me a sense of purpose, a deeper understanding of the importance of my existence. I had evolved from playing games to ending lives. This revelation connected me with the self behind the mirror, the id. This was the me society had subdued and nearly smothered to death, the me that was pure and honest in ways I had not been since I was a very young child. And though I still hid it for my own safety, I was no longer denying it what it needed. The inner me—the *true* me—needed hard violence and perverse sex. Without these things I would starve, just as surely as the fuck-demon would starve without human meat.

In an ironic twist, I was now living for death.

There was no real decision to come to.

I would just have to take things one day at a time and hope a decent plan would form. I tried to tell myself maybe being pregnant wasn't as bad as I was making it out to be, that women all over the world had learned to deal with it. I told myself I could always put the fuck-demon up for adoption. The thought of a cannibal child ripping and slashing its way through an orphanage gave me a giggle, but as much as I tried to put a positive spin on this, I knew I was just putting sprinkles on a turd sundae. This *was* the end of the world; maybe not for the single mom skanks, but for a promising young woman like myself, this was a painful, slow death.

But I was at an impasse. I couldn't take action without a course of action. All I could do was go on with my daily life, keep trying to poison the belly-beast, and see what happened. I knew this was just a countdown to ruin, but I was tired of sitting around thinking about it, allowing the same nagging thoughts to keep swirling through my mind. Maybe if I went on as if I wasn't carrying a time bomb, a way to defuse it would come along when I least expected it.

After yet another day of canceled school due to a student's death, we all went back to finish our final week before summer break began. The school had brought in temporary grief counselors and therapists, and a special memorial event was being put together for Caitlin, Derek and Dakota that would take place on our field, where the whole town could come out and talk about how fucking swell those precious teens were. There was a dark mood to the halls. The students weren't just lacking the giddiness that usually bubbles to the surface in the last days of the school year, they were devoid of even the most basic pleasantries and the humor of everyday life. A plume of fear and despair had left a gray stain on everyone and the teachers had to deal with their pupils' unhappiness as if it hung from their necks by chains. This was a rich hell I savored. I'd caused such powerful misery and instilled terror into the hearts and minds of everyone I knew. It was quite an accomplishment. I almost wished I had somebody to brag to. It was hard not to be grandiose.

Father now insisted on coming home. Apparently three dead classmates was the charm. This caused me some concern. For one thing I was trying to hide my pregnancy, and for another I had been rationing the pieces of Dakota in the fridge, eating just enough to satiate the fuck-demon, so they would last. There were still a lot of prime cuts in the freezer I did not want to toss. Could I risk leaving them in there? Father never did any of the cooking. Would he even look at them? I was fairly confident he wouldn't, but having the remains of one of my victims in the house with Father around would be hell on my nerves. But disposing of them would be wasteful. Worse yet, it would mean I would have to go out and kill regularly, getting my fix of human flesh from fresh kills instead of being able to stockpile cuts at home. This would have me out butchering new people every goddamn night. That would be a bit much. Besides, I didn't want to kill again just yet. I wanted this miserable town to cool and settle, to get back to some semblance of normalcy, so I would be striking just when the hairs on their arms had started to go back down. The murders would have more power if they were spaced out. Although, I had to admit, a nightly feeding would be fun, and daily murders would cause quiet a panic, bringing mass insomnia to our once sleepy town. But it was too easy to get caught that way. That kind of frequency was bound to max out my luck.

I decided to keep Dakota's parts in the fridge. If Father were curious about the strange containers and packages, I would tell him I was trying new recipes. It wouldn't be a lie. And as long as I kept his belly full he wouldn't ask questions. It would look strange if I ate different meals than he did, so I wondered what part of my latest victim he would like best. He'd never been one for organ meats, but he loved red meat, and I still had some choice cuts from Dakota's legs and ass. However, the flavor of human flesh is not identical to beef, so I would have to dice it up and make a stew or something to disguise the taste and texture, even though I had come to prefer Dakota served as medium-rare steaks. I enjoyed cooking, especially for Father. It was time to get creative.

I spent the afternoon watching *Salò, or The 120 Days of Sodom* and preparing Dakota's brain, which I had scooped out of her hollowed-out forehead. It took some time to get the skull fragments out of the mass, but it was worth the effort. I'd read about how monkey brains were considered a delicacy in some Asian cultures and, knowing man and ape were siblings when it came to our biological makeup, I decided to prepare myself a nice meal, this being the last day I would have the house to myself.

The Anyang tribe of Cameroon had once had a tradition in which, after hunting down a gorilla, the chief would devour the brain while his apprentice ate the heart. Other members of the tribe were not allowed to taste these treasures. Reading about this excited me, as I felt consuming this particular part of my dead friend would enhance me somehow. The brain is what makes a person who they are, what many refer to as one's spirit or life force. Eating it would be like eating Dakota's soul. The notion made me tremble with delight.

The only trouble I had was finding recipes. There is a dessert called monkey brains that is actually just cinnamon bread, and another dish which is mere sushi, and these kept coming up in my Google searches, frustrating me as I hunted for the real deal, coming up empty. Because of the gelatinous texture of the organ, I decided to prepare it as if it were squid. I did not want to fry it like calamari, for I worried that would hide the true taste which I wanted to savor, so I cooked it in a sauce pan using lemon, garlic and olive oil, then speared it on kabobs along with bell peppers and onion. It was rather tasty, so I devoured the whole brain in one sitting, and the fuck-demon gurgled its applause. It was getting hungrier by the day.

When night fell I once again watched the hidden camera footage of Amy and Ashton's first fuck, trying to come up with new ideas for its use. Plotting Amy's annihilation had come to inspire greater salacity than any of the extreme humiliation porn online, and I masturbated to the video again as my mind raced with ideas, one toppling over the next like a panicked mob. Here I had a racy film that would not only devastate her if it got out, but it could also damage her relationship with Brian if it was made clear this had happened before they broke up. Brian was too pussy-whipped to dump her for it, but it would rattle what they'd been repairing and take a few more tokens out of the trust jar. But I had additional dirt on her. She'd been screwing Brian behind Ashton's back. If this dirty secret got out somehow, Amy might lose Ashton, and that would make her vulnerable. The best victims are the vulnerable ones. Just look at Caitlin Blakley. Once Amy was emotionally broken, I could sneak into her mind in the guise of her one true ally, spotting her weaknesses so they could be better exploited. Amy was strong-willed and wouldn't deteriorate as quickly as little Caitlin had, but she was easily embarrassed and fragile when it came to her reputation. Exposing and exaggerating her promiscuity could crush her, as could the loss of her boyfriends—particularly Ashton, her trophy.

It was important to me for my best friend to succumb to grief, misery and failure.

The last thing I wanted was for her to die happy.

"I should have returned the moment I heard about your girlfriend," Father said.

He scooped another blob of chili from his bowl. The hot peppers and sauce gave a nice kick to the minced muscle tissue, which I had cut with ground bison.

"It's all right," I said. "You had to finish the project."

"Well, I still feel bad about it. Such a ghastly thing."

"It's terrible. I wish I'd had time to get to know her better."

Being gone so often, Father had never met Dakota, so I tried to downplay my friendship with her to minimize any cause for concern.

"You've had one rocky school year, kiddo."

You don't know the half of it, I thought.

"Yeah, I really have."

"I'll bet you're happy it's nearly over with."

I hadn't given it much thought. "I suppose I am."

"You'll be a senior next year. So much has changed. It seems it all happened while I wasn't looking."

I swallowed another saucy chunk of human flesh.

"So," Father said, "you're still eyeing NYU?"

"For my undergrad degree."

"Have you settled on a major? I know you were tossing a few around."

I shrugged. "Still uncertain for NYU, but for grad school I was thinking of criminal psychology or forensics. Maybe go to John Jay College of Criminal Justice."

"That's up in New York too, right?"

"Right."

He smiled. "My little girl in the big city, fighting crime." He seemed happy about this, even proud, but then his face abruptly darkened. "Well, I guess it makes sense that's on your mind, considering all that's happened."

"I guess you're right."

He put his spoon down and looked out the window into the foggy night.

"So much has changed," he said again.

I wasn't surprised when Father came home with a gun.

He went on hunting trips with his associates every fall, and had a Remington rifle in a glass case in his study. He was no stranger to firearms. But the gun he purchased this time was a pistol.

"This is a forty caliber Smith and Wesson," he told me, turning the gun from side to side. "It's a powerful gun but doesn't kick all that bad. No worse than a nine millimeter. In fact, it's a lot like one. It's accurate and easy to reload. It may seem intimidating, but it's one of the better automatics to fit a woman's hands."

I blinked. "This is for me?"

He nodded. "You're old enough, and responsible. I trust you with it. More importantly, I want you to be able to protect yourself when I'm not around. Maybe this madman has left town, and by God we all hope he has, but you can never have too much security."

He handed the pistol to me. It was surprisingly light.

"Are you comfortable having a gun?" he asked.

"Yeah. I mean, thank you."

"Good. I bought us passes to the gun range. Let's try it out. The most important thing about owning a weapon is knowing when and how to use it."

THIRTY-TWO

I gave Father a kiss on the cheek and he hugged me before taking hold of the handle of his suitcase to roll it toward his gate. His assistant had stayed behind in Atlanta during Father's brief return home, and had called the night before to tell Father there were two ideal buildings on the market they could acquire while keeping the project under budget. Father needed to come out right away to view the properties. He made his usual apologies and reminded me a vacation was on the horizon, and I assured him I would be fine, and I felt well protected with the security system and my new pistol, especially now I had learned to use it properly. I told him to get on the first flight out and he made a joke about me wanting to get rid of him.

The early flight gave me time to drop him off before my last day of school. It was a hot day in late June so I dressed in a breezy skirt and thin blouse, my hair pinned up to keep it off my neck. The school seemed resurrected. The end of the year had zapped everyone with a newfound elation and many of the students could not keep their composure. Laughter filled the halls like a song, everyone tingling with the joy of summer. The death and tragedy were not forgotten, and there was still a great deal of gossip floating around pertaining to the intense police investigations, but these dark realities were placed off to the side in favor of plans for the season and last day pranks.

"We have to get wild," Amy said.

"How so?" I asked.

"We should start summer off with a bang. I keep saying we need to take a road trip. Let's give it a go. It'll be good to get out of this town for a while, don't you think?"

I didn't care. While my hometown had once driven me mad with its repetition and tedium, the past few months in it had been rather entertaining. Still, going somewhere new with Amy could give me some time to unearth some more of her skeletons I could use against her. Maybe some prolonged girl time would sharpen my knives.

"Where do you want to go?" I asked.

"Anywhere that's not here."

I looked out at the sea of faces in the cafeteria—awkward starter bodies with bright eyes, braces, zits, beginner moustaches, sloppy eyeliner, dyed hair and too many piercings. Looking at this cluster of youth, I wished them nothing but suffering.

"Of course," I said, "we'll have to go to the memorial service first."

Our school's big festival for our trilogy of tragedy was tomorrow night. There was no way I was going to miss the misery I was so proud to have caused. I even planned to record it. I could say it was for those who could not be there, then watch it again and again to feed off the pain of my friends and neighbors.

"Well, *of course*," Amy said, sounding annoyed, even a little offended.

I veered her into happier territory. "I'll go on a trip as long as we have a good destination. I don't want to be in a car for hours without it paying off."

"Calm down, Miss Priss. I'm sure we can come up with something. The real question is should we invite boys."

I rolled my eyes. "The last thing I want is to sit around a cabin while you and Ashton screw and I get dumped with one of his crotch-stain bros."

She laughed. "Um, yeah. I don't know what you did to Keith but Ashton says he won't even talk about you."

I hadn't heard anything from or about Keith since our bathroom boogie, and I was happy about it.

"He's a lice breeder," I said.

"Don't worry, he doesn't have to come and neither does Ashton.

I was thinking more about Brian."

Amy was really juggling her cocks these days. I appreciated her deviousness and complete lack of consideration or empathy, and the way she took more from men than what she gave in return was high art. Still, the way she thought she was *oh so adult* for doing this made me want to crush her ribs until they speared her lungs. Though bored of her personal soap opera, I still paid close attention to the details and tried to keep her going with open-ended questions. I had multiple plans to betray her, but didn't want to strike until I knew where I'd hit oil. I did not want to lose her trust prematurely. Why hurt her a little when I could wait and hurt her a lot? True sabotage requires patience and cunning. Our relationship deserved a fiery finale.

"Does Brian know that I know?" I asked.

"Not yet, but I figured, maybe, what's the harm?"

"You guys getting back together?"

She shrugged.

"I was thinking more about some girl time," I said.

She nodded slowly, considering. "Okay. Well, we could do that."

"Just you and me, BFFs having a retreat. I'll miss the first cheerleader practice of the summer, but that's no big deal. There'll be plenty more."

She nodded with more enthusiasm now. "Yeah, that's not a bad idea. Maybe it would be good to leave the boys behind. I could use a break from all this drama."

"And hey, maybe we could find some new boys if we go far enough out of town."

She snickered close to me. "You're so naughty."

"Oh yeah," I said, smiling. "I'm bad news."

The memorial was hilarious.

It was an astonishing turn out. Everyone brought candles, and the music teacher played weepy ballads on the piano they'd rolled out of the auditorium. Dakota's father came and gave a small speech he barely made it through, choking on sobs between the words. I had to bite the insides of my cheeks to keep from laughing. Some students had also prepared short speeches, sharing pleasant memories of Caitlin, Derek and Dakota. I wondered how many of them were fake and only written so their speakers could get a moment in the spotlight. The town grieved as one sopping heart, and I stood as if I was one of them in my black dress, a candle flickering in my hands, feeling the black vibes of their anguish. A current of desire writhed through me as I daydreamed of bathing in their tears.

When it was over I walked to the parking lot with Amy, Ashton, Tanner and Brittany. They all wore heavy faces, obviously moved by what we'd just been a part of. Brittany's cheeks were flushed and her eyes were puffy. Tanner had his arm around her, and I wondered if there was something going on between them.

"Maybe we should go somewhere," Ashton said. "You know, have a couple of drinks in honor of our fallen friends."

"I could use a drink," Tanner said. "That shit was heavy."

Brittany sniffled. "I kinda wanna go home."

"Well, I'm up for hanging out," Amy said.

She looked at me, hoping I'd invite us all to my big, empty house. I wasn't totally against it (the memorial had gotten me in a jovial mood), but if Brittany was going home I knew that would mean I'd get stuck with Tanner, and I wasn't in the mood to deal with the meathead all night.

"Why don't we go to my house," I said, touching Brittany's shoulder. "I've got beer and wine. It'll be laid back, private. We could all use some cheering up."

She took a breath. "Yeah, okay."

I drove alone while Tanner took Brittany in his car, and Amy took Ashton in hers. Having left a few minutes ahead of my friends, I got to my house first. When I got inside I felt a little twinge, so I opened a bag of my homemade jerky to satisfy the fuck-demon. As I stood there chewing, I wondered if there was any real fun that could be siphoned out of the night. A sudden thought came to me and I giggled and shook my head at the absurdity of it. I couldn't wait for everyone to arrive and then shoot them all, as funny as that would be. But it sure made me smile imagining the shock on their faces just before their bodies twitched and shuddered from the impact of my bullets.

I heard both cars pull up and I opened the door for the gang. They looked brighter already, even Brittany. We got our drinks and went out to the patio. The light of the pool gave the night a mystic, azure glow as we toasted the dead by pouring a little of our booze on the lawn. Amy pulled me aside while the others shared stories about Dakota and Derek.

"I think I have just the place for our trip," she said. "It's a spa and hotel on the beach. We can get everything from facials to mud baths to manicures. Plus, there's a good nightlife, lots of clubs we could go to. And, it's a three-hour drive, close enough for easy travel but far enough away to be *anonymous*, if you know what I mean."

She gave me a wink. This was great news. I couldn't give less of a fuck about going to a spa, but Amy was excited by the prospect of meeting some new boys and letting loose. She had summer fever; it would be easier for her to drop her inhibitions. If I could get video of her in the hotel room with a boy (or maybe even two), I could use that footage to end both of her relationships. I could also combine whatever new footage I recorded with the old video of her fucking Ashton, and make a sort of *Slutty Amy's Greatest Hits* mix for everyone to enjoy online. Judging by Amy's newfound kinks, I doubted she would need much persuasion to take in some new man-meat.

"Sounds fun," I said.

"You sure you don't mind skipping that cheerleader event or whatever."

"It's tournament practice, and kind of a pre-audition for seniors. But I'm going to be head cheerleader next year. I'll be on the squad, for sure. I can tell Mrs. Morrell I have a family thing or something. She won't mind if I miss just one."

On Monday morning Amy drove over to pick me up for our trip. She wore a blue shoulder-strap dress and flip-flops. I was still getting ready in the bathroom, but we had plenty of time, so she came inside with her suitcase and massive purse and rechecked them to make sure she had everything she needed. I'd packed a medium-sized suitcase with clothes and shoes, and had my old duffle bag open on my bed, half-filled with other travel items. I still had to pack the beauty products I was using, as well as other toiletries.

As I was finishing up and gathering them, Amy called to me from my room, which was right across from the bathroom.

"Hey, Kim, do you have room in this bag for a few of my things? I kind of over-stuffed mine."

"Sure. Just leave me room for my bathroom stuff."

I heard her shuffling about for a moment, and then everything went silent. This gave me a weird feeling I cannot explain. I took my brush and hair dryer and carried them into my room to pack them. I froze when I saw Amy sitting there. She jumped at the sight of me, then forced a smile, trying to act like everything was fine, as if she wasn't holding what she was holding.

"Umm . . ." she said, but found no other words.

I'd been using the new gym bag, the ones the cheerleading team had been issued. The old bag I had used to carry sweatshirts and such in had been semiretired. The only reason I had decided to use the old one today instead of my new one was that my new one smelled like summer sweat socks and needed to be washed. I was surprised at myself. In the panic that had followed my first kill, I'd forgotten to dispose of one last item, one that had been tucked away in a small pocket of the bag. It was too late for Amy to hide it. It was open, exposing the cards inside and the information and pictures they held. Amy turned it over in her hand.

"This is . . ." Amy said, ". . . um . . ."

My shoulders tensed. The fuck-demon growled.

"You know what it is," I said, my tone flat.

Amy blinked, cleared her throat. "It's Mr. Blakley's wallet."

There was firmness to her now. She seemed to be trying to bring herself to reality, or what she thought reality was. She was reasoning with herself. There had to be a logical explanation. This couldn't be what it looked like.

"Yes," I said. "It's his wallet."

"So . . . why do you have it?"

I stepped forward and she flinched but did not get off the bed. I sighed as if I was about to get into a long story, and then I hit her in the face with the hair dryer, breaking both.

THIRTY-THREE

Amy's head snapped to one side and her hands went into the air as she fell toward the mattress. She wailed and grew frantic. The hair dryer's plastic had cracked, but the steel beneath had only bent. The impact of it had left a mark on Amy's forehead and a red sliver of a cut blossomed with blood. Instead of trying to fight me she tried to inch away, confused and unable to process what was happening.

"Kim," she said, "it's *me*. It's Amy!"

She simply couldn't grasp this. Her best friend couldn't be attacking her on purpose. There had to be some mix-up. I gently reached for one of her hands and she let me take it. I guided her as if I was helping her off the bed, and then I swung at her with the dryer once more. She didn't raise her other arm in time, but she did manage to duck and turn her head to the side, so all I caught was the top of her head.

"No!" she cried. "Wait! Stop!"

I started hammering her with blows, some of which she warded off with her flailing arms, the others connecting with her face and skull, bloody cuts appearing as bits of plastic sprayed like shrapnel. A crack had split the handle of the dryer and it was digging into my palm, but I ignored it and kept on attacking. Amy thrashed and rolled to the floor. Before she could get up I jumped on top of her, knocking her all the way down, and I bashed the back of her head and the dryer finally snapped in half. She tried to buck me off and I took the cord of the dryer and wrapped it around her throat and pulled it tight with both fists. Her hands went to the cord but she couldn't get her fingers beneath it, so she tried to reach back to me. She batted at me and clawed, but I held on. Realizing she couldn't bat me off her, she placed her palms on the floor and pushed up. Her panic gave her strength and she got to her knees. I wrapped my legs around her waist and sunk my teeth into her bare shoulder and bit down hard. Instinctually she tried to scream and this only robbed her of what little air she may have had left. I shook my head like a dog with a dead duck in its jaws, trying to rip a chunk of her off. She tasted so fresh and clean, like a milk-dribbling tit. It took time for me to break through the skin, but once I did the blood came fast and rich, filling my mouth with its savory flavor, making my eyes roll. Amy had a quick spasm and then she collapsed, taking me with her as she crumpled to the floor.

She did not get back up.

Well, this certainly sucked.

Amy lay beneath me, strangled, a mere residue of her former self.

I'd left the goddamned wallet in the goddamned bag. *Un-fucking-believable, Kim.*

How was I supposed to explain to her why I had it? In retrospect, I suppose I could have made up some weak bullshit about Caitlin using my bag at one point, but in the heat of the moment all I saw was black rage. I'd wanted to kill Amy for some time, but not like this, not under these circumstances. Her home life was not like Dakota's. She had two loving parents who would want to know where she was going when she packed a bag, and who she would be going there with. Her car was in my driveway and the spa had both of our names and information on file.

I dropped the cord and sat on her back as I caught my breath. *Think.*

There was a new body on my hands—the second one to die in my house. Our town's serial killer had struck again, just happening to choose another one of my friends. The cops would have to tie it back to me at this point, wouldn't they? I looked at the scratches

Amy had put on my arms. There would be traces of my skin and DNA under her fingernails. I'm sure there were traces of my DNA at Dakota's crime scene, but I had not been tested for a match. This, however, was a murder in my own home. I could move the body somewhere else, but her family knew she had gone to my house this morning. No matter what tall tale I spun, the authorities would investigate me with every tool at their disposal.

I am so fucked.

Amy's body moved just slightly and I heard a wheeze. I climbed off her and rolled her onto her back. Her chest heaved for air and I put my fingers to her wrist to check her pulse.

She was unconscious, but still alive.

I sighed with relief, but my alleviation didn't last long. Sure, the bitch was alive, but when she woke up she would be a big problem, perhaps an even bigger one than if she were dead. She would awake with bruises and choke marks, not to mention a gnarled, punctured shoulder. Certainly she would remember I had brutally beaten and strangled her after she'd discovered a murdered man's wallet in my possession.

Was it really such a good thing she was alive?

By the time she came to I had propped her up in the chair I'd taken from the office, tying down her arms to the arms of the chair and securing her feet at the bottom. I'd taken a dirty pair of my panties from the hamper and stuffed them in her mouth, then sealed it in with duct tape. I'd brought a lot of things up from the garage. I sat on the bed, facing her, watching her eyelids flutter open. It took her a moment to register what was happening. She blinked at me, then tried to move and looked at her bound arms. A look of recognition came across her face, immediately followed by terror. She struggled helplessly, her screams muted, tears flooding her bloodshot eyes.

I stood up, Father's hunting knife in my hand. A sliver of sunshine had crept through the part in my curtains and it hit the blade just so, making it gleam like a jewel in a movie. The blade reflected the light and it fell upon one side of Amy's face, marking her for death. She squirmed, trying to back up into the chair, working to get even a fraction of an inch further away from me. Her face was pink as a pig, slick with mascara tears and watery snot. Her forehead wasn't bleeding much, but a welt had formed and was already changing color, and the blond hair at the back of her head was crusted over with blood that had dried in dark clumps.

I shook my head. "Oh, Amy. What am I gonna do with you?"

She moaned against her gag.

"You've put me in a hell of a position here," I said, pacing. "Hell of a position."

She mumbled, trying to speak.

I approached her. "I can remove the tape if you want to talk."

She nodded.

"Just know, the moment you scream, I cut your throat."

She nodded again. I peeled back the tape and pulled the panties from her mouth. She took desperate breaths and I realized the sobbing had congested her nose, making it hard for her to breathe with the gag on.

"Please . . ." she said. "Kim . . . don't . . ."

"Don't what?"

"Hurt me . . . don't hurt me . . ."

"You've put us both in a crazy situation."

"It's okay."

"What's okay?"

"The wallet . . . I don't care about it . . . really."

"Oh?"

"For real. Whatever happened . . . it's none of my business."

"I see. And just what do you think happened, Amy?"

She shook her head, tears rolling. "Whatever happened with Mr. Blakley . . . however you got that wallet—"

"I killed him."

She closed her eyes tight, chest heaving.

"Still don't care what happened?" I asked.

"No!" She bawled. "I don't care! I won't tell anybody! Honest." She opened her eyes and stared at me. "Hey, *it's me*. We're best friends. You don't have to do this. You know I would never rat on you."

"Don't you want to know why I killed him?"

"No."

"No?"

"I'm sure you had a good reason."

I patted the blade in my other palm.

"Please," she said, "I won't say a word. It'll be like none of this ever happened."

I'd known Amy long enough to know she couldn't keep the smallest of secrets. Even if she meant what she said, keeping her big mouth shut was beyond her capabilities. And even so, there was no way she would let someone leave marks on her perfect body without making them pay for it.

I was stuck. Alive, she would call the police. Dead, her corpse would bring the police to my door. Even if I hid the body, they'd come right to me when she became a missing person. This was it. This was the end of the line.

Coming back to the bed, I sat down heavy, the weight of my predicament hunching me over. I sighed deep into my chest, cursing Amy, cursing myself.

Maybe I could set the house on fire and run away.

They'd still find you.

Maybe I could kill Amy and beat myself up, then call the police and say the killer left before finishing me off.

There's too much evidence against you.

Maybe I could . . .

There are human organs in your fridge. You've been closely related to everyone who has been murdered so far, and Amy is the closest one to you yet. You're guilty, you're pregnant and you're fucking doomed.

The reality of it all hit me with chilling devastation. I could almost cry—*almost*. There was no recourse here, no way out. My grim fate was inevitable. Everything from now until my arrest was just a countdown to the apocalypse. I suppose it had been inevitable all along. I was a murderer, necrophile and cannibal. How long could that possibly last? Even if I kept managing to leave no witnesses or clues, one way or another all killing sprees tend to end in incarceration or death. My youth and gender would only keep me above suspicion for so long. I was prison bound, a dead girl walking.

"Please . . ." Amy said.

"Shut up."

"Kim . . ."

I stood up.

Amy shook in her chair. "Kim, please!"

The handle of the knife was cold even though I'd been holding it for several minutes. When I placed the sharp edge to Amy's throat, she made a small clicking sound, finally shutting her mouth. I kept the blade in place, my face inching closer to her cheek. She whimpered and shut her eyes. My face fell into her hair and I inhaled deeply, taking in the aromas of coconut shampoo, expensive perfume and teenage blood. I nuzzled into her, and the energy of her trembling body warmed me like a radiator. I felt suddenly soothed, the closeness of her flesh, her *essence*, stabilizing me. It was a calmness the situation did not warrant. The tension in my muscles fled, and my mind escaped, adrift in the stagnant blood ocean that was my consciousness. The sphere was forming again. Its walls came together, curling like unwound scrolls of tanned flesh. It surrounded me. I was in a nest, a womb.

I pulled the knife away from Amy's throat and used it to push her hair out of her face. I planted kisses on her cheek and tickled her ears and neck with my nose. She shuddered beside me like a newborn animal, and I kissed her forehead. As I licked at the gash, there was a stirring in my stomach, and then something pressed against my insides. It was not pain exactly, just movement. The fuck-demon was awake. Like me, it was calm but ready for delights.

"I killed Derek," I told Amy.

She wouldn't open her eyes and she was holding her breath so as not to scream.

"I cut him into pieces, Amy. Then you know what I did? I cooked him into lasagna and served him to my friends." I waited for that to sink in. Amy gagged. "You should be honored, Amy. Here I am, telling you my secret ingredient."

She couldn't hold it in any longer. A choking cry bellowed out of her. I put the blade back to her throat and made a *shush* sound into her ear.

"I killed Dakota," I whispered. "Killed her mother too. In a way, I even killed Caitlin, by driving her fucking crazy."

I snickered. Amy swallowed hard, her nostrils flaring with every breath.

"Aren't you gonna ask me why?"

She didn't speak, so I pressed the blade closer.

She stuttered. "Wha-wha-why?"

I rested my head on her shoulder, snaked my other arm around her, and slid my hand down the front of her dress. It had a built-in bra that was easy for me to get under, and I caressed the soft meat of her tit. Goosebumps spread across her skin.

"I was bored," I said.

Sweat was forming at Amy's hairline. It smelled so rich and alive.

This moment was an electrical storm. There was no past or future here; there was only the raw, pulsing present, without restrictions or consequences. It was all so fucking *real*.

"Well, I'm not bored anymore," I said, roughly squeezing her breast. "All of this has made me happier than I've ever been. But something tells me this is the last hurrah. Better make the most of it, right?" I twisted her nipple. "We don't need a fancy spa. We can have our girl time right here."

Accepting my fate gave me clarity, and that clarity granted me serenity. If this was the end, I was going to go out singing. The revelation quaked in my body, warming my blood. My fingertips and toes tingled. I felt weightless. Was I still standing, or was I levitating?

After putting Amy's gag back in, I cut through her dress and tore it away, leaving her in her panties with the tatters of the dress under her back and ass. There was a TV mounted on the wall across the room with an attached DVD player. The movie I wanted was already in there. I turned everything on and started the video from the beginning, then came back over to Amy and started to undress. The video came on, and I took Amy's head in my hands to make sure she watched. Her eyes went wide when she saw herself and Ashton fucking.

Once I was nude, I went to my bedside table and slid open the drawer, took out the dildo, and brought it over to Amy. I popped open the lid and deftly poured the contents into my palm and held them up for her to see. She winced and looked away.

"Open your eyes."

She did as she was told and I held up the pieces one by one.

"Here are bits of Dakota's cunt. The finger is her mother's. And this . . ." I said, lifting the shriveled, blackened lump, " . . . is what's left of Derek's cock."

I put the finger and vaginal shreds back into the dildo and placed it at her feet. Derek's penis was slimy but stiff with rigor mortis. It smelled like dog farts and spoiled milk. I slid it across Amy's breasts. She recoiled, shaking her head violently and screeching through her gag. I ran it up and down the cream of her body, gliding along the ridges of her ribs, then down toward her navel. She tried to close her legs but she was bound too tight. I tapped the front of her panties with the dick.

A buzzing sound snapped me out of my trance. I turned and saw Amy's phone on the bed, the screen lit up. I picked it up, seeing she had a new text message.

It was Ashton.

Ashton: *Hey, sexy. Hope you N Kim have fun at the spa. Can't wait 4 U to get back so I can do things to U. XXX.* (winking smiley face emoji)

I gently placed Derek's dick on my comforter and texted Ashton back.

Me (as Amy): *Hey, babe. We haven't left yet. I'm at Kim's. If you want to get naughty before I leave, you should come over.* (kiss emoji)

Ashton: *For real?*

Me: *Kim and I were talking. We've always wanted to be part of a 3-some. You up for it?*

Ashton: *Are you FOR REAL?* (smiley face)

Me: *Come over and find out.*

I turned on the camera on Amy's phone and turned it around to take a selfie, making sure my face and my tits would be in the picture. I put my finger in my mouth for added sex appeal, then snapped the photo and sent it to him.

Ashton: *I'm on my way!*

I tossed the phone back onto the bed and looked at Amy. I picked up Derek's cock and came over to her.

"Maybe having boys with us wasn't such a bad idea," I said.

I grabbed her by the hair and ran the dead cock all over her face as she mewed. My sex flushed and dampened. Everything seemed accelerated, the colors of the world brighter than they'd ever been, every sound like heavenly music, every one of my senses heightened to the point of godliness. I put the dick in my mouth to hold it, picked up the knife, and slid it beneath Amy's panties. She flinched and the blade cut into her thigh and poked her in the groin, blood emerging from these minor wounds as the panties came off. I went back to the drawer and retrieved the sex lube I used when using the dildo. I splashed some in my hand and used it on Amy's sex to open her up.

I took Derek's rotting cock out of my mouth.

I waited by the front door so Amy wouldn't hear the bell ring. I had prepared everything upstairs. Wearing nothing but thigh-high stockings and high heels, I opened the door just as Ashton reached it. He gazed upon me with his mouth open, as if he were witnessing some sort of miracle.

"Are you ready for this?" I asked.

He nodded. "Oh, fuck yeah."

I moved aside to let him in and closed the door behind him. He put his hands on my waist and pulled me into him, putting his tongue in my mouth. I patted at the bulge in his jeans and his hand climbed to my breasts and squeezed them together. Knowing what I was going to do to him and his girlfriend, Ashton's hands felt better on me than anyone else's ever had before.

"Take off your clothes," I said.

He pulled off his t-shirt and I undid his belt. His shorts and underwear came off in one move, getting stuck at his ankles because he still had on his sneakers. His erection was already at full tilt. I didn't see what Amy thought was so special about it. He bent over and removed his shoes and I reached to the table where I had put the belt to Father's robe. It was soft, black cotton, long and thick. I held it up before him.

"What's that?" he said with a chuckle.

I raised my eyebrows. "No peeking."

He chuckled again—young, dumb and full of cum—and turned around so I could put the blindfold on him. The belt was thick enough to fully cover his eyes.

"Man," he said. "I wish I'd known you were so kinky, Kim. We could have done this a long time ago!"

I took him by his hard cock, leading him by it as we headed toward the stairs. He held onto the banister as we made our way up to my bedroom, where the third member of our ménage à trois awaited us with a duct tape blindfold of her own. When we got to the landing, I stopped him in place and lifted the rope off the railing where I had placed it.

"So," I said, "you say you like getting kinky?"

"You bet."

"Good."

I got down on my knees and slid the rope around one of his wrists. To keep him from getting nervous, I sucked his cock a little before tying his hands behind his back. Ashton showed no reservations about being in restraints. All he knew in this moment was excitement.

"Savage . . ." he said.

I took him by his cock again, opened the bedroom door, and led him inside. Amy tensed when she heard the door come open, but she made no noise. She'd worn out her throat from all the screaming she'd done earlier. I locked the door behind us and brought Ashton to the bed, sitting him down where the video camera could capture all three of us. I lifted the .40 S&W from the end table where I'd placed it, along with my other tools, including the flower-watering can. Amy moaned and Ashton turned his blind head from side to side.

"What was that?" he asked.

At the sound of his voice, Amy came alive. She roared through the gag, a mad woman.

Ashton stood. "Amy?"

I pistol-whipped him in the face and he fell back onto the bed but kicked out with his legs and got back to his feet. His body flexed as he tried to break the ties at his wrist. He reminded me of a guard dog on a chain.

"Sit down," I said.

"Fuck you!"

Blood was trickling out of his nostrils where I had struck him. I cocked the pistol and he froze.

"You know that sound?" I asked.

He didn't answer. He didn't have to. His Adam's apple rose and fell.

"Sit down," I said, and this time he obeyed.

"What's going on?"

"Don't worry. You're still getting your three-way, sort of. It's just kinkier than you were anticipating."

I lifted the blindfold. He glared at me and I stepped back so I wouldn't block the view. When he saw Amy, he cried with horror and I put the gun to his temple.

"None of that," I said.

He closed his mouth, still looking at her in total shock. His girlfriend was tied to a chair, gagged and blindfolded by duct tape. She was nude, beaten and bloody, and there was a dark mass shoved into her vagina.

"What the fuck are you doing?" Ashton cried, his face contorting with genuine grief. It seemed he really did care about her. "Why are you doing this?"

"It's all part of the fun."

"She's *not* having fun, and neither am I! Untie us, right the fuck now!"

"I don't think you understand what I mean by *fun*. But that's okay. I'll teach you."

I went to Amy and pulled at the duct tape around her eyes, tearing hair out of her head as I removed it. The two lovers stared at one another with panicked longing, both expressing sympathy and crying for help at the same time. It was cute.

"Okay," I said, coming back to Ashton. "Now, where were we?"

With my free hand, I reached down to his now flaccid cock.

"What are you doing?" he asked as I stroked him.

"Amy's going to watch while I fuck you."

"No . . ."

I raised the barrel of the gun so it was inches from his face.

"It's your choice," I told him. "Your dick goes in me, or this gun goes in your mouth."

He was shaking now. "I can't do it . . . not like this . . ."

"You'd better."

"I'm too scared!"

His face pinched when he said it, hating to admit it, his male ego fucking with him even in this dark hour. I pushed him so he lay down on the mattress, snickering at the tears coming to the football star's eyes. All jocks are like this—tough exteriors disguising the frightened little boy within.

"I'll give you a little help," I said.

I put his hanging vine of a dick into my mouth and worked on him. I could feel him controlling his breathing, and knew he was trying to keep himself from crying. He was doing his best to forget what was really happening and just enjoy the blowjob so he could rise to the occasion, his life depending on it. It took a moment, but he impressed me by growing larger in my mouth. He was powering through his fear to save himself. Once he was hard, I straddled him, facing Amy so I could laugh in her face while I fucked her boyfriend. His erection expanded me, plunging deep inside, and I quivered with lust, my body bursting into invisible flames. I grinded my teeth as I grinded on Ashton, hips pumping, skin prickling red. All the while I looked at Amy, savoring the hurt in her eyes. Her anguish soiled every inch of her body and she went limp—a dirty, old ragdoll of ruin. Ashton was getting bigger. He was about to climax. The arrival of his orgasm inched me toward my own and I clenched him with my pussy. I was high on all this sweet suffering. The smell of sweat, blood and vaginal juices made my nostrils flare. My insides rippled, my cunt consuming my lover in one deep chug, and as we came as one I pointed the pistol and fired, sending a bullet into my best friend's stomach.

THIRTY-FOUR

I'd brought hell to earth.

Blood gushed from Amy's gut and she shuddered, groaning and gurgling. Ashton was screaming. I climbed off him, wiped myself with the comforter, and when I stood up the floor, walls and ceiling seemed to close then expand, again and again, throbbing like a great heart. The cries of my prisoners circled and echoed, sounding like poltergeists in a haunted castle, and when I looked up, I was somehow able to see through the ceiling and roof to the brilliant summer sky where vultures swarmed in a tornado of feathers, each of them as hungry as the fuck-demon was. The little beast cried and shook within me, filling me with black light.

Ashton got off the bed and ran toward the door even though he had no way of turning the handle. He screamed for help and I shot him in the back of his knee. The kneecap shifted and he collapsed instantly. I felt hot and tingly as I approached him, like I was being poked with a tattoo needle. I reached over to the bedside table where I had placed the watering can. Normally I used this to make the garden grow, but today I had filled it with a mixture of hot water and lye. Ashton was lying on his side so I stepped on his shoulder to get him on his back, and held the canister at arm's length and rained down the lye on Ashton's face. He shrieked and writhed as it began eating through his flesh. I poured more on his chest, stomach and cock, sizzling the skin away. Once the canister was empty, I placed it back down carefully, and shot Ashton in the face to shut him up. I hit him dead in the nose, creating a hole that gave way to a large, bowl-shaped cavity, and blood poured from the wound with the force of a bathtub faucet.

Amy was still alive, but she was in incredible pain. She writhed against her restraints when she could muster the strength to, but mostly she just moaned and contracted like a halved worm. I put the gun down and picked up the hunting knife. It was a powerful skinning tool, a thirteen-inch long blade that was four inches thick. I put the tip of the knife into the bullet wound in her stomach, then inched it in and turned it, widening the hole. Amy squealed and made the wound worse as she gyrated on the blade. It slid out, and I brought the knife up over my head, then came down at her chest, stabbing her in one tit then the other, the knife slipping in and out of her body. Frenzied, I stabbed her in her shoulders and arms, the blade knocking off bones and dicing the flesh. I hacked at her thighs until the meat split. I turned the blade underhand and pummeled her guts, driving the blade as far in as it would go. I gnashed and chewed at these fresh wounds, tearing strips away with my canines, eating her while she was still alive. Blood poured out of Amy's gag and nostrils. Her body convulsed. I must have stabbed her thirty times. When her head fell back, I stabbed her in the throat and twisted the knife slowly, then sawed my way across her neck until I hit an artery. I put my mouth to the spraying hole and drank my fill.

Stepping away from my victims, I was overcome by a case of the giggles. I dropped the knife and doubled over, laughing to the point of tears. When I finally calmed down I went to the camera and stopped the recording. I didn't want to waste time. A neighbor may have heard the shots and screaming. I carried the camera to the office and uploaded the video to my computer, pleased with the high definition of the picture. I uploaded it to the porn website, then to YouTube and Facebook, each time labeling it: *Real Snuff.* I put the older porno movie of Amy and Ashton up on all three sites too, as well as all the pictures of Caitlin, this time using everyone's full names in the descriptions. Then I burned a copy of the murder movie to DVD, along with the older porno of Amy and Ashton. While it was burning I used a washcloth to get most of the blood off me, changed into a pair of jeans and a white blouse, and put on my boots. Emptying out my duffel bag, I put the three extra, fully loaded magazines into it and gathered items from the garage, randomly picking instruments of violence and bondage tools, just so I would be ready to enjoy whatever pleasures fell into my lap. I took the machete and the fully charged nail gun and put them in the bag. I threw in some chains and a lock, some cable ties, rope, and a few box cutters. I also packed a container, which held a long coil of Dakota's intestine. The hunting knife had a holster, so I attached it to my belt. By the time I was ready, so was the DVD. With a magic marker, I wrote on it: *The Death of Your Little Whore*. I put it into a bubble mailer, addressed it to its recipients, and put it in the bag, which I slung over my shoulder.

I picked up the pistol and left my house for the last time.

As I pulled Amy's car out of my driveway, I turned sharply and dinged Ashton's truck. Turning into the street, I heard sirens and wondered if they were for me. Instead of feeling fear, I felt giddiness. It coursed through me, opening me up, making me feel excited and yet serene. The fuck-demon was chewing my insides a little, a baby with a pacifier, but I was too amped up to pay it any mind. I was laughing again. Tears of happiness rolled down my cheeks and I turned on the radio static as loud as it would go, the mumbled voices all talking about me, praising me. I was a hero, a legend.

I got to Amy's house and stuffed the mailer with the DVD into their mailbox for her parents to find, then drove away. When I reached the corner I spotted my neighbor, Mrs. Maxwell. She was a retired housewife and widow with three daughters who visited her regularly, bringing along their noisy children. Her one constant companion, however, was a black, Scottish terrier named Buster, who she was walking this morning. I stopped the car and got out, placing my arms across the top of the vehicle to steady them. She turned just in time to see the pistol in my hands as it bucked twice, landing two bullets in her frail body. She fell to the ground, moaning. Buster spun in circles, barking his head off as I shot his owner in the back of her head. Her blood and brain matter popped into the air and the dog whined. I thought about shooting Buster, but didn't want to waste bullets on a dog.

I got back into the car and drove down the street. There were some children playing in a yard and driveway, the boys tossing a football while the smaller girls drew with chalk. I slowed down and fired out the window, dropping one of the boys, but the other ran toward the girls, screaming at them to run. One got to her feet but the other was too young to really understand what was going on. A bullet to her chest turned her *Frozen* t-shirt a syrupy purple and she collapsed. The other children made it to the door before I could get off more shots, and I hit the gas and drove on, turning onto the main road that led into town as neighbors started coming out of their houses to investigate the noise.

I wished school were still in session. It would have been perfect. All those youthful idiots lined up for slaughter, not to mention all the teachers who adored me as a shining example of what all students should aspire to be. But you can't have everything, and besides, I still had somewhere fun I could go. The trees blew about in the breeze like pompoms, cheering me on. Behind their green blur, thousands of disembodied eyes watched me from the shadows. As I drove, I popped the lid off the container and snatched Dakota's innards, chewing on them to satiate the fuck-demon's increasing hunger and give myself something to do with my grinding teeth. I reached a red light and there was no one behind me or at the other intersections, but there was a car on the left hand side of me, waiting to turn. I stared at the middle-aged man at the wheel. A moment later he turned to look at me and I smiled with a string of guts hanging from my mouth. His jaw dropped. I raised the pistol and fired, missing him but shattering his window, and he hit the gas, running the red light. A car emerged from the corner and slammed into him headfirst, causing both vehicles to spin as glass and steel burst in a kaleidoscope of shrapnel. The light changed and I drove past the wreck slowly to get a good look. The front of the man's car had compacted, sending the engine block into the front seat, and he was screaming as its hot metal burned him. The other car was equally decimated and the windshield was cracked into spider webs. A bloodied airbag obstructed my view of the inside.

I drove on, careful of the speed limit.

When I reached the park I got out and reloaded, then slung the bag over my shoulder and walked toward the field where my cheerleading team was tumbling and flipping. I saw Mandy Clark at the top of a temple, Mrs. Morrell blowing her whistle and waving directions like a conductor with an orchestra. I slipped my phone into the holder with the clip on it, which I used to hold it in place while I was working out. I started a Facebook update, looked into the camera and smiled for my viewers, and selected "Go Live." This made my video stream live for all to see.

"For all I've done," I said, "and all I'm about to do, I am not the least bit sorry."

I snapped the phone to the front of my chest, the camera facing out so everything would be seen from my point of view. Cocking the pistol for my audience, I put a round in the chamber. Sirens wailed in the distance and a shiver of joy went through me. I was so alive, so free. Birds sang the prettiest of songs. For the first time in my life, the darkness had completely disappeared. Everything was clear to me now, clear and pure as baby flesh. There was no monotony to dull my heart. Life was rich. There were no mixed emotions now, and not a single trace of doubt. My body, spirit and mind were harmonious in their joy, and what I did next came not from rage, but from a sense of childlike wonder. The world is an amazing place if you can tolerate it.

My teammates were too wrapped up in their exercises to notice me approaching, but I tucked the pistol beneath my duffle bag just in case. The field was alive with the jumps, flips and kicks of promising young girls. I spotted Summer Scott doing Leapin' Loras with Hannah MacDougall and Connie Hong. Four other girls were hoisting Mandy Clark up into a split lift. When I got to the sideline, Mrs. Morrell spotted me and her eyes sparkled, happy to see one of her star players had made it after all.

"Glad you could make it, Kim!"

"Me too."

I shot her in the chest and her clipboard flew into the air as she spun toward the dirt. Screams surrounded me in a mad chorus, and before the girls holding Mandy could respond to what had happened I opened fire on them, hitting one of them at the base of her spine and blowing out another girl's elbow. The group ran in all directions, dropping Mandy. She hit the ground with a thud and struggled to get back to her knees as I approached.

"Kim!" she cried. "Wait!"

A bullet shattered her mouth, sending teeth flying. She fell and clutched at her bleeding jaw and I came closer and shot her twice in the heart.

A man I did not know was on the other side of the field, some kind of assistant coach or volunteer dad. He was calling to the girls, trying to get them out of harm's way. I opened fire on him but missed as he darted behind the bleachers, leading a line of cheerleaders to shelter. The field was a raging sea of panic. Terrified girls were bolting toward the parking lot while others tried to hide behind trees and trashcans. Even at a distance, I could smell their sweat and tears and my heart swelled with love for every drop. I shot at random, taking some girls out while missing others.

One of the cheerleaders stopped to pick up a girl of about five, who was standing in place and crying, someone's little sister come to watch. This moment of heroism slowed her, giving me time to aim, and I shot her three times in the back and she fell hard, landing on the little girl, crushing and pinning her. I aimed the barrel at the child's head and killed her too.

On the other side of the park was a baseball diamond where some college-age boys were playing softball. They ran toward the parking lot, calling to the cheerleaders as they went to their cars, offering to help the girls escape. Though they were further away, I still opened fire at them, emptying my magazine. Bullets peppered the tall blond boy's chest and he collapsed. His chubby friend caught one in his throat and fell backwards over the hood of a car. The others ducked and dodged and climbed into their vehicles.

I reached into my bag for another magazine and reloaded after spotting Summer at her car, fumbling with her keys. The windshield popped as I made holes appear, and she ducked for cover, shrieking as glass sprayed. I walked toward Summer, shooting at another girl as she ran past, landing a round in her shoulder that sent her back into a tree. Summer was trying to crawl under her car, but was stuck halfway. I leaned down, dropping the pistol for a moment, and took the nail gun out of my bag. It gleamed in the sunshine. I lifted the skirt of her uniform and blasted nails into her ass as she kicked and screamed. The sirens were louder now, closer, and there were a hell of a lot of them. When the nail gun clicked empty I threw it aside, picked up the pistol, and stuffed it into the groove of Summer's snatch. I pulled the trigger and her crotch burst open. Her thrashing ceased and I stood up, noticing three cheerleaders running to the small, concrete bathroom building. Cars were screeching out of the parking lot now. I could hear people crying into their cell phones, calling for police and ambulances, others begging their parents for help. Many girls had fled to the woods and others had hid themselves well enough I could not find them.

I went after the three cheerleaders as they ducked into the

bathroom.

The heavy door slammed behind me.

One of the fluorescent lights flickered above like bug zappers, revealing cracked tile and concrete walls. The trash bin was stuffed with paper towels, with more piled around the bottom of it in a soggy halo. Two of the stall doors were closed tight, the other hung wide open. I smelled feces, used maxi pads and dried urine.

And I could hear stifled whimpers.

I got down on one knee and looked under the stalls, seeing no feet. Outside, sirens were roaring and I heard fast tires crunching over the pebbled lot. I put down the duffle bag and fired a shot into the ceiling. The girls screamed in unison.

"Open those fucking doors," I said.

Nothing.

I fired a single bullet into one of the doors, and the opposing one came open. One of the junior cheerleaders was inside—a little redheaded thing with poofy pigtails and braces that reminded me of Caitlin, even though this girl was much younger. Standing with her arms tucked into her chest, she hunched to make herself even smaller. Her body was shaking like an old washing machine.

"Come on out," I said.

Aside from her convulsions, she did not move. She gasped as I entered the stall and grabbed her by one of her pigtails to drag her out. Piss soaked the front of her shorts as she cried, not fighting back. I flung her to the floor, put my gun into the bag, and brought out one of the box cutters with a new razor in it. Snapping her head back by her pigtail, I sliced at her face and she squirmed beneath me in a frail effort to get away. The razor opened up her face in several places, shredding what was left of the baby fat in her cheeks and nicking her ears and forehead. When she held up her hands to protect her face, she did so palms up and I slashed them. I caught her by one nostril and tugged, ripping it in two. In seconds her head was bloody pulp. Tossing the box cutter, I got some cable ties from the bag and then dragged the girl to her feet, slammed her into the bathroom counter and bent her over. I bound her hands with the ties, then spun her around to face me. She closed her eyes at the sight of me, screeching, her gory face being captured by my camera at close range.

"I'm letting you go," I told her. "Go out there and tell the police I have two hostages in here. Understand?"

She was bawling too hard to get words out.

"Nod your head if you understand."

She did. I released her and the girl ran out the door, nearly tripping on the curb. I slammed the door shut again, looking for something to barricade it with. I had the lock and chain I had brought, and there was a metal pull handle on the inside of the door, but nothing else to latch the chain around to seal it shut. The trashcan was lightweight. It would roll, offering no resistance.

Fuck it.

I took the pistol from my bag, and as I rose up again a sharp pain went through my guts. For a moment I thought I had been shot or stabbed and I spun around, looking for an assailant who was not there. I felt a sensation like claws pulling across my uterus and knew I was being attacked from the inside.

"Not now!"

Mustering all my strength, I went to the locked stall and kicked at it, hearing the two girls behind the door.

"Open up or I start shooting. Bullets will tear through this door like tissue paper."

I gave them a second. The latch clicked and the door slowly swung inward on its own. The girls were still standing on the toilet together, holding onto one another, trembling. One was a stout blond girl; the other, a spindly black girl with braids. Both were flat chested and wore no makeup. I knew these two. They were in my grade and on my team. They had been in some of my classes all year. But they were not popular enough for me to remember their names.

"Out," I ordered.

They stepped down gingerly. Outside, someone was talking through a bullhorn.

When I got the girls out I had them sit on the floor, back to back. I wrapped the chain around them as tight as I could get it and snapped the ends together with the lock. The girls sobbed but did not resist me or try to snatch the gun away. I stood over them, admiring my prizes.

"What a day, ladies. What a day."

The fuck-demon ripped at me and I couldn't help but bend over. It felt like a blender blade was spinning within me, and I pictured the beast whirling in a cyclone. There was still some of Dakota's intestine left, so I dug into the bag for it and wolfed it down in just a few bites. When I belched I tasted bile. My stomach contracted and I had to sit down. I heard an authoritative male voice coming from beyond the bathroom, distorted and amplified. It was assuring me things did not have to end violently, that no one would hurt me if I let the girls go. I could barely decipher the words. It was like they were in the wrong order or the speaker was going back and forth between English and some foreign language I did not know. There was static blanketing the voice, and the more I listened the more it faded into the background as the brown noise filled my head. The puddle of blood on the floor from where I had cut up the redhead was growing wider and wider. Like creeks jetting out of a lake, it sent the blood trickling through the grooves in the tile, making patterns in the floor. I struggled to decipher their codes. Beneath the tiles, I could feel the pulse of the earth.

I turned to the black girl, realizing for the first time she was Caitlin.

"What's it like?" I asked her.

She sniffled. "Wha-what?"

"Being dead. What's it like to be dead?"

Caitlin hung her head and cried. Beside her, her father slouched against the chain, looking ridiculous in the cheerleading uniform. I laughed.

"Hey, Mr. Blakley. How about one more good screw? You know, for old times' sake?"

He cried too, sounding like a girl.

"There's not much time left," I said, feeling the stir in my guts. "The baby's coming."

As if to remind me, the fuck-demon spun once more, sending hot knives of fire through my abdomen. My vagina closed tight and I felt something trickling out of it. I turned on my side, hoping it would ease the pain, and when it dulled I opened my eyes again and saw Father sitting there, chained to Amy's mutilated corpse. He was naked and his erection was jutting straight up, bloody pre-cum at its tip.

"Are you hungry?" I asked him.

He said nothing.

My eyes filled with tears even though I felt no emotion, and when I batted the tears loose I saw the chained cheerleaders were watching my every move. I was popular, beautiful, a better cheerleader than they were. They wanted to be me so badly. I wondered how much they would be willing to sacrifice to slither beneath my skin.

Since I had brought it along, I wanted to use the machete for something, but when I took it from the bag I found it was dull and grass-stained. I let it clamor to the floor and the girls flinched.

"A pound of flesh," I said to no one in particular. I wasn't even sure what I meant.

"Please . . ." one of the girls said.

I wasn't sure if it was the black girl or the blond. Their little bodies had fused together into a squirming mass with two heads and four legs. I undid the button on the holster and slid the hunting knife out. It was still caked in Amy's blood. I wondered if the chained blob's black flesh would taste any different from the white parts, like chicken's white and dark meat. Looking at these conjoined twins, I realized I was as horny as the fuck-demon was hungry. I could tell the little bitches wanted to fuck me too. They were chained up, just like all the slaves in all the porno films I watched. God, they were asking for it. Just look at how they were dressed.

I got to my knees and moved toward the blond, the knife glowing in my hand. I felt my phone bob against my breast and I smiled, remembering I was still filming. This was my last stand, the final act of my one-woman show. I hoped everyone was watching, because I was going to eviscerate these girls while they were still alive. I was going to pull their organs out with my teeth and fuck myself with their bones. This was one thing all the maggots of this world deserved to see.

As I tried to get to my feet, a lightning bolt of suffering shot from my stomach down to my groin, then split into separate rivers that jolted through my legs, cooking the blood in my veins and paralyzing the muscle tissue. I fell over, landing in the blond girl's lap, gagging from nausea and dizzied by vertigo. Pain exploded through me in a dirty bomb of nails and teeth. I twitched with my back against the girl and her screams pierced my eardrums. But I knew they were not truly *her* screams. The fuck-demon was using her as a microphone for screams of its own. It wanted to make sure I could hear it over all that radio static.

My day of ecstasy and beauty had come to an end. Now there was only agony. The comfortable blood bubble had burst and the protective layers of my sphere crumbled like sand. I leaned back into the girl and dropped the knife so I could undo my button and zipper. I kicked out of my sneakers and breathed a steady percussion like I had seen in Lamaze videos during Mr. Blakley's class. Pulling my jeans over my hips, I saw my panties were soaked with blood. I tugged myself out of my jeans and panties and leaned back against the girl again, my feet planted on the floor, my legs spread wide.

It didn't matter it was several months early, because this was no normal fetus.

I pushed, but instead of feeling the fuck-demon shift downward, I felt it crawl deeper in, rebelling against my efforts to spit it out and be free of it.

It doesn't want to be born.

But there was no way I was letting it stay in. When I went to prison, there would be no more human meat meals, and the fuck-demon would chew its way right through me. But that was only one of the problems I had with it continuing to gestate. My main concern was the same one I'd had since I had first read that pink dot on the applicator.

I did not want to be a pregnant teen.

There is no greater shame than that. Nothing would embarrass me more than having my secret revealed, which it would be once I was brought into custody. Father would be so ashamed of me. My teachers would all look down on me and my friends would whisper about me behind my back. Despite my constant thoughts of suicide, I felt I was a fairly strong young woman. But I knew I couldn't take this shame. It would crush me.

I pushed again, bracing myself against the twins.

In protest, the fuck-demon started cutting me up, much as I had sliced the redheaded girl I had just released. Claws like straight razors opened my uterine walls and tiny teeth peeled the sinew away. It no longer cared if it killed me. It could survive on its own because it was actually ready to be born, but fighting me just for the fuck of it. If I didn't take swift action, it would eat its way through me.

I had no choice.

All thirteen inches of the blade entered my belly.

I used my entire body to drive the knife home, digging into the swelled lump in search of the fuck-demon. There was a stinging pain from the impact, but it was nothing compared to the shredding jaws of the little monster, and its attack ceased as it bounced around my uterus, trying to dodge the knife as I jabbed it in and out, hunting my prey. I could feel its panic and I laughed as it begged me for its life, calling me *mommy* for the first time as it pleaded for mercy. It sounded like all the rest, saying *please* and *you don't have to do this* and *don't kill me*. It was so funny that I became hysterical. I stabbed and stabbed, my body having gone numb to defend itself, working with me so we could destroy the beast within us once and for all. Convulsions coursed through me like an orgasm. I tasted blood and bile. My bowels voided. And as I stabbed at the dancing demon the girls who cradled me screeched and cried, awed by the beauty of this anti-birth.

I barely noticed when the others came piling into the bathroom.

There was muffled yelling. I saw blue slacks and big belts with all sorts of tools dangling from them. Slick, polished shoes splashed through the gore. *So much blood.* People in white came toward me just as my cushioning was removed from behind my back. I heard a rattle like chains and the sweet sobs of young girls.

Words spun in the air like the buzzing of flies.

"Oh, Christ . . ."

". . . one crazy bitch."

"Get those two out of here . . ."

One of the men in blue slacks ran to a stall and I heard vomit splash into the bowl. I laughed but only heard a wet click in my throat. Everything was brighter and more colorful than it needed to be. It hurt my eyes and I closed them. When my eyes reopened a moment later, the woman in white was fiddling with my body. I saw gauze and shining, steel tools. Her face was a blur of old flesh, no nose or eyes. She said something about *fading* and tried to take my hands from the knife but I held it tight and twisted it, feeling something pop and tear loose.

I've got you now.

A crowd fell upon me then, everyone yelling and reaching for the knife, and I heard the woman say something about not pulling, and then the knife came free, dragging everything out like a fishing hook, all that remained splattering out into the cruel, flickering light of our world.

Acknowledgements

Thanks to C.V. Hunt and the Grindhouse Press team for all of the work they put into this demon-seed of a book. Fist-bumps to Bryan Smith, Edward Lee, and Ryan Harding. Additional fist-bumps to all my fans, friends, readers, reviewers, who make it possible for me to write insane horror stories for a living. Thanks to Thomas Mumme—always. And thank you to everyone who buys and reads this novel.

Huge appreciations to Jack Ketchum. Rest well, Dallas.

And special thanks to every mean girl I knew in high school.

I WAS A TEENAGE CANNIBAL

The birth of *Full Brutal*

I was sitting in a hotel lounge in Virginia. It was Scares That Care's charity horror convention, 2019, and I was talking with friends when author Aaron Dries walked by us, stopped in front of me, and gave me the kind of look your dad does before he goes into one of his lectures.

"We need to talk," he said.

I looked back and forth, as if for an explanation. "Um, okay."

"I read your book."

"Which one?"

"*Full Brutal.*"

"What did you think?"

Aaron took a deep breath. "I loved it…" He smiled. "What the fuck is going on inside of your head?"

It's a question that comes up a lot regarding this novel, and it's a fair one. It's not like *Full Brutal* is a horror story about a haunted house, psychics, or some sexy, misunderstood vampire. Hell, it's not even your standard serial killer book. *Full Brutal* is not a conventional horror novel. It's something far more disturbing.

Before starting the book, I had decided I wanted to create a character who was horror incarnate—evil concentrated down to its purest form. Naturally, the novel would therefore contain murder, but I didn't want it to be a mere serial killer novel. The slayings in

Full Brutal are but one part of its inhumanity and only begin after cruel manipulations, psychological torture, betrayals, and orchestrated sexual assaults. Our lead character quickly learns she must do worse and worse things to others in order to get her kicks, so her stealthy attacks get exponentially more vicious and depraved.

The character of Kim White revealed herself to me slowly—that pretty, young face coming out of the shadows only to expose how much darker it was than them. I decided early on that she would be a pregnant teenager who believes her unborn child is trying to eat her alive from the inside, and that the only way to satiate its hunger is by feeding it someone else's flesh, forcing Kim into cannibalism. But as the story progressed, Kim's deviancy blossomed before my eyes, and so it became a story of not just cannibalism but also of every callous act I could imagine someone doing to others.

When I began writing the novel I was suffering from depression. I have bipolar disorder, so when depression barges in it burrows deep and turns my mind black. One only needs to read the first few pages of the book to see how my mood was reflected in the writing. Kim is despondent and engaged in suicide ideation. But as Kim's assaults on those around her began, her spirits brightened because it became a fun challenge for me to have her outdo herself with each successive act of sadism. Each of her actions had to top the last in depravity and extremity. And all while her actions escalated, at the same time, her mental state was further deteriorating. She wasn't just sadistic. She was going insane. My own negativity was utilized creatively, sending Kim into a mental spiral far worse than anything I've—thankfully—ever come close.

One of my favorite things about this book is everyone has at least one scene where they had to stop reading for a while. Some people are triggered by Caitlin's rape. Some are more disturbed by Kim's autosarcophagy. For others, it's her hypersexual acts of necrophilia. There are so many atrocities to choose from. Every reader I've talked to brings up *"that one scene"* which made them put down the book and go take their dog for a walk or watch cartoons to decompress from their time in Kim's horrible world. It's a rare thing for an author to be proud that their readers had to step away from their novel, but this is one of them. If *Full Brutal* didn't repel people, then I simply didn't write it correctly. This book had to push. This book had to *hurt*.

And the best part is that this has become one of my most celebrated works, even winning the 2019 Splatterpunk Award for

Best Novel. So while everyone had to take little terror breaks, they also kept on reading. They all needed to know just how brutal Kim would go, and how deep into the black bowels of madness the novel would take them. The true power of *Full Brutal*, I think, is that it tests the morality of the reader. While Kim is the worst human being imaginable, you find yourself rooting for her in a way, not because you would ever want these things to happen in real life, but because you want to know what the crazy bitch is going to do next.

I'm sometimes asked if Kim was only imagining her baby was a flesh-eating ghoul or if there really was a monster in her belly trying to chew its way out. Some ask if she was ever really pregnant at all. I have my own take it on it, of course but, just as with those scenes which made people take a break, I prefer to let the reader decide what upsets them the most about this book. It's just scarier that way.

Because this ain't your Mama's horror novel.

This is *Full Brutal*.

—Kristopher Triana

Kristopher Triana is the Splatterpunk Award-winning author of *Gone to See the River Man, Full Brutal, The Thirteenth Koyote, They All Died Screaming,* and many other terrifying books. His work has been published in multiple languages and has appeared in many anthologies and magazines, drawing praise from Rue Morgue Magazine, Cemetery Dance, Scream Magazine, and many more.

He lives in New England.

Shop: TRIANAHORROR.COM
Kristophertriana.com
Twitter: Koyotekris
Facebook: Kristopher Triana
Instagram: Kristopher_Triana
TikTok: Kristophertriana
Podcast: krisandjohnwayne.com

Made in United States
Orlando, FL
27 February 2025

58961782R00155